"I must [...]
"You we[...]
Quinton. [...]
would be angry when you found her
here."

"You made that plain enough," said Edward, looking down at her from his great
height. "As to Mrs. Quinton, I don't suppose you had much choice; she's as persistent as a river in flood, isn't she? Poor
creature. When a worthless young man gets
into a scrape there's always some soft-
hearted woman in the background, suffering far more than he does."

Mary swallowed this allusion without
resentment. "You may call me a soft-
hearted fool if you will; your own heart is
not as inflexible as you pretend. You can
show compassion, even to a papist, though
I know very well what you feel about
them."

"I doubt it," he retorted. "You are not
placed as I am. Make what you can of my
actions, but don't waste your time trying to
assess my feelings. However you do it, the
sum will come out wrong."

The flat contradiction brought her up
short with a shock of pain. Just as she was
beginning to feel closer to him he had
eluded her again, stretching the distance
between them quite deliberately, and leaving her more lost than she was before.

The Second Husband

Sheila Bishop

ace books

A Division of Charter Communications Inc.
A GROSSET & DUNLAP COMPANY
360 Park Avenue South
New York, New York 10010

THE SECOND HUSBAND

Copyright © 1964 by Sheila Bishop

An ACE BOOK,
by arrangement with the author

Printed in U.S.A.

The Second Husband

FOR ANNE

1

After Captain John Dacre was killed fighting in Ireland it was clear that a second husband would have to be found for his widow.

A young woman of twenty-eight could not fend for herself and bring up four children; she needed a man to protect and control her. There was some money: just enough to give her a false illusion of wealth and to entice the fortune-hunters. Left to her own devices, she would run into debt or get into mischief—not that Mary had ever shown signs of indiscretion, but then she had met so few temptations, safely married at fifteen to the son of a neighbouring squire down in Sussex. Now he was dead, and her family must make new plans for Mary.

So in the autumn of 1576, after a decent interval of mourning, her lawyer brother Guy Freeland fetched her up to his house in Holborn, and put the case to her, padded with a good deal of long-winded prosing that he mistook for tact.

"I've no wish to marry again," said Mary Dacre. "Not yet. I was too happy with Jack."

"You've given him eight months of grieving, that's long enough. The best tribute you can pay to his memory——"

"Don't tell me again, my dear Guy, I have it all by heart. The best I can do for Jack's memory is to

give his children a brand new stepfather who will
knock some sense into the boys, and prevent me
from frittering the girls' dowries."

"I did not put it so crudely," objected Guy,
which was certainly true, as he had taken forty-five
minutes to make these points clear.

He studied his sister, trying to hide his exasperation. She was rather small; dark, curly hair con-
trasted with vivid blue eyes; her skin had the delicate glow of light shining through alabaster. This
colouring, and her smallness, made a particular appeal: she looked younger than her age and decep-
tively fragile. Guy was not taken in. Mary had been
a little mule in the nursery, she was a mule still, and
she had developed an irreverent gift for mockery.
With a certain cunning, he changed his tactics.

"It's all very fine to jest about your daughters'
dowries," he proclaimed heavily. "You owe a duty
to their future, even if you won't consider your own.
That elder girl of yours—she's rising twelve and a
well-grown maid, you'll have to look around for her.
Now I have a friend, a man of some consequence,
who wants a match for his heir. The boy's fourteen;
if we could strike a bargain it would be an excellent
prospect for your Jane."

Mary frowned. "I don't like child betrothals."

"How can you say so? You were contracted at
eleven, and you say yourself that no marriage could
have been happier."

"Yes, but I'd known Jack since we were babies;
there was never a time in my life when he wasn't
part of it. To yoke two strange children together like
cattle—that's entirely different."

Not that Guy would see the difference, she
thought, rather wearily. It was one of the sad things

about growing older, you realized the wide gaps which separated you from the people who had seemed nearest. How she had admired Guy once; the exciting elder brother who kept a ferret in his bedchamber and wore a real sword. Now the sturdy country boy was a prosperous townsman, his head stuffed with legal conveyances, and his horizon bounded by money. He was putting on weight and the fashion for wide ruffs did not suit him; he seemed to have too much jowl and too little neck.

Mary's mind returned to her problems. Jack had been the youngest of a rich, landed family; she had lived with him in one of his father's manors. Now he was dead, she had her jointure, and there was a settlement on the children, but old Sir Roger had thought it quite unsuitable for her to stay on at Ramsdene; he had said she would be lonely. What he meant was, she would let the farm go to ruin. So she and her children had been carted off to the great house, where she had endured eight months of interference from a singularly stupid mother-in-law.

Mary's own parents were dead. Her brothers and sisters would willingly have her to stay—as a temporary measure, while they chose her a new husband. It was an uncomfortable situation. At first she had hardly cared, letting herself be dumped around like a piece of furniture. Jack was dead, cut down in a skirmish with the Irish rebels, and nothing that happened to her would ever matter again. Lately the pinpricks had pierced more sharply through her numb perceptions, and she had begun to worry about her children. This homeless state was bad for them all. So she let Guy go on talking about his friend whose son might be a suitable match for Jane.

"He's a gentleman of great reputation. A good old family, somewhat reduced, but that's of no account, for he's in a fair way to restore all their former honours. He's made a reasonable fortune, entirely by his own merits; he has friends in the very highest places, and he'll be able to give his boy a splendid start in the world. Indeed, Jane would be lucky to marry the son of such a father."

"Well, what's the name of this paragon?" enquired Mary. "Have I ever heard of him?"

"Yes, you have heard of him." Guy took a simple pride in produing his effect. "It's Edward Garnham."

And Mary was impressed, she could not help it. "Edward Garnham! I didn't know he was a friend of yours, Guy."

"He's a bencher of my Inn, though he does not practice at the Bar, being fully occupied in the Queen's service. You know he's Walsingham's most trusted lieutenant."

"What manner of man is he? I've always fancied he must be unlike other people."

"He's a deal more able than most."

"Is that all?"

"What else do you—— Oh, I take your meaning! It's hard to tell, he never speaks of the past; I suppose he carries the signs of a special glory for those who can interpret them. You may judge for yourself, he's coming to dine tomorrow."

Mary felt she was being rushed; Guy was trying to force on this betrothal he had planned for Jane. All the same, it would be interesting to meet Edward Garnham. He was a man who fired the imagination.

She had her two elder children with her at

Holborn: Jane and the ten-year-old Roger. The little ones, Clemency and Greville, had been left in Sussez with their grandparents.

Next day she persuaded Jane into her new green taffeta dress; it was slashed with primrose satin and stiffly boned. The bodice was very tight. Jane, a lively child who was bursting out of all her clothes, did not appreciate this finery.

"I'd far sooner wear my old red dress," she grumbled, as her mother's expert fingers pulled at her laces.

"I dare say. Your uncle has guests coming, so you must do him credit. Do hold your stomach in, Jane."

"My uncle has guests every day."

"They aren't all so famous as Mr. Garnham."

"Oh. What's he famous for?"

"He's a martyr," volunteered her cousin Nan, who was sitting on the bed.

"Don't be a fool," said Jane scornfully. "You have to be dead to be a martyr. This man's still alive, I suppose? Or am I wearing my green taffeta to dine with a ghost?"

"No need to snap at poor Nan," said Mary. "And Mr. Garnham has been reckoned among the martyrs. Keep still while I do your hair."

"But I don't understand——"

"If you will only keep still I'll tell you the story."

You could always captivate Jane with a story. Docile, she lapsed into silence, hardly bothering to fidget and squeak until her mother brushed her brown, glossy curls.

"It happened eighteen years ago," said Mary, "in the bad times when Queen Mary was on the throne. You know that during her reign nearly four hundred Protestants were cruelly slaughtered because they would not give up their religion. Well, Edward Garnham was quite a young man then, a graduate of Cambridge University and very learned. He was himself a zealous Protestant, but he saw how hard the choice must be for people who had no skill in studying theology. So he wrote some pamphlets, explaining the arguments in simple language that anyone could follow. One of his friends printed them, others passed them around, and they did great harm to the papist cause. The author's name was soon an open secret; Mr. Garnham was arrested and ordered to reveal his associates. He refused, and they tortured him."

"How?" asked Jane.

"He was racked, five or six times, I believe. He never betrayed any of his companions, never gave an inch. When they saw it was hopeless they put him on trial for heresy. He was sentenced to death —to burn at the stake, like all the other martyrs."

"But they didn't burn him after all?"

"No, through God's mercy, for it was then Queen Mary died, just in the nick of time for Edward Garnham. The Lady Elizabeth—our own great Queen —succeeded, and Mr. Garnham was released, and rewarded for his courage. He's been in Her Majesty's service ever since; he has an important post under Mr. Francis Walsingham, the Secretary of State."

"He must be very brave," breathed Jane.

Yes, he must be very brave. Mary was herself deeply moved by a mental picture of the young prisoner lying in his cell maimed and exhausted, waiting for a horrible death. It was almost a shock, when they joined the company, to meet the confident and distinguished public servant, in an extremely well-cut doublet, who was telling his hostess how to plant a herb garden.

Edward Garnham was forty; one of those tall, fair Englishmen whose looks improved as they got older. He was built with the compact resilience of an athlete, and his features had a firm, clear edge. His mouth, uncompromising above the small, clipped beard, gave a hint of his inner character; Mary could imagine this man defying his tormentors in the spirit of Luther's famous declaration: "Here I stand—I can do no other."

For the moment it was all a matter of social civility. There were several other guests, as well as Guy's tribe of children and their cousins, Jane and Roger Dacre. The room was full of noise. Mary and her sister-in-law, Ann Freeland, made the usual admonishing, motherly faces at their young. Presently they went in to dinner.

When grace had been said Mary found herself sitting next to Mr. Garnham with no idea of what to say to him; eight months of mourning had left her out of practice for these gatherings. He did not give her any lead, and they both took refuge in the business of handing dishes and plates. Turbot and carp, roast hare, leg of lamb and gallardine sauce, spinach and dressed artichoke passed round the table in a steam of savoury smells, overpowering on a hot September morning.

Mary imagined Mr. Garnham would want to talk about his son and her daughter; she made some remark about Guy's children, and asked if he also had a large family.

"Three only, madam. I've a girl of fifteen and two sons."

"Do you send them to the country for the summer?"

"They've had a spell at my house in Essex. They returned last week; the plague season is over for this year. Nicholas and Harry are back at Paul's."

"That's the most notable school in London, isn't it? Your boys are fortunate."

It struck her that he would find Jane very poorly equipped by London standards. Girls didn't go to a grammar school, of course, but his daughter probably learnt all the fashionable subjects from half a dozen visiting masters. She made a tentative enquiry.

"Susan?" he said. "I should be sorry for the masters who wasted their knowledge on her, it would be like pouring water through a sieve. And what should she want with algebra and the rest? She can read her Bible, write a letter and cast up accounts; that's all a woman needs."

This was about the limit of Mary's own education, and Jane's, but she was nettled by his sweeping condescension.

"Some women are more aspiring," she retorted. "Didn't your wife want more for Susan, Mr. Garnham?"

"I doubt it; she cared nothing for books herself. Susan was nine when she died, and she had not noticed any deficiency."

Mary had not realized he was a widower, and was glad that the phrasing of her question had not given her away. It was odd that Guy had not warned her; he was usually full of hints and details. She ate a mouthful of salad, idly watching Garnham as he cut up his meat. He was a little clumsy about it, which was unexpected, propping his hand on the table. Had he hurt his wrist?

The question answered itself with a sickening pang of horror. When a man had been bound on the rack, each limb dragged slowly and deliberately away from his body, stretched to the agonizing tautness of a bowstring, he would never be entirely free from the threat of rheumatic swelling in the joints. He met her glance. His eyes were sea-grey and aloof; she felt that he was reading her mind and daring her to pity him. She flushed and looked down at her plate.

Garnham sipped his wine. "So you are an advocate of learned ladies, Mrs. Dacre. I wonder why? Have you studied Greek and Latin?"

"Not a word of either," she admitted.

"And you have done very well without them. Which proves my case."

"No, it doesn't," said Mary, rallying. "Just the contrary. You are getting the better of this argument, sir. If I had been properly taught I should be the victor."

He laughed. It was extraordinary how the sudden flash of gaiety changed his expression, bringing out a latent charm. He made no particular reference to Jane until the end of the meal, when he asked Mary whether her children had seen any of the sights of London. She told him they had arrived only three days ago; so far they had done nothing.

"My boys have a holiday on Saturday," he said. "If you would care to meet us for a tour of the City I should be honoured to escort you."

Mary accepted. She was not going to commit Jane to any formal betrothal, but it would be stupid to throw away the chance of a new family friendship which might lead to something closer in the future.

2

The Garnhams and Dacres met on Saturday, just inside Newgate Arch. As Edward presented his children to her, Mary's interest centred on the elder boy who might possibly become her son-in-law. She was faintly disappointed. Nicholas Garnham was too tall for his age; he moved with an awkward slouch. The English fairness that blazed so effectively in his father made him seem merely negative, and though his features were good, she hardly saw them; he gave her a brief, stiff bow, and then retired into the background.

Well, boys of fourteen were seldom at their best with strangers; it was too early to judge. His brother, Harry, at eleven, was more engaging; he fastened on to Roger. Mary could tell that they were two of a kind: tough little animals with a keen sense of enjoyment.

Susan Garnham was pretty, apart from an obstinate mouth and her clothes, which were deplorable. She was swathed in thick, reddish-purple kersey, and the elderly brim of her hat obliterated her small face. Mary wondered who dressed the poor child.

"I propose we should go first along Cheapside," suggested Garnham. "Tom, you'd better bring up the rear and see we don't lose any stragglers."

"Very well, sir," said the last member of the group, a dark and extremely good-looking young man of about twenty. His status was not explained.

They strolled down Newgate, past the Shambles, and into the wide expanse of Cheapside, the finest street in London, perhaps in Europe. Mary had been there before, on occasional holidays with Jack, but it was all new to Jane and Roger. They never stopped exclaiming and asking questions.

Was it called Cheapside because of the Market? Was the Market held here every day? What did they do when it rained? Who bought all the glazed pots and the pewter spoons and the little birds in cages? Surely there couldn't be enough people in London to want them all?

"And who lives in those splendid houses, sir?" asked Jane. "Do they belong to great noblemen?"

"No, to solid citizens—though there's enough wealth in those fourteen houses to buy up most of the lords at Court. That's Goldsmiths' Row."

Jane gazed respectfully at the gabled buildings, four storeys high, the homes of the jewellers and merchant bankers: even a little girl in the country had heard of Goldsmiths' Row.

Garnham and Tom shepherded the party across the street, between the coaches and waggons, to look through the doors and windows of the jewellers' shops at the scintillating treasure inside: cascades of pearls, dark lustrous rubies, clocks and ornaments winking in the sunlight, and delicate gold chains, each link shaped and painted like a tiny flower. There was a continual sauntering crowd round the windows, including several foreigners chattering away in their own languages. This free display was one of the glories of London.

When they left Cheapside they struck south through a warren of little streets, so narrow that the dangling shop signs nearly met overhead. Now they were in the old, unchanging heart of the capital, beautiful, chaotic and teeming: a city of timbered houses and pale stone churches clustering round the mighty bulk of St. Paul's Cathedral.

It was difficult to keep together. In Watling Street they lost Nicholas. The young man called Tom saw him loitering behind, and shouted his name. Nicholas peered about him and came uncertainly towards them. Mary realized that he was very shortsighted. She was sorry for him, though she was beginning to feel sure that he would not do for Jane.

"For heaven's sake, Nicholas, stop wool-gathering," said his father tersely.

"I'm sorry, sir," muttered the boy.

Mary had gathered that the young Garnhams were very much in awe of their father.

By now they had reached Fleet Street, a paradise for the young and simple. Jane and Roger were spellbound. They saw a strange tropical fish, alive and swimming in a tank of water; the story of Jael and Sisera performed in dumb-show, a sword-swallower and a man doing card tricks. Best of all, a motion or puppet-show.

Even when they had exhausted Fleet Street the children were still avid for more. Harry wanted to go to Eastcheap, where they had the best cook-shops. Susan thought Jane ought to see the Royal Exchange. Roger wanted to climb to the roof of St. Paul's.

Edward Garham settled the matter without consulting anyone. "Tom, you can hire a boat and take them downriver to the Tower and back."

Roger was delighted. "Shall we pass under London Bridge? Will our boat capsize?" he asked hopefully.

"Not at this tide," said Garnham, smiling. He turned to Mary. "Madam, if you have had your fill of wonders I thought you might prefer to rest at my house in Warwick Lane. You can trust Mr. Fletcher to see that Roger doesn't fall in the Thames, however hard he tries."

The young party set off, highly elated, and Garnham escorted Mary up Ave Maria Lane, across Paternoster Row at Amen Corner, and into Warwick Lane. This was evidently one of the streets where a gentleman could live; it was better paved than some, and the refuse had been swept out of the gutters.

Garnham's house was one of the largest; he took her in, and she looked round curiously. It was rather dark, which was inevitable; perhaps that made it seem cold and a little cheerless. The furnishings were rich, there was no lack of money here, but the general effect was impersonal, as though many of the pieces had been ordered unseen by a busy man whose main interests were outside his home. A dumpish, elderly matron appeared, jangling the keys at her waist and reciting a nervous welcome through a mouth that was too full of teeth. Garnham introduced her as Mrs. Sims, his cousin and housekeeper. One riddle was solved. Mary knew who had chosen Susan's clothes.

Mrs. Sims ushered Mary upstairs to the great chamber and sent a servant for some wine. After a sign from Garnham she left them alone.

Now, presumably, he would come to the subject

of Nicholas and Jane. Instead, he went on talking about London. Did Mary think she would like to live in a town?

Mary said truthfully that she thought it would be very pleasant. There was a pause. He got up and fetched something from a locked casket.

"I have a small trifle here, madam, that I should like you to accept—I hope it suits your taste."

It was a hat-brooch of exquisitely wrought gold and crystal, carrying the unmistakable elegance of Goldsmiths' Row. Mary was surprised. Was it the custom to blandish the mother of a prospective bride with such a valuable gift? She murmured a few words of admiration without actually taking the trinket. Garnham leant over and put it on the table beside her. In doing so, his hand brushed her shoulder and remained there, his fingers curling in a deliberate pressure through her sleeve. She had a close view of his grey eyes, intent and exploring, under curiously heavy lids. For an astonishing moment she thought he was going to kiss her. Then she moved abruptly, and his hand dropped away.

So Edward Garnham was the kind of man who became amorous at the slightest opportunity. She would never have suspected that. What disturbed her more was her own reaction. When he touched her she had felt a sudden and terrifying pleasure. Her whole body had seemed to quicken and then melt, she could hardly resist the impulse to slide back against the cushions like any casual wanton and let this stranger make love to her.

Aghast, she took a tight pull on herself, sitting rigidly stiff, her hands knotted in her lap. Garnham had gone to stand by the window. He said something she did not hear; she forced herself to concentrate.

"Your brother tells me that you are ready to consider a marriage."

"As to that, he may have exaggerated." Her own preoccupations were shelved in the need to think and act for Jane. "I'll be frank with you, sir. I could not agree to a definite betrothal. We must let time pass while the acquaintance ripens. I see no reason for haste."

"There I fear we differ, madam. I don't wish to seem importunate, but I should be grateful for an answer, one way or the other. Having resolved to marry again, I should like to sign the contract as soon as possible."

"*You* are resolved to marry!" She stared at him, completely astounded. Already confused, her wits were not working as well as usual. She had come here to discuss a marriage for Jane—and now, apparently, she was being asked to hand over her precious child to a widower of forty. It was monstrous.

"There has been some mistake," she said. "Guy told me it was Nicholas—but if you are to be the bridegroom there is no point in going any further. I could never consent to such a match. The disparity in age is far too great."

Garnham flushed. "I am sorry you should think so, madam," he said in a very hard voice.

Surely anyone must think so, Mary told herself indignantly. It was a ridiculous suggestion—so ridiculous that her common sense gave her a jolt, and she felt a qualm of uncertainty.

Garnham had also been putting two and two together. "You spoke of Nicholas," he said. "I don't see how this concerns him, unless—you can't suppose that I was asking for your daughter? What kind of besotted gull do you take me for?"

Mary gulped and said nothing.

"It is you that I am trying to marry, Mrs. Dacre. Perhaps you still consider the disparity in age too great," he added as an afterthought.

"We were at cross-purposes." She stumbled on the words in her haste and embarrassment. "You must know very well that I did not mean—that I could never be so discourteous."

There was a gap of twelve years between them, enough to have made her protest sound peculiarly insulting. There had been another implied insult, whether he realized it or not; that tentative caress, which she had taken for a piece of lecherous by-play, had been the perfectly honourable approach of a man who believed she was willing to marry him. She had made the most appalling fool of herself. But it wasn't her fault, and she was beginning to grasp what had happened.

"Mr. Garnham, did my brother lead you to imagine that I was anxious to marry again?"

"Yes. I thought he was going to plead my cause. What did he say to you?"

She told him. He looked incredulous for a moment, and then began to laugh.

"I should have thought Freeland was far too sober for such a puckish flight of fancy. Oh, it's true I've talked at times of making matches for my children, as we all do. But he was well aware of my present intention. What can have possessed him that he should serve us with such a trick?"

"He knew that I would refuse to meet you as a suitor." In a flood of mortification she burst out: "I could kill Guy for this! It was outrageous to place you in such a position. And I assure you, sir, this is no matter of personal antipathy. I should decline any offer that was made to me."

"I see." He came back and sat beside her on the settle, studying her thoughtfully. "May I know why you are so set against marriage?"

"It's barely eight months since my husband died," she said. "I loved him very dearly."

"Yes. I understand. Indeed, I am truly sorry for your loss." Some kind of condolence was unavoidable, yet she was convinced that he meant it, and that he had put aside his own claims and interests and was concentrating on hers.

"I suppose you know," he said, after a short silence, "that they will give you no peace until you do agree to marry? A young and beautiful woman can't manage alone in this world of ours, that's a plain fact and there's no escaping it. And the hard necessity may not be as evil as you think. Has it never struck you as strange that though our religion enforces such strict laws of chastity and fidelity, it has never asked us to keep a vow to the dead? Isn't that because God knows what is right for His creatures on this earth? Every grown man and woman should have a partner, every young family a home with two parents. If we ignore the pattern we are incomplete, and we suffer for it."

"It may be so," she whispered. "I had not seen it in that light."

"At least I can claim that I've tested my own argument, for I have tried to live alone, and found there were too many disadvantages. Which is why I am now seeking a wife. Mrs. Dacre, I haven't the effrontery to tell you that you ought to marry me;

you must have plenty of suitors. Let me speak to
you as a friend: I think you must learn to recognize
that you do need a husband, and then choose the
one you prefer."

She was too deeply concerned to brush this off
with a glib reply. An outside opinion always
sounded more convincing than good advice from relations. And this man was very persuasive. Had
Guy bargained for that when he threw them together in such a clumsy way? He could hardly have an-
ticipated the other result of her encounter with Garnham: that brief physical contact, and the primitive
and pagan elements that had blazed up like sparks
in a dry rick. Poor Guy, he would be scandalized.
Garnham, she decided, would not be scandalized at
all. Hadn't he said there were too many disadvantages in remaining unmarried?

She watched him cross the room to fetch her a
cup of wine. His looks went well with his heroic reputation. She tried to conjure up a picture of Jack,
and nothing came. He had deserted her. He had
insisted on going to the wars, got himself killed, and
now he wouldn't even protect her from the in-
terloper who wanted to take his place. She was
fighting back her tears. To sit and weep like a silly
kitchenmaid—that would be the last humiliation.

"I trust Roger was satisfied with the Tower,"
said Garnham. "The Traitors' Gate has a most
gloomy aspect from the river, and that's what small
boys relish."

He talked on, calmly. Mary drank her claret, listened, and was grateful for the neat way he had regained an ordinary social footing. He would not
pursue his courtship this afternoon; he was too
chivalrous, and far too intelligent. He could afford

these virtues, they were in themselves a recommendation.

While she clung with an obstinate loyalty to her memories of Jack, Mary knew already that she was going to marry Edward Garnham.

3

Mary tried half-heartedly to resist the pressure of circumstance. After a fortnight she gave in. She would have to take a new husband sooner or later; what was the pont of nursing her bereavement for a few months longer, merely to strike a bargain with some other unknown suitor in the end? It seemed wiser to marry Garnham while she had the chance. She liked and respected him; he would give her a home and make a good stepfather for her children.

The contract was signed, the banns were called, they had nothing to wait for. On a fine October morning they were married at St. Sepulchre's, his parish church. The service was suitably quiet; after the wedding breakfast Mary's children remained at Holborn and Garnham's went back to Warwick Lane, where very soon they would all seven have to settle down together as one family. In the meantime Garnham was taking his bride to his house at Maringale Bois in Essex, which she had not yet seen.

They rode out by Aldgate through the affluent suburb of Stratford-le-Bow, past Bethnal Green, and into the Forest.

In London you hardly noticed that autumn had come; here it was visible on every side, triumphant and in no way sad. The tall trees were shedding their summer thickness; the delicate, dark lines of

the branches seemed to flower against the sky,
lemon and russet and amber. They met a party of
hunters, and then some boys gathering nuts, whistling and calling to each other. Most of the time the
only sound was the crisp scuffle of dead leaves under their horses' feet. Garnham's groom kept his
distance; he had Mary's maid riding pillion behind
him, and was leading a packhorse. Mary breathed
in the warm golden smell of autumn in the country.

"I'd rather spend my wedding-day like this,"
said Garnham, "than mewed up at a banquet.
Thank God we escaped the junketings that are inflicted on the young."

"Oh yes," she agreed. "Have you ever remarked
how marriage-feasts are haunted by all the cronies
the bridegroom doesn't want to see? So determined
to make a fool of him if they can. When Jack and I
were married half the bright lads in the neighbourhood planted themselves under our window,
beating drums and singing bawdy songs till three in
the morning. Not that it made any difference."

She stopped, horrified. Of all the inappropriate
memories to drag out at such a moment.

"I'm sorry," she muttered. "I didn't think what I
was saying."

"Why should you be sorry? After so many years
with Dacre you can't banish him in a few weeks. I
haven't yet earned any right to be jealous."

"You are very kind, sir." Her gratitude demanded some return. "You must tell me about your
—about Elizabeth."

"There's little I wish to tell. My first marriage
was not so happy as yours."

She was surprised, having decided that he had
spent six years trying to mend a broken heart. It

would be easier to live with a man who was not always harking back to an idyllic past. But she must play fair with him; she mustn't make comparisons either.

Garnham had changed the subject and was now talking about his house.

"I hope I haven't given you a false impression, you may be disappointed. Maringale Bois means so much to me I am apt to glorify it. There's no great mansion, just an old manor house, and one that's seen hard times. My grandfather was a gambler; he milked the estate of everything he could get, and even then my father could never catch up with his debts. His troubles nearly broke him. I'm glad that I was able to square accounts at last—mend the roof and replenish the stock, so that he and my mother had some years of unclouded peace before they died." Even so, he added, there was nothing at all grand about Maringale Bois. Mary, catching the note of diffidence, was determined to like his home, however ugly or shabby it might be.

It was getting on for dusk when they rode down a long chase to a break in the trees and a village green, with a few cottages and a tiny wooden church. Straight ahead, on a rising slope, stood the Manor. It was over a hundred years old; you could see that it had once been fortified: there was still a moat spanned by a narrow bridge. The building itself was compact and satisfying. Between the weathered beams the butter-coloured plaster was grooved with intricate patterns. There were new brick chimneys springing from the tiled roof, and the windows, though small, were all of glass, sparkling in the sunset. No Italianate flourishes here, certainly—there was something far better; a harmo-

nious and simple dignity, perfectly in tune with the
Essex countryside. This was a proper setting for an
English gentleman.

Garnham looked at Mary anxiously.

"It's a beautiful house," she said. There was no
need to pretend, her delight was spontaneous. "I
don't wonder you love it so well."

He was obviously pleased. They crossed the
bridge to the main door. Garnham dismounted,
lifted his bride out of her saddle and carried her
over the threshold.

The hall was freshly panelled in pale oak and
augmented by a little carved gallery. There was a
pack of servants, bobbing and staring. One old man
patted the bridegroom fondly and called him Master Ned. When Mary had met them all Garnham
took her upstairs to the great chamber: a fine, airy
room with a massive king post holding up the roof.
Beyond it, another fine room, dominated by an
enormous bed.

Mary lost interest in the house and began to
worry about herself. It was absurd, at twenty-eight,
to feel so lost in a situation that most girls had en-
countered before they were eighteen: the first moment of isolation with a stranger. For her it had
been different, when her parents chose Jack—I
must not think of Jack, she told herself, as Garnham
took her cloak and gloves and laid them carefully
down. He turned back to her; if he was nervous he
did not show it. They had made a bargain, and they
had got to get used to each other in the most civilized way they could manage.

With a smooth dexterity he collected her into his
arms and kissed her mouth. He was gentle but un-
mistakably possessive. She was his wife now, and it

was her duty to give him whatever response he
asked for. Unfortunately, Mary found that her body
was weighted with lead and she could not feel anything at all.

Garnham stood back, surveying her with his level
glance. "Are you afraid of me?"

"No." And that was true. She was a sensible
young woman who knew what life required of her;
this freezing constraint had nothing to do with fear.
But she could not get it out of her head that she was
doing something wrong, alone in a bedchamber,
being embraced by a man she hardly knew. She did
not feel able to explain this fantastic notion to her
lawful husband, so she repeated, "No, I'm not
afraid of you, sir."

"Good. Do you think it would seem easier if you
called me by my name?"

Smiling a little, she said, "Edward."

"Mary."

They looked at each other. Then Edward kissed
her again, and this time the sparks blazed up as
they had that afternoon in London. She was suddenly alive with sensations, including one that was
both incongruous and prosaic. She realized that she
was ravenously hungry. Feeling a surge of confidence, she said so.

Edward laughed, and agreed that it was high
time they had supper. They went down to the
parlour, and Mary was further heartened by a hot
and very well-cooked meal. When they had finished, and the servants had left them, Edward got
up and came round to her chair, taking both her
hands in his firm grasp.

"If you are ready, my love, we'll go to bed."

Mary was ready. The strangeness was no longer disagreeable. And she had stopped thinking of Jack.

They spent the next week very contentedly. Edward enjoyed showing Mary everything at Mangale Bois, and she soon gathered how much he had done there. The original structure remained, but all the improvements dated from the last twenty years. Besides putting in the chimneys and the glass he had added the gallery, panelled some of the walls and chosen new furniture with a thoughtful care she had missed in his London house. He had laid out a formal garden, with an arbour and a terrace, fashionable conceits which did not interfere with the serious business of farming. There were no separate enclosures; the Lord of the Manor and his tenants cultivated neighbouring strips of land, waging together an incessant war against their deadly enemies: the deer and the bracken that tried to break in from the forest. Edward had a sound pair of oxen for the plough, a few head of cattle and sheep, pigs grubbing for windfalls in the orchard, a flock of geese and four hives of bees.

This was a world that Mary understood. She talked to the gardener and the dairymaid, inspected the stillroom, and made ambitious plans for preserving more fruit next summer. Edward watched her with a growing affection.

"I believe I did well in settling for you. Even though I might have waited for a lady who knew Latin and Greek. Or made a bid for your young daughter."

"You'll never let me forget that, will you?"

"I'll never forget your confusion when the truth finally broke through. Trying so hard to cancel

what you'd said of the disparity in age." He gave
her a challenging look. "Am I too old for you,
Mary?"

It was a question no man would ask unless he
was certain of the answer.

They were sitting on a bench at the end of the
garden, gazing across at the sunwashed walls of the
house. A maidservant was beating the dust out of
a rush mat. The stable cat woke up, stretched
languorously and went to sleep again. It was very
peaceful. Behind them, and all around, the Essex
woodland: beech and oak and hornbeam rioting in
their October gold against a blue sky.

"There was a time," she mused, "when the gap
between us was infinitely wide. I can remember the
fervent discussions of your trial when I was ten
years old. How incredible a glimpse of the future
would have been."

Edward had stiffened; she did not notice, absorbed in recollection.

"My parents conformed," she said. "It wasn't
very noble, but I'm afraid there were many like us
who went to Mass every Sunday for fear of the pen-
alties. I think my mother had it on her conscience;
she taught us the Protestant faith in secret. Someone gave her a copy of your pamphlet; when we
learnt that you were in prison she was so greatly
distressed. And then when the news came that the
Queen was dead there was such rejoicing, the bells
pealing and the bonfires, everyone foretelling what
good things would happen now that Elizabeth was
Queen. In the midst of it all my mother said, 'That
young man won't burn.' I couldn't understand why
she began to weep."

"And what am I supposed to make of that affecting story? Do you expect me to be grateful?"

She gaped at him, startled by the sting of hard contempt, so unlike anything she had heard from him before. His face had become pale and remote, the eyes hidden by those heavy lids.

"Edward, I don't know what I've said——"

"Don't you? Hasn't it struck you that I might have grown weary, over the years, of being always tethered to that one event? The man with the martyr's crown dangling over his head, an object of curiosity, a freak at a fair. I saw you studying me the day we first met, wondering how many of my joints they'd wrenched apart. As though no one had ever been racked before. You'd think I might have cut a different figure by now, but I am only esteemed for the sweet syrup of pity my story brings to those who took care never to taste anything sharper at first hand. I suppose there are fools who envy my good fortune. Let them feed their fancies on some other victim. I've no use for them."

He got up, brushing aside her little gesture of entreaty, and walked away between the trees.

Mary's first impulse was to burst into tears and rush back to the house, hurt and ill-used because he had been so wantonly unkind. The next moment she wanted to run after him into the wood, forcing on him that very gift of pity which he obviously hated. Instead, she stayed where she was, trying to work out what exactly had provoked this outburst.

She was staring at a rose-bush. It came into focus, heraldic with a late cascade of crimson flowers. Moving automatically, she went over and started to nip off the dead heads. If Edward wanted her he knew where to find her. She would not violate his privacy.

Presently her patience was rewarded. There was a hesitant step on the path behind her.

Speaking in her normal manner, she said: "This is an excellent soil for roses. I never saw any so fine."

"Mary, forgive me. You must think I'm a savage, so brutal and ungracious—can you believe that I am truly sorry?"

He was so close that he was touching her, she could feel the vibration of his heart-beats. She fumbled for his hand.

"It's of no account. I fear I have been very clumsy, probing into matters I don't fully understand."

"No one can understand." The words had a quiet desolation. "If I could tell you, make you see what it was like—but that's impossible. I can't bear to think of that time, of the anguish and horror. . . . You'll perceive that I'm not as brave as you thought." He drew a long breath, and continued, with a rigid detachment: "I should warn you that I sometimes have nightmares, when I feel my flesh being devoured by the flames. You are to pay no attention to anything I say in my sleep. I find it wiser to ignore this weakness, and you will have to do the same."

"It shall be as you wish," she whispered.

So that was the explanation. Mary flinched at even the small amount of pain that he could communicate. No wonder he would not discuss his ordeal, and rejected any stupid attempts to recall it. People treated him like the heroes who survived at the end of the plays and legends, unchanged by any number of harrowing disasters. It was not so in real life. Edward had been permanently scarred by suffering. This was the lifelong sacrifice he had made for his religion, and she was in no way equipped to ease or share it. All the eager compassion in the world was not enough. A very young bride might have seen herself as a ministering angel; Mary had too much experience to make that mistake.

Edward said: "I hope you can learn to bear with my moods. You are very good. And very beautiful," he added, almost to himself.

She was, in fact, pretty and graceful, nothing more. Jack had thought her beautiful because he was in love with her. It was some encouragement that Edward, even in the stress of his afflictions, shared the same illusion.

She had begun by regarding her second marriage as an answer to the problems of being Jack's widow. At the end of one week she was embroiled in the quite distinct problems of being Edward's wife.

4

They returned to London next day. As they left the country behind, Edward grew more and more silent. He might be brooding over his work. Or daunted, possibly, by the prospect of finding seven children in his rather cramped town house. Still, the boys would be at school all day, and Mary thought she could manage the girls.

"I hope Roger is accepted at Paul's," she said.

Although St. Paul's was a fee-paying school, no amount of money or connections could get a boy in unless he reached the required standard in both English and Latin.

"I'll take him round tomorrow," said Edward, "and have a word with the high master. I don't think you need fret, my dear. Roger's got his wits about him, and he wants to succeed. Unlike my brat."

"Harry?"

"Oh, Harry's well enough. I meant Nicholas. He's idle and careless, doesn't do a stroke of work— heaven knows how I'm to get him to Cambridge."

He had mentioned none of this before and it struck Mary that for the past week he had ignored everything outside the immediate present at Maringale.

When they got to Warwick Lane the house certainly did seem full of children. Mary's four ran at her, hugging her and bubbling with delight, their voices pitching higher and higher. She was vaguely aware that Edward's trio were greeting him with far more formality. Extricating herself from the clinging arms, she tried to make a friendly approach to her stepchildren. Nicholas stood on one leg and stammered. Susan made a stiff curtsey and ducked away when Mary kissed her. Only Harry came bouncing up cheerfully to ask: "Did you bring us any pies from Maringale? Old Meg always sends up a hamper." Harry, at least, was uncomplicated.

Mary decided to get her younger children to bed early with bowls of bread-and-milk. Clemency was seven and Greville five; they were almost feverish with excitement.

"We're going to live in London, live in London! Isn't it a fine, strange place, Mother? Did you know there's a man comes round the houses every day with tubs of water, and people pay for it? Fancy having to buy water."

"It costs a lot of pennies," announced Greville, "so I'm going to give up washing."

"Oh no, you aren't my lad." Mary reached for the soap.

Greville was sharing a bed with Roger; the two Garnham boys were next door. The three girls were to sleep in Susan's room, Clemency in the truckle bed. While Mary was unpacking the cloak-bags, Greville careered about on his hobby-horse, blowing an imaginary trumpet.

Susan appeared in the doorway of the room that had once been her private domain, looked critically at the clutter, and said: "Can't you keep him quiet? My father doesn't like us to make a noise."

Impudent little hussy, thought Mary, caught at a disadvantage and conscious of a slight apprehension. Edward was the master of the house and still, in many ways, an unknown quantity.

"Greville, do stop that braying. I wonder where Aunt Ann packed your nightrail, Clem."

Clemency was looking out of the window. "I can see the little tiny courtyard at the back. How odd it seems to have no proper garden. And no animals. I wish I could have brought the dogs, and the donkey, and the little lame squirrel that my father rescued from the snare." The loss of her pets and the alien surroundings overwhelmed the tired child; her face grew scarlet, her eyes grew ominously bright, and she bellowed, "I want my father!"

It was two years since Jack had gone to Ireland; his children had got used to living without him and this had lessened the shock of his death; they had not seemed to mind their mother's second marriage. Poor Clemency would have to choose this moment for a belated orgy of grief.

Mary cradled the little girl in her arms, trying to distract her from the heart-rending picture of her father lying in a cold churchyard, all alone, with no one to care for him any more. Trying also to control the stir of pain in her own heart, and hoping Edward would not come in to ask what was happening. Susan brushed past them and began to rummage in a chest. Presently she turned, holding out a dilapidated rag bundle, stitched in a vaguely human shape, with button eyes and a red woollen mouth.

"Would you like to take this to sleep with you, Clemency?"

Clemency choked back her sobs sufficiently to ask, "Is it yours?"

"Yes, my dear old Lob. My mother made him for me when I was two."

"Where is your mother?" Clemency was vaguely puzzled. "She's not here, is she?"

"Of course not," said Susan briskly. "She's in heaven, with your father."

For some reason this seemed to exorcise all painful images. Clemency said her prayers and went contented to bed, clutching the tattered Lob.

When they had tucked up both the children, Mary said to her stepdaughter: "You worked a marvellous cure, Susan. How very kind of you to think of it."

Susan turned aside, awkwardly. "You don't have to thank me. I know how she feels, that's all."

"Yes, I'm sure you do, my dear."

Mary was touched by compassion for this ungracious little creature in the ugly dress who fought against expressing her emotions. She would have to approach her obliquely and with care, but it should not be too difficult. There was plenty of affection there.

They sat down nine to supper in the parlour: Edward and Mary, the five elder children, Edward's cousin Mrs. Sims, and Tom Fletcher, the handsome dark boy who had come with them on their tour of the City, and who lived in the house; he was Edward's secretary. He was engaged in passing on obscure scraps of information which made sense only to Edward. There were allusions to pamphlets and passports and Orders in Council; severe strictures on some misguided person who thought he could get what he wanted by offering Edward a bribe. Mary listened, ignorant but fascinated. Presently Edward came down to a homelier level, and asked his sons how things were going at school.

Harry volunteered that the usher was a brute who treated them all like galley-slaves, but he was getting the hang of Euclid now, and he had won two fights.

"Splendid. You look to me remarkably healthy for a galley-slave. And, Nicholas, what's the news with you? Have you been studying the extra Latin I set you?"

"Yes, sir. I—I've caught up with the others, sir. Mr. Cade marked me alpha for my last essay."

Twelve years of bringing up children made it clear to Mary that Nicholas was lying. That slippery, nervous brightness was its own worst enemy. What did Edward make of it? He merely said that Nicholas must bring his books home on Friday, he would like to see them.

This unsettled Nicholas, who was helping himself to pease-pudding. Missing the plate by inches, he deposited a large spoonful on the table. Edward began to say something sharp, caught Mary's imploring glance, and restrained himself.

"Never mind, Nicholas," she reassured him. "Here, mop it up with this napkin."

Nicholas had no luck. Reaching for the cloth, his sleeve caught another dish, and a cannonade of sausages shot onto the floor, to the explosive giggles of the younger children.

"Well, pick them up." Edward's tone was dangerously quiet. "No, don't put them back in the dish! Good God, boy—do you have to be taught sense as well as manners? Fourteen years old, and you might be five. I don't know why Greville was put to bed early, for I'm sure he's more fit for a place in the parlour than you are."

The giggling had stopped. They were all

munching their supper and trying not to notice the unhappy Nicholas. Uncomfortably, Mary changed the subject by speaking to Roger about his first day at Paul's.

"Your stepfather is going to take you in the morning and present you to the master, so you'll be well supported."

"What's that?" Edward was still contemplating Nicholas, who was pursuing the last sausage underneath a chair. "Take Roger to school? I'm sorry, love, I forgot to tell you, I have to wait on the Secretary of State. Roger must go along with the other two. Provided Nicholas doesn't get lost on the way."

Mary felt deflated and unreasonably annoyed. She knew from the way Roger's mouth was drooping that he was downcast. He was not naturally timid, but a great London school must be an alarming place to a country-bred child, and no doubt that young monkey Harry had been regaling him with gruesome and exaggerated stories about life at Paul's.

"Would it help matters if I was to go with Roger?" suggested Tom Fletcher. "If you could spare me, sir?"

"That's a very good notion," said Edward. "You couldn't have a better escort, Roger. Tom was at Paul's, too, and a great man in his time; he carried away all the prizes."

Roger was considerably cheered. "I should like to go with Mr. Fletcher," he said politely.

"You don't have to call him Mr. Fletcher," Harry told him. "Tom's one of the family."

The subject of these tributes flushed with a diffident pleasure which Mary found rather surprising;

he had seemed such a very self-possessed young man.

"Where did you acquire Tom Fletcher?" she asked Edward later, when they were alone.

"He's my apprentice."

This must be a joke. Mary laughed, slightly mystified.

"There's more truth in that than you think." Edward sat back, stretching his long legs towards the fire. "Tom was bound an apprentice when he was little younger than Roger. I came across him eleven years ago when I had to arrest a villainous printer who'd published a seditious libel against the Queen. The fellow was sent to prison; I questioned his people and dismissed them, all except this little chap who had nowhere to go. His father, a poor coppersmith, had died of fever. The mother had farmed Tom out and then disappeared."

"How could any mother be so wicked? You wouldn't think it possible."

"He was like a stray dog. I hadn't the heart to turn him over to the constable, so I brought him back here to Elizabeth; at least we could give him shelter for the night. The next day Susan went down with measles. You can guess the sequel. All the children took it—and the nursemaid. By the time we'd done, Tom had been with us so long that I wanted to keep him. I could see he was wonderfully gifted. He'd taught himself to read at the printer's; I sent him to school and then to Cambridge. When he came down I decided to employ him as my secretary, and got Walsingham's permission to train him in the Government service. He shows every promise of going a long way, in spite of his humble birth; there are plenty like him these days, after all. So you see he's my apprentice—in two senses of the word. I fancy there are rumours that he is my bastard, and though that's utterly false, I do indeed love him like a son. I could wish that Nicholas had some of his quality. But what's the use of wishing?" He yawned. "Ah well, it's back to the grindstone. And I must be early astir in the morning."

Mary was up at six to see her menfolk dressed and fed before they set out for the day. Tom went off with the four boys—four because Greville was starting at a little school round the corner; Mary had meant to deliver him there herself, but her younger son was so disgusted at the idea of being taken to school by a woman that Tom had again stepped into the breach. Edward left a few minutes later, very handsome and elegant, for his conference with Mr. Francis Walsingham, the Secretary of State. The house now belonged to the women.

Mary told Jane and Clemency to finish unpacking and fold their clothes neatly away in the press. Perhaps Susan would see that they did it properly?

"And don't stand for any nonsense from them," she added. "I am very sorry to rob you of your privacy, Susan, by landing two young stepsisters in your room, but there was no other way we could all squeeze in. I'm sure you'll have them eating out of your hand, for you have a way with children." If this was diplomatic it was also quite sincere. Susan was good with children.

She was thawing visibly this morning, which was a blessing. A resentful stepdaughter of fifteen would be very trying, thought Mary, steeling herself to cope with someone who had more reason to resent the new Mr. Garnham.

Edward had told her about Eulalia Sims, her life

with a husband who had pilfered her dowry, ill-treated and finally deserted her. She must have been thankful to become the virtual mistress of her cousin's house during the six years that he was a widower. Now she was relegated to the position of a poor relation or waiting-gentlewoman; it could not be pleasant.

But Mrs. Sims seemed almost eager to hand over her responsibilities.

"You'll want the keys," she said, giving Mary the chain to hang at her waist. "I trust you'll find everything in order. So glad to have you here, my dear. You are so pretty, just what was needed, it will make all the difference—my cousin seems a new man."

"I thank you," said Mary, touched. "I hope we shall all deal comfortably together. You must guide me, cousin; will you tell me first about the servants?"

There were four women: a cook and a kitchen-maid, a chambermaid and a laundress; they were all good maids, though Hannah was apt to be saucy. A long digression, with examples of Hannah's sauciness. "And Ben, the serving-man, as well as Mr. Garnham's groom, though he sleeps round at the stable. . . . Now, what else? The linen? You would wish to see the linen?"

It was all brought out for her to inspect.

"A trifle thin, I fear," chattered Mrs. Sims. "We have done our best—sides to middle—but it's old stuff; Mr. Garnham has bought little since his wife died. Alack, what am I saying? His first wife . . ."

She chattered on. Mary sounded her about the children.

"Does Susan have many festivities? The boys and

girls in London are so gay."

"Oh no!" Mrs. Sims was quite shocked. "Her father would consider her too young. And, indeed, Susan would not choose to go into the kind of company you speak of, she has been strictly brought up and cares nothing for worldly vanities."

More's the pity, thought Mary. Susan, she felt, needed more attention than the threadbare linen.

When she had been shown the kitchens and talked to the maidservants, Mary went upstairs to sort her own belongings. She could hear the girls talking through the open door. Jane was prepared to admire Susan, which was a very good thing.

"What does Mr. Garnham do?" Jane was asking. "He isn't a lawyer like my uncle?"

"He is a lawyer, but that's by the way. All his time is given to serving Her Majesty. He holds a court appointment, and he is an assistant to the Secretary of State."

"Oh. That sounds very splendid. What does he have to do?"

"He has to keep a record of the foreigners that come into the country, why they come and where they go, in case they are enemy spies. And the same with Englishmen who wish to go abroad. He has to report to the Privy Council. That's only part of his work; there's a lot more, I don't understand it all, but he is deep in the confidence of Mr. Walsingham. He knows everything that goes on. Last year there was a man wanted to murder Lord Burleigh, and my father caught him; he was hanged at Tyburn. My father," said Susan proudly, "is much concerned with the safety of the Realm."

That was probably as good a definition as any. Like many of the Queen's servants, Edward held a couple of nominal offices under the Crown which, combined with the pension he had been granted when he came out of prison, assured him of a steady income. In return he carried out whatever orders the Privy Council gave him, and these, in 1576, with the growing menace from Rome and Spain, were chiefly concentrated on preserving the safety of the Realm.

All through the day Mary wondered how her boys were surviving the perils of their new schools. Greville came home clutching a hornbook on which he could identify the letters of the alphabet; he was speechless with pleasure at his own great learning. Roger came in later with his stepbrothers, full of the wonders of Paul's. It was so big, and there were so many people—but he didn't mind that; the other boys, prompted by Harry, had made him welcome, he had a host of friends already. The Latin? Oh, that was easy stuff, he'd done it all before.

Mary's heart lightened, and presently soared, when Edward walked into the hall and kissed her as though they had been separated for a year.

"How is it with you, sweetheart? Mr. Secretary says I am the image of a bridegroom. A little unbecoming, don't you think, at forty?"

"But very pleasant," she murmured, fingering the velvet of his sleeve.

Edward rather spoilt this tender moment by going to the foot of the stairs and shouting, "Nicholas!"

A face appeared in the shadows above them. "Sir?"

"Was it you borrowed my chessmen while I was away?"

"Oh. Yes, sir."

"Why haven't you returned them?"

"I—I don't know where they are."

"Find them, then," snapped his father. He turned back to Mary. "If anything vanishes in this house you may be sure that young jackdaw has borrowed it. Whatever can be broken, he breaks, and the rest is left lying around till the maids throw it away."

"Boys of his age are always careless." She hoped to placate him.

Edward had caught sight of Nicholas trying to slip downstairs unnoticed in his search for the missing chessmen.

"I suppose you don't recall where you had them last? No, to be sure, that's too much to expect. You never take much account of other people's property, do you, Nicholas? Well, get on! Don't just stand there gaping. You are going to find those pieces if it takes you all night, and you won't have any supper until you do."

Nicholas shifted miserably from one foot to the other and stared at the ground. Incompetent at the best, his father's lethal jibes obviously reduced him to a state of paralysing stupidity in which he could hardly think at all. He muttered that he did not know where to look next.

"You can try all the most likely places, can you not?" Edward spoke with the cold, pretended sweetness of extreme exasperation. "Good grief, Nicholas—I said the likely places! What would they be doing behind the arras? Do you think the mice play chess?"

This kind of scene was typical, as Mary discovered in the next two days, of Edward's attitude to his elder son. It seemed that poor Nicholas had a

fatal effect on his temper. Although Edward kept a
firm control on all his family, he was ready to put
up with a good deal of lively impudence from
Harry, and he was kind to Susan. He took a genuine interest in his four new stepchildren, and they
were delighted with him: this tall, fair man who
would look, so Jane informed her mother, "just like
St. George if he wasn't so old." Mary accepted this
remark in the right spirit, and was grateful to Edward for his sympathetic handling of her first
husband's children. If only he would spare a little of
that sympathy for Nicholas.

Of course the boy was infuriating. Unpunctual,
untidy, clumsy and lazy, he was doing badly at
school, and his many failings did not include the
tough, attractive devilry that most fathers would
forgive. He disliked fighting and did not care for
sport. He was a lonely figure, ambling along with
his thumbs through his belt, whatever interests he
might have hidden by an expression of clouded
vacancy. It must be galling for Edward to be sad-
dled with such an heir, and Mary was sorry for
them both. All the same, there was no blinking the
fact that Edward's continual savage comments were
doing the wretched boy more harm than good.
Nicholas was afraid of his father and showed it;
that, Mary thought, was the real trouble. Edward
had no use for cowards, and the resulting vicious
circle disclosed a side of his character she was not
anxious to recognize.

So that on Saturday when he suggested an
evening's music, her first thought was that this
would be another occasion for Nicholas to make a
fool of himself. It was an activity which had so
many pitfalls. Her pleasure was spoilt by the dread

of hearing again that slashing contempt when Nicholas inevitably lost his place or played a wrong note.

"The chest of viols, sir?" asked Tom.

"No, I think we'll try Byrd with the broken consort. What's your choice, Mary—the lute? Susan, you can have the cithern."

"I'd rather play the dulcimer."

"I dare say, but we don't require one. You'll manage well enough."

Jane was watching Tom get out the instruments. The pear-shaped lute, the beautifully carved cithern or guitar. Then the shawns, the sweet reed-pipes. He lifted the lid of the virginals in the corner. A broken consort, combining wind and strings, gave harmonies of the richest and most varied texture.

"Couldn't I play too?" asked Jane.

Edward looked enquiringly at Mary.

"She isn't fit for it yet. You can stand beside me, Jane, and follow the score."

Cousin Eulalia picked up her sewing, and the two younger boys sat on the floor, prepared to make an audience. Nicholas appeared in the doorway.

"Come along," said his father. "We need you here."

"I thought you meant to sing madrigals."

As his voice was breaking, no one could expect Nicholas to sing, and he had probably been hoping to escape the evening's entertainment. Mary took the sheet of music that Susan offered her; it had been carefully pricked out by hand, and looked rather alarming. Like every educated person, she had been taught to play at sight anything that was put in front of her; she wondered how far Nicholas could meet this test. He was standing beside her, vaguely holding his own copy.

"Do you know this?" she asked him.

"We have played it. Some time back."

He dropped the paper, and did not bother to pick it up, nor the pipe that lay on the table. She tuned her lute, waiting instinctively for a sharp word from Edward. But it was Edward who took up the pipe, while Nicholas, most surprisingly, went to sit down at the virginals, flexing his wrists.

It was an unusual instrument for a boy, and what happened next was so astonishing that Mary could hardly believe her ears. Nicholas touched the keys, and from his fingers there sprang an exquisite current of sound, every separate note like a drop of crystal, infallibly true and clear, filling the room with magic.

Entranced, she nearly forgot to join in. From where she stood she could watch Nicholas, leaning forward a little, his whole body subject to the strong and effortless rhythm of his hands. All the time they played she was conscious of the part borne by the virginals. He did not try to dominate; in that polyphonic pattern no instrument must override the rest, and Nicholas was far too good a musician to indulge in vulgar display, yet somehow he was holding them all together, and he was using his right to improvise with a flawless choice that must be quite instinctive.

When they finished she was feeling dazed; she had not quite caught up with her own impressions.

"That had a pleasing effect," remarked Tom with satisfaction, lowering his pipe.

"Pleasing!" echoed Mary. "It was celestial. Nicholas, I had no idea you were such a fine performer."

None of the family had seemed to notice anything out of the way. Edward greeted her remark with a rather satirical gleam of amusement, but only said: "We were a trifle thin in the middle. That was my fault. Where did I go astray, Nick?"

Nicholas twisted round on his stool. "You were in too great a hurry, sir. There should be more resonance in the slow passage, a kind of grandeur." He spoke with certainty, as though to an equal.

"Yes, I think you are right," said Edward meekly.

"He wasn't even reading the score." Mary was pursuing her thoughts aloud.

"He doesn't need to," Susan told her. "He only has to play a piece once and he has it by heart."

Roger was very much struck by this. "Do you mean it's all there in his memory? No wonder he hasn't any room for Latin declensions!"

His doting mother could cheerfully have boxed his ears.

Edward laughed outright. "That arrow goes home, Nick. Roger can see through you, if no one else can." And then, as Nicholas flushed: "Well, never mind that now. Shall we try our piece again?"

On a second playing, as the complicated melodies became familiar, Mary found her enjoyment growing. Celestial was the word—I know why they play harps in heaven, she thought, plucking from the lute-strings her own contribution to the consorted glory.

After that Nicholas played to them alone on the virginals, a simple theme by Tallis on which he embroidered his own variations. Moving round to sit by the fire, Mary could see him in profile. He was transformed, alive with intelligence and ardour. She realized for the first time that he was very like Edward. And Edward never took his eyes off his son.

They forgot how late it was, the children were eventually packed off to bed in a hurry, with admonitions about getting up in the morning.

"I couldn't have believed it," said Mary after they had gone. "I never heard a boy of his age play so well. And few men to equal him, either."

"Nick isn't such a dunce as he makes out. Perhaps you will now acquit me of being a monster?" Edward appealed to Tom. "Mrs. Garnham has been suffering agonies on Nick's behalf; the poor unfortunate simpleton, badgered beyond reason over the faults he is too dull to correct. And I am cast as the villain."

Cousin Eulalia clucked reproachfully. Tom grinned, and said, "You are the victim of a grave injustice, sir."

"You are talking nonsense," put in Mary, nettled because he was, in fact, a shade too accurate. "In any case, I don't follow your argument. His talent for music does not prove him a scholar. It's a different matter, surely?"

"His music is a gift from God, far exceeding any other buried talents he may have—I'll grant you that. But it isn't the whole story. What you heard tonight didn't fall on him like a mantle from the skies, and it didn't come by dreaming in idleness. It needed hour upon hour of hard striving—patience, energy and self-command. Wait till you've heard him practising; my cousin can tell you, he drives us nearly demented."

Cousin Eulalia had gathered up her silks. She paused on her way out. "Yes, indeed. Those scales!

Dear Nicholas is such a persistent boy."

"It's worth it in the end," said Tom. He was helping Edward sort through a bundle of sheet-music.

"Well worth it," agreed Edward. "And that's the point. Nicholas may have no great taste for Latin or mathematics, but if he devoted one quarter of his energy and ability to his lessons he could be sure of a safe, level place in the school—I never asked that he should reach the top. Tom, you're asleep on your feet; off to bed with you, I'll deal with this.

Tom bowed and said good night. The room was quiet and still now, with only the rustle of paper, and Edward's quick, neat movements as he slapped together the pile of music.

"I find it very strange," said Mary. "If Nicholas is capable of achieving so much why does he waste his time and bring down your wrath on his head every day of the week?" She thought of the miseries Nicholas endured; boys were odd, intractable creatures; this one was beyond her. "You don't think his weak sight affects him—but you must have considered that already?"

"Yes, when he began schooling. It made no difference. He was a promising scholar then. There's no great mystery, my dear. I know very well what's wrong with Master Nicholas. He has only one desire, to earn his living as a paid musician, and since he can't do that, the rest of the world may go hang."

"Get his living by music! No, I suppose he can't do that; it's hardly a profession for a gentleman. It seems a pity, though. Tallis and Byrd are men of some standing."

"They are also men of some genius," said Ed-

ward drily. "Nick may think he can surpass them.
I don't. They are the exceptions. Most of those fellows are lucky if they can find refuge as the household servants of a rich lord; they rate a little above
the yeomen and far below the usher. I've more ambition than that for my heir. How could he keep
pace with the friends he has known from his birth,
or support a wife and family, on the pittance he
would earn? How could he maintain Maringale
when I am dead? He'll have to make terms with life,
as we all do. Music can remain his chief recreation;
anything more would be folly."

"Yes," she said. "Yes, I accept that. I wonder
merely whether you may not overreach yourself.
You are very severe with the boy, and it does not
always answer."

"There are reasons why I have to take a special
care of Nicholas."

"What reasons?"

He did not answer.

"Edward, what do you mean? What are you
trying to protect him from?"

"Aren't there enough dangers that beset a boy
growing into manhood? The world, the flesh and
the devil. We needn't dig any deeper, Mary. My
office requires me to ask many questions of many
people; I have an inveterate dislike of being questioned on my own account."

She felt as though a door had been shut in her
face. Not slammed, but pushed home with a firm
civility. She would not get any more out of him, not
at present; she was still finding her way with him,
very much of a beginner.

He smiled down at her, saying inconsequently,
"How small you are," as though this was some rare

and delightful quality for which she deserved great credit.

Mary allowed herself to be distracted.

5

It was pleasant to walk to church with Edward at the head of their young family, three fair Garnhams and four dark Dacres, all in spruce white ruffs. Their well-groomed Sunday burnish reminded Mary of the King's daughter in the psalm: they were like the polished corners of the temple. It was pleasant also to meet Edward's friends in the exchange of dinner and supper parties, though this was a slow and infrequent process, because Edward had so little time for these junketings. Almost every waking hour was consumed by his work—that mysterious work which took him off to the Council and the Court, and to many less salubrious places that she was left to guess about.

When he came home he would often hurry through a meal, preoccupied, with a bundle of papers beside him, and then retire to his study and write endless reports for the Secretary of State. Mary had an uneasy sensation that she was further from Edward now than she had been during their first happy week at Maringale. The sheer weight of every-day cares was building a wedge between them instead of a bridge. However, she stifled her faint sense of disappointment, and set about the business of housekeeping in her new surroundings.

One day in November Edward and Mary were

invited to a christening party in Clerkenwell. Lady
Foyle was the daughter of a wealthy merchant who
had bought the large estate next to Maringale Bois;
that was how Edward had come to know the family.
Blanche Piggot had risen in the world through a
series of ascending marriages. Her first husband
had been a country squire, her second a courtier
and her third was a prominent general who was
connected with half the nobility. The new baby was
Sir Gilbert Foyle's heir, and the christening would
be very grand. When the day came Edward said
he could not go. He had some urgent work on hand,
it was impossible to play truant.

"James and Margery Radcliffe will take you in
their coach; you'll be well escorted."

Mary was very disappointed, though she was getting used to this kind of setback.

"I shan't enjoy it without you," she said. "I'd as
soon stay at home."

"Nonsense. You'll have to go. The Foyles are our
nearest neighbours in Essex, and Blanche is Susan's
godmother. Though I freely admit—she's an odious
woman, like all these spoilt heiresses. There's no
love lost between us."

"If you dislike her why did you choose her as a
godmother for Susan? A sacrifice to Mammon?"

"That's was Elizabeth's wish. She and Blanche
were sworn allies, and much good it did either of
them. But there it is; we must keep in with the
Foyles."

There was always a constraint when Edward
spoke of his first wife, which he hardly ever did. It
now turned out that Lady Foyle had been a partisan of Elizabeth, which would not tend to make her
very cordial towards Mary; did Edward imagine

this would encourage her to brave the party alone? How extraordinary men were.

Mary would have liked to take Susan with her, but Susan was frightened of festivities, frightened even of new clothes. She strained her hair back flat against her skull, in spite of Mary's hints, and met all outsiders with a curious indifference. She warmed to animation only among the small events of domestic life; she was at her best with the younger children, Clemency and Greville, whose arrival had given her a great new interest. As though she was still essentially a sister, a daughter, and nothing more.

So Mary resigned herself to going alone. She put on a new dress of sapphire velvet with enormous winged sleeves and a lace ruff that was stiffly wired to stand up behind her head like a frame. The colour intensified the brilliant blue of her eyes, and the huge hooped farthingale accentuated her tiny waist. Mary was vain enough to know that she was looking very pretty and a credit to her husband. She went down to his study to be admired, only to find he had already gone out.

She had to make do with a paean of praise from Cousin Eulalia, Susan, Jane and the maids. The one note of dissent came from Clemency, who said flatly: "You're so boned and padded you don't feel real. I like you better when you are being my mother."

Mary laughed, and hugged her, and then they heard the clatter of the Radcliffes' coach in the lane outside.

James Radcliffe was Edward's closest friend, an extremely clever scholar with a private fortune and a plump, sweet-tempered wife who gossiped gaily

all the way to Clerkenwell. Radcliffe leant against
the window and grumbled about the traffic. London was so jammed with coaches and waggons it
would be quicker to walk.

The christening was like any other, with an
added veneer of wealth. The church was hung with
tapestry and the font was made of silver; one of the
sponsors was an earl. But the baby let out the usual
lusty roar when the water touched his forehead, and
everyone said he was getting rid of the devil. He was
wrapped in his chrissom robe, while hypocras and
comfits were handed round among the congregation.

After this they adjourned to the Foyles' town
mansion, all packing into the state bedchamber,
where the mother was still lying-in. Her bed-curtains, specially ordered for the occasion, were made
of white satin, embroidered with pearls and gold
thread.

"They must have cost hundreds of pounds,"
murmured Mrs. Radcliffe.

Mary could well believe it. The whole gathering
had a rarefied magnificence: the clothes, the jewels,
the scent, the clear, positive voices which were un-
mistakably the voices of conscious power. The
Radcliffes found a number of friends and presented
them to Mary; there were also various remote and
splendid figures who intrigued her very much, and
she wished Edward had been there to identify them
for her. He undoubtedly knew them, for besides
being a personage in his own right he had access to
the Court, which was a closed world to her and
always would be. There was a magic ring of
aristocratic ladies who belonged to the Palace, but
the wives of ordinary gentlemen did not accompany

their husbands to the Court of the Virgin Queen.

In due course Mary and the Radcliffes paid their respects to the lady of the house. With the contrariness of fate, Blanche Foyle was as dark as a gypsy, a flamboyant creature, luxuriating in her wide white bed and inspecting the gifts that had been brought for her baby: caudle cups and silver bells; corals and apostle spoons. No one would have guessed that she was thirty-five, the mother of two previous families, with a son at Oxford.

When she heard Mary's name her mouth curved in a slow smile.

"So you are the new Mrs. Garnham. I'm happy to meet you, madam. And what has become of your bridegroom?"

"He was kept away by the pressure of public affairs, madam. He charged me to convey his apologies to your ladyship, and to offer you his congratulations with my own."

"Oh, this burden of public affairs! You've married into a sorry profession, madam. On my word, I pity you."

"You need not, my lady," said Mary crisply.

She produced her tribute, a small silver platter with a design showing Moses in the bulrushes. Lady Foyle received it with the correct amount of rapture, and then asked: "How is Susan? You must bring her to see me, if she can conquer her aversion to going out in company, poor lamb. There, at least, is a disposition that may still be moulded, if you have enough zeal."

Mary made a noncommittal answer. She was beginning to see why Edward disliked Blanche Foyle. After a few more guarded pleasantries she curtseyed and moved away.

The room was crowded; Mary and James Radcliffe found themselves hemmed in a few yards from the bed, so that they could not help catching the comments that were flying about a few yards behind them.

"History repeats itself."

"Garnham makes a habit of marrying beautiful women and then neglecting them. What a dog in the manger the fellow is."

There was an eddy of laughter, flippant rather than malicious, from the group of intimates who surrounded Lady Foyle, and through it her own scornful verdict: "This is a fair pattern of the marriage, after a mere matter of weeks. Didn't I prophesy how it would be?"

Mary felt the blood racing under her skin. It was stupid to mind what they said, these worldly strangers who knew nothing of the deep affection and tenderness that Edward gave her when they were alone. Yet she could not deaden the stab of humiliation; she knew that her face and neck were scarlet, as she twisted the fronds of her feather fan and tried to pretend that she had not heard.

Radcliffe slipped a consoling hand through her arm. "Pay no attention to their spite. It's chiefly founded on envy."

Someone else had noticed her distress. Sir Gilbert Foyle quelled his wife and her faction with a warning frown, and came over to speak to Mary, a handsome, grey-haired soldier with an assured charm of manner.

"Will you give my regards to your husband, madam, and tell him how sorry I am that he wasn't here to see my son baptized? Not that I expected him—anyone with a grain of sense must know that

Garnham has other fish to fry today. He's dealing with Matthew Austin, I take it?"

"Yes. That is, I think he may be, sir."

Edward seldom told Mary where he was going but it now struck her that his important engagement had probably been at the Tower. Matthew Austin, an elderly Catholic with many ties on the Continent, had been accused of acting as an agent of the King of Spain. He had certainly been living very comfortably on Spanish pay—he had taken it, he said, with the laudable intention of tricking the Dons out of their money and giving nothing in return.

"Do you think Austin will talk, sir?" Radcliffe asked Foyle.

"Yes, I fancy he'll prove an easy nut to crack, a greedy, self-indulgent villain, not a fanatic."

"He's past sixty, and his health is poor. They dare not go too far."

"Well, Garnham can judge his power of endurance better than most men. He won't embarrass Mr. Secretary with a corpse they didn't bargain for."

Mary, as she listened, found herself grappling with an aspect of Edward's work she had been too simple, or perhaps too soft, to contemplate before. She was left with a horrible suspicion of what he was doing at the Tower.

When Foyle was distracted by some other guests, she asked Radcliffe outright, "Is Edward torturing that old man?"

"Edward doesn't apply the instruments himself," said Radcliffe, shocked.

"But he is there, in the cell, watching?"

"Someone has to put the questions; they can't

leave it to the ignorant warders."

"How can he bear to be a witness, remembering his own anguish——"

"Surely that gives him an undisputed right to be present? You could call it poetic justice." He saw her repugnance, which he mistook for feminine sensibility. "The examining of prisoners is an ugly necessity; no need for you to trouble your head over it."

Mary did not argue with him. Lady Foyle's sneering remarks were forgotten now; she wanted to get away from the party, but for another reason. She was very silent on the drive back to Warwick Lane.

When she got in she was told that Edward was already home and in his study. She went there at once. He was sitting at his table, with a sheet of paper in front of him, but it was quite blank; he had not started to write.

She looked at him: the fine bones, the character-lines of restraint and control, the traditional fair colouring of a heroic knight in a legend—he reminded her children of St. George. And the grey eyes that welcomed her had seen such a different sight an hour ago. Was it possible?

"How was the christening, my love? Plenty of pomp and display, I don't doubt?"

"Yes, it was done with all ceremony. . . . Edward, there's something I must ask you. They said —Mr. Radcliffe and Sir Gilbert—they said you were at the Tower, plying that wretched Austin with questions, while he was being tortured. Is it true?"

"Yes, it's true." His voice was low and faintly defensive. He shifted a little in his chair.

"I hoped they were mistaken. I didn't want to believe—Edward, how could you play such a part? You of all men?"

"It was my duty to be there. Not a duty I relish —and certainly not one I should choose to discuss with you. I'm afraid you may find it displeasing, but don't brood over it, Mary. It's no concern of yours."

"Everything you do is my concern."

"I think not," he said coldly. "I have authority to govern your actions; you hold no jurisdiction over mine. That was implicit in our marriage vows. However, since this subject affects you so strongly, I'll try to set your doubts at rest. There's no reason to stand there like an avenging angel; you'll hear me just as well if you sit down."

She moved to the nearest stool. "Go on."

"You must keep a due sense of proportion," he said. "Torture is a vile and brutal business; every civilized man abhors it. Yet in this imperfect world we often have to use methods we detest. Look at the sufferings caused by the most righteous war."

"War is inevitable and it does have some rules of chivalry. I don't see how deliberate cruelty to one helpless prisoner can ever be justified. It seems iniquitous to me—and altogether horrible that *you* should condone such a pratice."

"Why am I singled out? Because I am your husband? I bring the reek of blood too close to you, is that it? You don't care for the touch of a butcher's hands?" The words carried an undertone of rigid anger, and those hands—graceful and carefully tended—gripped the edge of the table, white to the knuckles.

"Edward, you must know what I mean. After all

the agonies that have haunted your memory for the
last eighteen years how can you inflict the same
pain on any other creature, no matter how good
your intentions may be? Did it ever lessen your
hurts to know that the Catholics honestly thought
they were justified in torturing you?"

"My God, haven't I warned you to leave my past
alone, you impudent little shrew?" He was suddenly so furious that he had to pause and master his
breathing. "In any event, your whole argument is
false and irrelevant. No one, not even a Catholic,
can believe he is justified in defying Magna Carta
by wanton acts of tyranny. I was a loyal subject of
Queen Mary, I had committed no sin of any sort
against the State. All I did was to champion the
faith I was brought up in, which happened to be the
lawfully established Church of this realm, ratified
by the Queen's two predecessors before she ever
came to the throne. When they arrested me it was
not for treason, nor even for heresy; they simply
wanted the names of other men who had answered
the same call of conscience. For this I was racked
five separate times. Do you dare to suggest that
such things are done in England now? That there is
any resemblance between Austin's case and mine?"

Mary, shattered by this attack, still clung in her
mind to the real resemblance: that both he and
Austin had been subjected to an outrage which she
considered totally wrong in itself. But she had no
chance to interrupt.

"If you think we are hounding a misguided saint
into martyrdom you must be far more ignorant
than I supposed. Or else wilfully stupid. Don't you
know what they are after, men of Austin's kind, and
what they mean to do? They are ready to murder

the Queen, with the Pope's blessing—there's a reward promised in their heaven for that bloody deed.
And if they succeed they'll bring in the Queen of
Scots, with a foreign army to support her, and all
the glories of the Holy Inquisition. It will be twenty
times worse than the last reign. If you are too young
to recall that, at least look towards the future. Do
you want to see Roger and Greville burn at Smithfield? Do you want to see Jane and Clemency raped
by Spanish mercenaries? Because that is what you
will see, my dear, unless we can catch all the insidious devils like Austin and get their secrets from
them, and I don't care what means we employ to
rid England of such vermin."

The voice that outlined these terrible prophecies
was now calm and passionless, and this somehow
deepened the impression of a man who had mea-
sured his enemies and was implacably armed
against them.

"There's one more fact you should know," he
added. "I hate the Catholics. To me they are all
tainted stock, every man, woman and child, and I
wish they could be swept off this fair island into the
sea. But I have never abused my power as an Officer of the Crown. Interrogation by force is re-
served for those who are suspected of treason. In the
course of my career I have had to prosecute many
ordinary papists for minor offences. I have persecuted none. I hope you have the grace to admit
the distinction."

Mary did not answer, too stunned by Edward's
whole attitude. She had not met anything like this
before and the effect was physically disturbing.
Here, behind the quiet phrases, was obsessive hatred, deadly and unsheathed.

He had walked over to the press, picking up a
bundle of papers.

"Still not satisfied?" he enquired. "Perhaps you
are contemplating a sermon on Christian forgiveness? Let me advise you to wait until you yourself have something to forgive."

He reached out and gave the door of the press an
irritable slam. Then, as she watched him, he reeled
back and almost fell, clutching his left arm and
gasping with pain.

She jumped up. "Edward—what is it?"

Swearing, he pushed past her and opened the
door which led into the hall. Nicholas was there
with his satchel; he broke out of his usual inertia.
Catching one word from Edward, he vanished at a
run, calling: "Tom! Tom, come quickly to my
father!"

Edward sat down, still nursing his arm, which
seemed to be hanging at a very queer angle.
Bewildered, Mary went towards him, but before
she could offer any help Tom was in the room, deft
and competent.

Coming up behind his master, he said, "We'll
soon have it back, sir." He grasped Edward firmly
by the shoulders; there was some delicate pulling
and pressing, a most disagreeable click, and then,
apparently, it was all over.

Edward was wiping the sweat from his forehead,
and saying: "A neat piece of carpentry, Tom. I
thank you."

Nicholas reappeared with a cup of wine which he
had managed not to spill.

"Good boy," said his father gratefully. He swallowed the reviving draught in two gulps.

"Is the pain very bad, sir?"

"It's passing off now."

"What happened?" Mary asked Tom.

"Mr. Garnham has a loose joint that works adrift from the socket every now and again—one of his old injuries. Simple enough to set the limb in place if you have the knack. I think I could teach you, madam, so that you would be prepared for any future occasion."

Still gazing into the empty cup, Edward forestalled her reply.

"You may find, Tom, that Mrs. Garnham considers this to be a judgment on me, for being so cruel to the papists. I dare say she thinks that a few sharp twinges are very salutary."

"How can you say so?" protested Mary, cut to the quick. "You know it isn't true."

She caught an incredulous murmur from Nicholas, and was aware that he and Tom were studying her with blank indignation, as well they might, if she had really been the heartless monster that Edward suggested.

He was pursuing his own resentment. "Maybe you imagine that I can stage these dramas at will, in order to excite pity? This one seems confoundedly opportune."

There was no way of countering that bitter derision, which would twist everything she said. Edward's son and protégé had both drawn closer to him, instinctively showing their allegiance. Mary felt their silent reproach smoulder to a point of actual hostility.

They were bound to Edward by years of unquestioning hero worship. Outside that invisible unity, Mary was isolated, a lonely alien. More than that, they had contrived to put her in the wrong, as though she was the one who had broken every law of humane conduct.

She could not fight against such odds, nor stay here where she was so plainly unwanted. Accepting defeat, she got herself out of the room with what shreds of dignity she could cling to for protection.

6

It was still two hours till supper-time. Mary climbed automatically out of her rich sapphire dress and put on an old milaine fustian which she wore every day. She needed some violent outlet for the emotions that had been roused by the scene in Edward's study.

She went downstairs, through the cheerful kitchen where the maids were gossiping and the pans sizzling over the fire, and into the sanctuary of her stillroom. Fetching the pestle and mortar, she began pounding almonds for the supply of marchpane she made every week. The activity helped her to think.

Am I an unnatural wife? she wondered. Was it wrong to believe in the ultimate value of mercy because Edward had once been the victim of men who showed him none? Some women, if their husbands had been so ill-treated, would be crying out for the blood of every papist in the country. That's how he expects me to behave, she thought; they all do. Well, I may be ignorant and untaught, but I have principles too, and I can't alter them. With her smattering of education Mary had breathed in that air of mental independence which had infected all Englishwomen since the Queen began to reign. Entirely subject to their husbands, there was a private fastness where they now called their souls their own.

With the vigour of frustration she crushed the white nuts until they danced under the pestle in smaller and smaller fragments. The desire to break something gave her a faint indication of those impulses which she found so dangerous in Edward.

Presently the maids' chatter in the kitchen stopped, and Mary heard a man's footsteps on the stone flags. She waited, watching the door. The man who came in was Tom Fletcher. She greeted him with a mixture of relief and disappointment.

"Could I have a word with you, madam?"

"By all means, Tom." She could guess, without much pleasure, what he wanted to talk about.

He leant against the table, and contemplated his feet. He was extremely handsome, with his dark eyes, white teeth and cleft chin, the hallmark of a particular masculine attraction. At the moment he was very much embarrassed.

"I hope you'll forgive me if I seem to be impertinent, but I think you have formed a mistaken picture of Mr. Garnham's part in the interrogation of prisoners. He doesn't enjoy it, I assure you."

"Did I accuse him of enjoying it? You have no right to draw such an inference merely because I dislike the whole business." She studied the keen young face, unclouded by any doubts. "Do you attend these sessions too?"

"I was there today. And there have been two similar cases since I became Mr. Garnham's secretary. You should understand, madam, that this method is only a last resort, when there are vital secrets at stake. Even then the Council is most reluctant to use force."

"I'm glad to hear it."

"No more glad than he is, I assure you. Anyone can tell you that he finds it a desperate ordeal. He is so overcome by compassion for the prisoners."

She was taken aback. This was not what she had gathered from Edward himself.

"It's true, I promise you," said the boy. "He implores them, almost begs them to make a voluntary confession, and if that fails he'll strain every ounce of wit and subtlety to dig out the facts as quick as he can get them, with the very least infliction of pain. He says that if you can surprise a man with an unexpected question he'll often give way through confusion rather than fear. And once they start talking they don't stop. As for that old rogue today—he was no hero. They'd no sooner got the boot on him than the whole story came pouring out, and a great deal more than he was willing to invent—you never heard such a hodge-podge. The warders were inclined to jeer at him, wanting a bit of sport. Mr. Garnham tore them in shreds, told them what he thought of savages who mocked a fellow-creature in his hour of degradation. Then he comforted the old man and tried to lighten his despair."

Mary was astounded. Why couldn't Edward have explained? Was he too proud?

Tom was helping himself to blanched almonds out of the jar. She smiled at him.

"You're very much attached to my husband, aren't you?"

"He's given me everything I have," said Tom simply. "He took me in when I was destitute, sent me to school and to Cambridge, opened countless windows on worlds I should never have known otherwise. That morning he came to Zadok Rowley's shop where I was apprenticed I'd never seen such a godlike being. Rowley was arrested, we were all dismissed, and I was obliged to admit the fact, so shaming to a child, that I had no one who cared for me and nowhere to go. I shall never forget how kind Mr. Garnham was. Not only ready to shelter a pauper brat, but able to perceive that the brat had feelings like any ordinary mortal. He gave me the sense of being someone in my own right; it was the first of many gifts. It's through him alone that I've grown so far from my wretched beginnings. I'm not a gentleman; he's provided me with the means to pass for one and something that counts infinitely more: he's shown me, by example, what a gentleman should be."

And the example had not been wasted, she thought. Whatever his antecedents, this charming and intelligent boy of twenty-one had acquired the qualities that were supposed to go with gentle birth.

"I'm glad you've told me this," she said. "I'm still groping to understand the nature of his work; you have helped to sweep away some delusions. I'll make my peace with him this evening."

Having formed this good resolution it was damping to discover that Edward had gone out, leaving the curt message that he would get his supper at a tavern. He did not return until after midnight.

She was lying awake in the dark, feeling guilty because she had rushed to condemn his treatment of Austin without the slightest evidence of what had really happened. What right had she to accuse him of cruelty when he was reluctantly doing his duty as a servant of the Council? She had put the ugliest interpretation on the whole story. She must make it very plain that she did not dread "the touch of a butcher's hands." That remark echoed in her conscience.

When the door opened softly she sat up, pulling back the bed-curtains.

"Edward, I've waited so long."

He stood still. The candle he was carrying threw up his shadow on the arras; he looked immensely tall.

"You ought to be asleep."

"I couldn't sleep until you came home. Dear heart, I'm sorry I preached at you in that arrogant fashion. I should have known better——"

"Oh, for heaven's sake! Can't you let the topic die? I've had a heavy day, and I think I might now be permitted to get some rest."

"I only wanted to tell you I'm sorry——"

"I haven't the smallest interest in anything you want to tell me. Now will you leave me in peace."

Mary's heart shrivelled into a tight lump. After the pictures Tom had conjured up of Edward's chivalry the bleak words came like a slap in the face.

He snuffed out the light and got into bed, turning deliberately away from her.

"Does your shoulder still ache?" she whispered, clutching at any excuse for his rejection.

He did not reply. She lay tense in the blind, unyielding silence. The tears were swimming down her cheeks on to the pillow. However hard she struggled he must know that she was crying. He did not relent. It seemed that he had no pity to spare for her.

The next morning it was just as bad. He would not speak to her. Mary had never lived with a man who sulked. Her father had been a roaring, genial

autocrat. During her first marriage she and Jack
had argued and teased each other; their very rare
quarrels had come and gone like lightning. She was
not prepared for this glacial stranger who stared
past her as though she was invisible. She was
thankful when he left the house.

Miserably she settled to the daily chores; order-
ing the meals, scolding Doracas, the chambermaid,
for neglecting to sweep the stairs.

Tom had gone out with Edward; an hour later he
was back.

"Mr. Garnham sent me with a message,
madam."

"Yes?" There was a flicker of hope, but the
message was not an olive-branch.

"He's invited a Frenchman and his wife to stay;
I was to warn you of their arrival, and ask that you
make ready to receive them."

"A Frenchman and his wife?" repeated Mary,
bewildered.

"Yes, madam. They are Huguenots, escaping
from Catholic tyranny. They landed this morning,
without money or possessions. Mr. Garnham often
gives refuge to such people until they can find somewhere else to go."

"But, Tom—where are they to sleep? Perhaps
Mr. Garnham has forgotten that this house is full to
overflowing."

Tom was disconcerted. Manlike, he and Edward
had both forgotten. Until recently there had been
eleven people living in the house; now, with the ad-
dition of Mary, her children and her maid, there
were seventeen.

For a moment they could neither of them think
what to do.

"I'll move out and fend for myself," Tom volunteered. "One of the neighbours will take me in. Then Roger and Greville can make shift in my room, and you may give theirs to the guests."

This seemed the best solution. There was a great deal for Mary to do while Tom went off to fetch Monsieur and Madame d'Aubais, who were waiting at an inn near the Custom House. At least it took her mind off her own troubles. She collected an army of helpers: Cousin Eulalia, Susan, Jane and two of the maids. Clemency ran about, meaning well and getting in their way, as they trailed to and fro with sheets and warming-pans, Tom's belongings, the boys' belongings—there were an enormous number of things to move about in different directions.

Roger and Greville's room seemed very small and shabby, and the four-poster bed sagged downhill on the uneven floor. It was an old one Mary had brought from Sussex, and it had not been improved by its present owners, who used it as a carrack of the Queen's Navy or an Irish fort. She prodded the feather-bed; it was decidedly lumpy. Still, these unfortunate foreigners would hardly be critical.

"They've come," called Clemency, who was keeping watch. She bounced with excitement. "The French lady and gentleman have come!"

Mary went down to greet her unknown guests.

Etienne d'Aubais was an ugly little man whose high, bald forehead shone as though it had been polished. He bowed and kissed Mary's hand, thanking her in careful English for her kindness.

"I am most happy that we can help you, monsieur. I dare say you would like some refreshment? Your wife will be the better for it."

Madame d'Aubais was a brittle, tightly boned lady with jet-black hair under a fashionable hat that had become pathetically tousled on her travels. She followed Mary mutely into the parlour, and subsided into a chair.

Mary offered her some soup and a glass of wine.

"It is French, no?" asked the visitor.

"Canary, madam. I think you will find it sustaining."

Madame d'Aubais sipped the wine suspiciously. As she revived her glance darted about the room, sharp with discontent.

"It is very dark here. I did not know London would be like this. Who is that shouting in the road?"

"A street-crier, selling coals. He'll soon move on."

"I hope so. I cannot abide any loud noise. I must tell you, madame, that I have been accustomed to very different environs, and after two days tossing on that terrible ship I shall die if I do not get some rest. That rude peasant must be instantly told to go away."

"He is going, Margot. You'll rest peacefully here." Her husband patted her hand, and said in an aside to Mary, "She is worn out; she has suffered so much these last weeks."

"Donc, it faut encore souffrir." Madame d'Aubais's voice rose to a querulous whine, and they began a conversation in French, apparently thinking their hostess could not understand them.

Here they were wrong. One of Mary's uncles had studied on the Continent and brought home a Genevan wife. Tante Jeanne had taken a fancy to her pretty niece, and taught her quite enough French to follow what was going on. She listened with mixed emotions, her face a polite mask.

"We should never have come here, Etienne; I knew it was a mistake. That man is not a fit acquaintance for persons of our rank. He is a bourgeois, some sort of clerk——"

"An Under-Secretary, *ma mie,* and that is far grander than you think. He is an important servant of the English Queen, and a great Christian hero. He is also extremely well born."

"Then why does he live in this mean house in a common street? Why did we ever come to London? The whole city stinks, and I know we shall find fleas and lice in the bedding."

"This house doesn't stink, and there will be no lice. See, there are fresh rushes on the floor, and scented pomanders. . . . *Cherie,* don't you think we should accept God's will, and be grateful to these foreigners who are so good to us?"

D'Aubais looked worn to desperation himself, but he went on soothing the nearly hysterical woman who clung to his arm, gentle and cheerful, without a trace of irritation. Mary got up and slipped quietly out of the room.

The door was open, and Tom was standing just outside, scarlet with indignation.

"Of all the impudent bitches——"

"Softly, Tom. They'll hear you."

"Much I care!" But he continued his tirade in a whisper. "To come here begging her bread, and then say ours is too coarse for her. You'd think any fool could read Mr. Garnham's quality in his bearing. And how dare she suggest this house is lousy?"

"Well, we do have fleas," admitted Mary. "As fast as I get rid of them you all bring them in again from the town. I suppose the French gentry keep aloof from the herd and don't work for their living. One thing's certain: I'll have to put the d'Aubaises in our bedchamber, even though it means more changing of sheets. I can't lodge them in that wretched garret."

"Why should you turn out for them, madam? It would serve her right if she slept in the cellar."

"I'm not thinking of her. It's Monsieur d'Aubais who would pay for their discomfort, poor little man. He has eyes like a sad spaniel."

She set off on another bedmaking expedition, and was transferring some of her own possessions to the boys' room when Edward came to find her.

He said, very stiffly: "I'm sorry to have thrust this visitation on you without warning, madam. I hope you are not too much put out by the extra labour."

"Not in the least, sir," she replied, with equal formality.

"I feel bound to care for such people when I can." He noticed the odd assortment of things she was carrying. "Where are you going with all that gear?"

Mary explained, with a slightly excessive patience, as though she was speaking to an idiot, that the duty of being kind to foreign Protestants was rather more difficult now that his house was so crowded.

"I'm afraid I never considered—it was stupid of me." He was taken at a disadvantage, and could only repeat, "I'm sorry you've had so much trouble, madam."

"That's of no account." She was so riled by his distant civility that she could not resist an acid comment. "I am perfectly willing to care for any victims of persecution; perhaps you expect me to reserve all my pity for the Catholics?"

Edward flushed. "Your conduct is always impeccable. I am sure you derive great satisfaction from being so virtuous." He turned abruptly and walked away.

"Why did I have to say that?" she wondered. Now she had made him more angry than ever, and he would go on punishing her in this way that hurt more than any amount of violent raging. Despondently she forced herself back to the job in hand.

Madame d'Aubais was persuaded to lie down. She was soon asleep, and she slept soundly through the day, quite undisturbed by the vulgar street-criers under her window. She emerged in time for supper in a much calmer mood, her sallow face alert as she tried to assess the exact social position of these English barbarians.

Such a plain house, with no gates or forecourt; so few attendants—the single waiting-gentlewoman turned out to be some sort of cousin; it was quite wrong that the secretary should sit at the same table and call his patron's children by their Christian names. Full of misgivings, she went on probing. So Monsieur Garnham was an advocate? This was very low. But he had access to the Royal Palace and went there constantly? *Tiens!* Her eye was caught by the painted coat of arms above the mantel. Edward's quarterings were impressive. She did not know what to make of him.

Mary was amused by her growing confusion. She herself had never before realized how far England had broken from the feudal traditions which had encrusted the whole of Europe for centuries.

Madame d'Aubais was shocked to learn that the boys went to school with the sons of ordinary shopkeepers.

"It is not the custom in France for gentlemen of illustrious lineage to mingle with such base and inferior persons, or allow their children to be polluted. Are there no tutors in England?"

"The nobility employ their own schoolmasters," said Edward. His good manners were unruffled by this impertinence. He shot a repressive glance at Harry, who was nearly exploding with giggles at the idea of being polluted by his particular friend at Paul's, whose father happened to be the Lord Mayor. "Most private gentlemen are now agreed that their sons get the best grounding at a grammar school."

"And this prepares them for your universities?" asked Etienne d'Aubais, who had been trying unsuccessfully to interrupt his wife.

"Yes. There are schools established in all the large towns. In the country it's different; until lately my stepson was taught by his grandfather's chaplain."

"Your stepson?"

The visitors had assumed that their host and hostess were the parents of the whole brood of children. Edward and Mary both began to explain; the relationships were complicated, especially as they had all been talking English. Without thinking, Mary switched into French.

"Ah, now I comprehend." Margot d'Aubais added, with her first sign of approval: "You speak very correctly, madame. Yet your husband informed us this morning that you had no command of any language but your own."

Mary had been pleased to note Edward's astonishment at her fluent French. She said: "I am still capable of surprising my husband—on a variety of subjects. We have been married two months."

"Then we must offer our felicitations. So you are a bride? I should not have guessed."

Mary's gaiety was quenched. No one would guess, she reflected sadly, from the manner of her bridegroom. She stared at her plate, while the conversation flowed around her, and was only roused by a quiet voice at her side.

"Therefore you understood every word that my wife and I exchanged in this room this morning. Madame, what am I to say? Such a shabby return for your charity——"

"You have no call to reproach yourself, monsieur," she said quickly. "Your wife was tired, your situation was preying on her mind; who knows how I might act in her place?"

"You are very generous. It is true my poor Margot is out of tune with the world. She has endured such a terrible weight of affliction."

The little man started to describe Margot's sufferings, the loss of the luxurious home and the secure position she had been brought up to regard as a right; how could any woman face such trials without complaining? Mary was convinced that Margot was a natural complainer who would have invented her own hardships if they had not been provided by the Catholics. Her husband did not seem to reckon that he had an reason for grumbling. He had been threatened, degraded, imprisoned, rescued and hunted like an animal. Several of his family had been murdered in the Massacre of St. Bartholomew four years ago. She had gathered these details from Tom: d'Aubais did not mention them. He spoke of religious persecution as though it was a tragic malady rather than a crime, and apparently bore no malice. Mary had never met anyone so amazingly tolerant. She found herself liking him very much indeed.

For his sake she did her best to like his wife. It was an uphill struggle, and the evening passed very slowly.

When the party finally broke up, Edward and Mary were left to the rigours of their temporary bedchamber. It really was no more than a garret, being sliced out of an angle of the gables, with the whole of one wall at a steep slant, and the bed taking up most of the floor-space. Edward, robbed of his dressing-closet, could not find anywhere to put things down. It was extremely awkward for two people in the middle of a quarrel to be penned in such close quarters. They ignored each other as best they could, nearly collided at the basin, and apologized with a stony politeness.

There was a thick beam running across the centre of the room. Mary had hardly noticed it before, as her little boys could pass easily underneath it, and so could she. To Edward, well over six foot tall, it was a menace. Inevitably, he banged his head, and the unnatural silence was shattered by a string of highly articulate curses.

"I fear this lodging is very uncomfortable for you, sir," said Mary with a small, pleading tremor. She had got to the stage of feeling that everything was her fault.

Edward stopped swearing and looked straight at her for the first time that day. Then he announced, with a portentous gravity, "It is not the custom for gentlemen of my illustrious lineage to be knocked on the head by a base and inferior beam."

She blinked at him, and gave a gasp of relief. "Edward——"

He made a sudden movement towards her and hit his head again. Ducking under the beam he seized her, they stumbled, and collapsed, helpless with laughter, on the edge of the bed.

"Edward, isn't she the silliest woman you ever met?"

"It's only her folly that makes her tolerable. Did you see her examining her plate and wondering how a humble attorney could have a family crest?"

"She's hunting everywhere for lice."

"I hope they bite her. My darling, I must have been out of my wits to land you with such a millstone."

"I don't care. So long as you aren't angry with me any more."

"I've been a brute," he said slowly. He wasn't laughing now. "It was a disgraceful display of bad temper, and I haven't a word to say in my defense. My gentle little love, are you going to forgive me?"

"So that I can derive more satisfaction from my virtue?" she quoted in her turn.

"Don't," he implored her. "I deserve that, and much worse, but if you knew how I loathe the devil that possesses me—Mary, be merciful."

"Dear heart, I was just jesting. I didn't mean to hurt you."

She could not bear the note of supplication which obscured her image of the strong, self-confident man whom, in spite of his faults, she was learning to love with a heart-searing intensity unlike anything in her previous experience. She put up her hand to ruffle his hair, which was as fair as a child's, and to trace the taut line of the cheekbone above the beard.

The old warped timbers of the bed creaked and listed still further at the edge where they were sitting.

"This is a monstrous piece of furniture," murmured Mary. "Madame d'Aubais would think very poorly of it."

"I don't propose to share it with Madame d'Aubais," said Edward in his dryest manner. Then he said, "Beloved," with an urgency that swept away the events of the last two days, and with them all doubts and reservations.

7

Etienne and Margot d'Aubais remained at Warwick Lane for a month. The Garnhams found him a delightful visitor, his wife drove them nearly mad with her pride and affectations. D'Aubais was trying to find work, and it was not easy. London was swamped with Huguenot immigrants. The poorer sort could set up in their old trades; the gentlemen were mostly reduced to giving French lessons, a fate which horrified Margot, and when she heard that Etienne had actually accepted a post as tutor she made a scene that rocked the whole house.

But there was no help for it. They had to eat, as her husband told her reasonably, and they could not live on charity for ever. So they went off to Chelsea, and Mary had her house to herself again.

It was Christmas; there was a sparkle of gaiety in the air, and the working life of London came to a standstill. There were feasts, masques and games—and, of course, the exchange of family presents.

Above the chorus of gratitude from the other children there was a special degree of awestruck rapture from Nicholas. His father had given him a splendid and most expensive lute for his very own.

He played it almost without stopping for several days, and when Edward finally told him they could not bear another note he carried it about the house with him as carefully as though he was nursing a baby.

"Like enough he'll take it to bed with him next," said Harry. "And I shall have to sleep on the floor."

"At least it wouldn't kick all night as you do," retorted Nicholas.

He was very different from the inky, sullen boy who trudged drearily home from Paul's in term-time. During the holiday he could concentrate on his music. When they went out he was frequently asked to play; everyone praised his talent, and his father was proud of him. All of which was very good for him. He was quite without conceit.

"Can you desert your lute for an hour," Mary said, "and escort me to Blackfriars? I want to take a pot of quince marmalade to old Mrs. Trotter, she's been ailing over Christmas."

Nicholas came willingly enough. There had been an early shower, and now it was a light, shiny day and the city was washed clean. Above the steep roof-tops the church spires, too many to count, glittered needle-bright after the rain. The pigeons wheeled about them, and down below there were little groups of citizens in their best clothes hurrying off to their jollifications.

"London is beautiful today," she said.

"I like it best when the bells are pealing for some great procession. You hear a fanfare of trumpets a long way off, and then another, and perhaps the Tower cannon. And the marching feet, very grave and solemn, come nearer, keeping time with the drums. Each harmony enhancing the other, like a broken consort."

How strange, she thought, his whole perception of beauty and excitement is translated into sound.

"Do you hear tunes in your head all the time, Nick?"

"Oh yes. In my dreams too. I dreamed a most marvellous melody the other night, and when I woke it turned into "Three Blind Mice". . . . I dare say you think I'm a fool, madam, but, you see, music is the only skill I shall ever have."

She hoped he would not say so to Edward, and was beginning to expostulate when she was interrupted by a cry from the other side of the road.

"Why, Mary! Mary Dacre!"

There was a tall woman in a blue cloak, attended by a servant. "Eleanor!" called Mary. They hurried to meet each other.

Eleanor Quinton came from the same corner of Sussex as the Freelands and Dacres. She had married and gone to live in Derbyshire, but there was still that well-forged link that comes from a shared childhood. She had written to Mary after Jack was killed.

She murmured something about him now. "Dear Mary, my heart bled for you, but I knew you wouldn't give way to vain repining, nor would he have wished it. I am happy to see you looking so well—and so fine. What brings you to London? I suppose you are staying with Guy? This young man must be one of your nephews, for I know it can't be Roger."

"This is my stepson."

"Your stepson! Then you are married again—I had no word of that. The most excellent news, you must tell me everything." This was rather difficult, as she went chattering on without a break. "Gervase and I are with his cousins near Westminster. You must dine with us, one day next week

perhaps, so that we may meet your husband. I hope
he is as handsome and brave as you deserve. She'll
have to say yes to that," turning to Nicholas, "since
he is your father."

Nicholas blinked at her, completely out of his
depth.

"He is exceedingly handsome and brave," said
Mary, smiling. "And a great deal else besides."

"I must speedily make his acquaintance. You
haven't yet told me his name."

"Edward Garnham." Mary felt a surge of pride
in announcing her new husband's name, aware of
the impression it always created.

Mrs. Quinton was certainly impressed. There
was actually a gap of several seconds before she
found her tongue: "Edward Garnham? So that is
who—indeed, you are moving in exalted circles,
small wonder that we haven't met. It isn't likely
that our paths would cross. Yet you can surely visit
me, when there is a day to spare—I don't know,
poor Gervase is much occupied with a troublesome
lawsuit. Lord save us, I mustn't stand dawdling
here, I'm late already."

After twittering a few more inconsequent fragments she embraced Mary, asked rather vaguely for
her address, and went bustling off down the street
at a great pace, her servant plodding behind.

"What an odd lady," remarked Nicholas.

"Oh, she was just the same as a girl. She
progresses by fits and starts, you soon learn to take
her measure."

Though surely there had been a curious under-
current at the end of that conversation? Could
Eleanor possibly imagine that the Garnhams,
puffed up by the glories of his official position, were

too grand to associate with country squires? How
foolish people are, thought Mary, remembering
Margot d'Aubais. She must ask the Quintons to
dinner and allay any doubts. She poured all this out
to Edward when she got home from Blackfriars.

"Eleanor was most anxious to meet you, though
she seemed somewhat overcome when I told her
your name."

"I can well believe it," he said, unexpectedly
ironic. "And did she still want to meet me? Or did
she run like a hare?"

"She was in a hurry—Edward, how did you
guess? What do you mean?"

"Mrs. Quinton is a Catholic recusant."

"I had no idea! Are you certain of it? Her own
family, the Brasseys, go to church every Sunday.
You must be mistaken."

"The Brasseys conform to save paying the fine.
They contrive to face both ways. The Quintons are
all declared papists. This Gervase has kept out of
mischief so far, but his brother's a priest in Rome."

Mary was astonished by his detailed knowledge
of the Catholic gentry. Was this an essential part of
his work, probing for disloyalty, even where it had
never existed? At least she had solved the puzzle of
Eleanor's abrupt retreat. Knowing what Edward
thought of the Catholics, Mary began for the first
time to wonder what the Catholics thought of him.
Was he a sinister person to be avoided and feared?
A bogey to frighten naughty children? It was a disagreeable notion.

Edward said: "We can't have friends in that
quarter. I'm sorry, Mary."

"No," she agreed slowly. "I can see how you
would dislike the acquaintance." And Mr. Quinton

would dislike it too; he was probably telling his wife so at this moment. How troublesome men were. "I must visit Eleanor by myself. I'm sure she will understand."

"It's you who don't understand," said Edward after a short pause. "You cannot visit her at all."

"Why not? She is one of my oldest friends." It had not dawned on her that he would try to cut her off from ordinary men and women simply because they were Catholics. There was no suggestion here of treason or Spanish plots, no other possible objection. "Why shouldn't I see her if I wish to? There are papists admitted at Court, you mix with them constantly there, and in other men's houses."

"That's beside the mark. I can treat them with civility on common ground. I have to. Which is not the same as seeking them out deliberately and suing for their goodwill. You might as well foster a nest of vipers and have done with it. They are a pernicious breed, there's not one I would admit to my house, and I won't have you contaminated by their company."

"You are making a mountain out of a molehill," snapped Mary, thoroughly irritated by this extravagance.

She forgot she and Eleanor had got on very well without each other for years on end. All the Brasseys belonged to her youth, to memories of the beloved dead, her parents and Jack. Eleanor had been there, that wonderful Christmas long ago, when Mary and Jack had found the beans in their slices of the Twelfth Night cake, and put on the paper crowns of the chosen King and Queen of the Revels, as a new generation of boys and girls would be doing all over England tonight. Why should she break with her past, just because Edward felt this morbid hostility towards the most innocent Catholics?

"You fling out these wild accusations without a grain of substance to support them. What harm has Eleanor ever done to anyone? What is it to you how she says her prayers? Give me one good reason why I must not meet her."

"I'll give you the best of reasons. Because I have forbidden you to do so."

"If that's all you can say——"

"All? Is it so slight a matter? Do I have to remind you that you once made a promise to obey me?"

Mary was trembling with anger. It was intolerable of him to speak to her in that peremptory way, as though she was a child to be taught her duty. Jack had never told her to obey him. (In fact, though she would not admit it, she had been the stronger of the two, which was not the best preparation for marriage with Edward.)

"Come," he said, quite gently. "You aren't going to quarrel with me over Mrs. Quinton; she can't be so important to you, for I never heard you mention her name until today. If you insist on visiting her against my wishes you'll be putting yourself completely in the wrong, and that would be fatal. I know this much about you, my dear—you'll never fight successfully in a bad cause. You have too keen a conscience."

And of course he was right, that was what made him so infuriating. She had promised to obey him; even, she supposed, when he was prejudiced and dictatorial.

He reached for her hand and held it lightly, in an almost pleading gesture which he could well afford, since he knew he was winning.

Reluctantly she felt her independent toughness dissolve at the coaxing in his voice and the caressing friction of his fingers on her wrist. It was physically impossible for her to be angry with Edward when he used these weapons. Better give in gracefully, and enjoy the last day of the revels without thinking too hard. Yet through the hours of dazzle and gaiety her mind retained its critical faculty. It struck her that whenever they disagreed Edward thought he could solve their problems by making love to her. Which might be charming at the time, but it wouldn't produce a cure.

The next morning they all came down to earth with a bump. Christmas was over for another year. Edward was brisk and preoccupied. Tom, distinctly pale, with dark furrows under his eyes, was in no state to play the model secretary, and Edward was being rather sharp with him when they left the house on official business. The boys dragged gloomily off to school. The girls were listless. Too much rich food, thought Mary, sending them to help Hannah with the household washing.

The rooms looked bare now that the kissing-rings and evergreen garlands had been taken down, but they had left some traces: Mary was retrieving bits of shrivelled holly from behind the settle in the great chamber when Ben announced: "Mounseer Dobey."

She was delighted to see him. He had travelled by boat from Chelsea to buy books for his pupils in Paul's Churchyard.

"You come in a most welcome hour to cheer us. We are all out of sorts, and the house is full of dead leaves. You'll stay to dinner? Now there is no sense refusing—as if we should let you go and eat by yourself at an Ordinary."

You could press Etienne d'Aubais to accept a free meal without insulting him. He had independence and dignity of the right kind, but no false pride.

A smile beamed all over his broad, thick features, and spread upwards to the hairless dome of his forehead.

"Tell me your news, monsieur. How is your wife?"

She is well, I thank you. Though a trifle melancholy in remembering the past at this season."

"Yes. I noticed when you were here on Sunday."

"Poor Margot, she cannot comprehend that the English do not care how we celebrate Christmas in France. Why should they?"

That shrew is making trouble again, thought Mary. Not one man in a thousand would bear it as patiently as he does—and she is too great a fool to know how lucky she is.

She said, "I marvel how some women are blessed with husbands they do nothing to deserve."

D'Aubais gazed into the fire. "If that is said on my account, you are mistaken. I have little to recommend me as a husband. I am a fat, ugly fellow, a pauper and an exile, and I have given my wife no child."

"How can you speak so ill of yourself?" she responded indignantly. Though what he said was basically true, it seemed trivial beside the qualities that she discerned in him—toleration and loving-kindness, an inward peace that seemed intensely precious. She asked abruptly, "Do you hate the Catholics?"

He looked slightly baffled by the change of subject. "The Catholics? Not any more. That is the way to self-destruction. Hatred does more harm in the end than the crimes that bring it to birth. No, I do not hate the Catholics."

"Edward does."

"That may be. His sufferings have been more acute than mine. They never tortured me."

"They killed your brother and sister. Forgive me if I am too blunt."

"Do you think I ever forget? Yet I must not forget either that we are all children of God, and that if I give way to hatred I too am a murderer."

"I know," she said; "that's what I find so terrible."

The Frenchman surveyed her doubtfully. "I am a little confused. What is the connection between my failings as a husband and Edward's bitterness towards his persecutors? Is it that you have troubles within your own marriage—but I should not ask such a question."

Mary was seized by a longing to confide in him. She was sure that this little man, unimpressive and even comic at first sight, was spiritually more mature than anyone she had ever met.

She began to tell him how Edward was haunted by the horrors of the past—which did not prevent him condoning those same horrors when they were inflicted on his enemies. Of his saying that all papists were tainted, every man, woman and child, and he wished they could be swept into the sea.

"And however much I love and respect him, and try to be a good wife to him, I can't escape the certainty that there is something very wrong here."

"He has been in hell," said d'Aubais in a low voice. "In effect he is still a prisoner."

"Yes. That is why—I wonder if I can make you see? There are people who would say that he, above all men, is justified in his hatred. Because he was bound on the rack, while they pulled his arms and legs as though they were tearing up a plant by the roots—indeed, it sickens the mind to think what they did to him."

She paused, twisting her handkerchief, and forced herself to speak dispassionately. "If that was the whole story I should not wonder at his desire for vengeance. I should not care to judge him. Only there is more. Afterwards, as you know, they tried him for heresy. He stood his ground. He knew what was in store for him, and he was willing to accept a martyr's death. Isn't that the ultimate victory of a Christian warrior? I was brought up to believe that those who reached the heights of martyrdom were granted a divine charity, a supernatural grace. When I married Edward I thought he would be different—oh, I can't say how. Perhaps I expected him to look on life as you do. Instead, his sufferings have brought him nothing but misery and the temptation to hurt others. As though, after all his faithful service, God has denied him the light of consolation." Would d'Aubais think she was being blasphemous or merely stupid? "Am I talking like a simpleton? Is my picture of the saints just a pious falsehood that they serve up to us in church?"

"No, it is a very clear picture. There is one detail you have overlooked. Edward was not martyred."

"That doesn't alter the fact that he was fully prepared for death, subjected to every torment but the last. He lay in his cell, day after day, waiting for them to fetch him. Surely it was in their solitary meditations before they ever got to Smithfield that the souls of the martyrs were perfected?"

"Have you never asked yourself why he was spared?"

"That's no mystery. Queen Mary died, and he was released——"

"I did not mean the exact circumstance, rather the workings of destiny behind it. Four hundred Protestants went to the stake; why, among so many, was Edward Garnham chosen to receive an extension of his life on this earth?"

She said nothing, unable to see where he was heading.

"This crown of martyrdom," pursued d'Aubais, "what does it signify? Why should such dreadful agonies be regarded as an emblem of God's favour? Because the aspiration is allowed to give the most extreme proof of his faith and courage? That is not enough. There is a supreme quality which you see to be lacking in your husband, in spite of his devotion, his tremendous valour. For no man is a true martyr unless he can repeat the prayer of my great namesake."

The door flew open and Clemency came running in to announce that dinner was ready, her stepfather was home—and she had been at the washtub all the morning; Hannah had let Jane starch the boy's ruffs and they had come out as stiff as a board. Soon the family was congregating round the parlour table, and Mary had no further chance of a private conversation with d'Aubais.

During the afternoon she thought over what he had said, tantalized by the obscurity of his last remark, and wondering who his great namesake could be. Some early French bishop, probably, of whom she had never heard.

That evening she saw a way of getting the question answered. Edward mentioned d'Aubais; it was easy to throw out an idle comment.

"It's an outlandish name, that: Etienne. Have you ever come across it before?"

"Yes, and so have you. In English we call it Stephen."

Then, of course, she identified in a flash the prayer that Edward could not bring himself to say.

"Lord, lay not this sin to their charge."

8

Now the boys were back at Paul's, Mary soon
noticed that Nicholas was slipping down into his
old state of apathy. He was more slovenly, more incompetent than ever, and she was sure he was not
doing any work.

Roger, pressed for details, admitted that his stepbrother had a wretched time at school. He was the
victim of the ushers, who could not overcome his
stubborn resistance to learning, and vented their
antipathy in savage tirades and clever jeers that
made the sycophants titter. He was sent to the high
master; continually harried by detentions and
homilies.

"Though I don't think he cares," said Roger.
"He's a stoke."

"A what? Oh, a stoic. Poor Nick." He was certainly afraid of his father, in the moral rather than
the physical sense, yet no amount of angry condem-
nation would make him take the obvious way out of
his troubles.

"So long as he refuses to study his masters will
give him no quarter. Why must he persist in this
hopeless rebellion? Do you know, Roger?"

She thought the children might have some idea,
but Roger was as mystified as she was.

"Most of the other idlers play the clown," he

said. "Or think only of archery and football. Nick
isn't like that."

"Has he any friends? He never brings boys home
with him, as you and Harry do."

"The fellows mock at him for being clumsy.
There's no malice in it. But he lurks in corners, and
won't join in with any fun that's going. So how can
he make friends?" asked Roger reasonably.

It was pitiful, thought Mary. His own contemporaries were the one set of people who wouldn't
mind how badly he did his lessons. Yet he couldn't
come to terms with them either, and they dismissed
him as a dull dog. At home he spent most of the
winter evenings in his room, plucking melancholy
tunes from his lute. Once or twice, when he came
down to supper, Mary suspected he had been
crying. She was desperately sorry for the lonely boy,
but he evaded all her efforts and shrugged aside her
enquiries with an indifferent yes or no that led to a
stalemate.

Edward, who was busy preparing a report for the
Council, did not seem to notice what was happening, until one evening, just after Candlemas, he had
a caller, a serious, soberly dressed man who was
closeted with him for nearly an hour. When Edward came upstairs to join Mary in the great
chamber he was looking decidedly grim.

"That was Cade, the usher from Paul's; he came
as an emissary from the high master. It seems that
Nicholas has fallen so far behind in his studies that
if he doesn't improve within the next month they
will be obligated to expel him."

She had not foreseen anything so drastic. "Is that
the best solution they can offer?" she objected. "It's
a confession of weakness. What good will it do to

anyone if they send him away?"

"It would free a place for a more deserving scholar. They have no choice; it's all laid down in their rules, and I should be grateful that the high master has been courteous enough to warn me."

"What do you mean to do?"

"Use the last card in my hand."

Harry had been sent to fetch Nicholas. When he arrived, slouching and untidy, his appearance did nothing to reawaken confidence.

Edward wasted no time in preliminaries. He delivered the school's ultimatum. "So now we know what you are, despite four years of the finest education in England—ignorant, lazy and unbiddable. Have you anything to say for yourself?"

"I'm sorry," muttered Nicholas automatically. He did not sound particularly interested.

"You have a good reason to be sorry," Edward told him bleakly. "I doubt if you perceive what you stand to lose. Being thrown out of Paul's might well ruin your entire future, and I could do with some show of concern."

Nicholas shifted his feet. "I've said I'm sorry. What else do you want me to do?"

"What else do I want——Good God!" Edward was struggling to control his feelings. In a rigidly calm voice he continued: "I want you, if it is not asking too much, to stand still and pay attention while I am speaking to you. You seem to have little conception of what it means to be expelled—however, we needn't consider that now. You still have a chance to redeem yourself, and I am going to see that you profit by it. I know what's the matter with you, Nicholas. You are so besotted by your fancies of becoming a musician, your brain is so

swamped with music, that you have lost all sense of
proportion. You neglect and despise every other
form of learning, and you won't heed the consequences. You've let this passion of yours turn into a
vice, and vicious habits have to be broken. This
mad self-indulgence has got to cease. There'll be no
more dreaming over the lute, or mooning round the
virginals in Verney's shop, pretending you belong
there. No more parading your talents. You'll devote
your whole mind to your books, and satisfy your
masters that you are fit to stay on at school. Until
that is safely accomplished I shall not allow you to
play another note."

"You can't mean that!" Nicholas seemed completely bereft, unable to grasp his father's arguments. He blinked myopically and pushed back a
lock of hair, tousled hair from his forehead. "You
can't deprive me of my music, sir. I'll work harder,
I swear I will. Not that it will make any difference,
but I promise you I'll try—if only you'll give me a
different punishment."

"What use would that be?" asked Edward, exasperated. "Nicholas, haven't you understood one
word I've been saying? I'm not trying to punish
you, though you certainly deserve it. I'm trying to
ensure that you make some headway with your
schooling before it is too late. You are in my charge
and I am acting solely for your happiness, whatever
you may think to the contrary."

"You don't give a straw for my happiness!"
Nicholas was beside himself, in such a frenzy of despair that for once he had the courage to answer
back. He flung himself onto a stool and hunched
there, shaking, with the primitive abandon of a
child, screwing his fists into his eyes. "How can I be

happy? What is there left for me without music? I've nothing else in the world—nothing. I wish I was dead."

Edward took one long step towards him and caught him by the shoulder.

"Get up," he said.

Flinching under the cold command, Nicholas got up.

Still gripping his shoulder, Edward stared down at his son.

"You wish you were dead, do you? God has given you so little to be grateful for? You can stop whining over your injuries while I remind you of a few advantages you seem to have forgotten. You were born into a state of life that thousands would envy. You have a good home, a loving family, the chance of growing up to serve your Queen in some honourable employment and being well rewarded for it. You take it for granted that you have a stout coat on your back and plenty of food in your stomach. Do you know that there are people in this city tonight, half naked and starving, herded in stinking hovels without a blanket or a fire? Would you like to tell them of your poverty? Would you like to go downstairs and tell Tom? I think he might find your suffering hard to swallow. When I came across Tom he was four years younger than you are now; his mother had deserted him, he had no friends and no money, and he thought I was going to hand him over to the constable. But he didn't say that he wished he was dead. That humble journeyman's brat had more pride than you. And more guts. I'm thankful he didn't hear you talking such blasphemous rubbish. I'm sufficiently ashamed of you as it is. . . . Now you can go and get on with your Latin."

Nicholas went on standing there, limp and miserable. He tried to stammer out some sort of apology.

"I wasn't intending to whine—I know I'm lucky, having enough to eat and all the rest, but it's so difficult to feel grateful—you don't understand."

"I understand that your own misfortunes seem worse than other people's," said Edward, not unkindly. "There's nothing uncommon in that. So don't try to convince me that your burdens are too heavy—I'm in no mood for lies and excuses."

Nicholas looked more dejected than ever. There was an apprehensive flicker of the eyelids as he mumbled a few words, inaudibly.

"Well, what is it?" asked Edward. "Have you anything you wish to say?"

"No, sir." Accepting the tone of dismissal, the boy turned and went slowly out of the room.

Edward glanced at Mary. "Now you'll say I was too stern with him. He was on the defensive."

"If you were I think he drove you to it. You may be right to use this method as a last resort, but I wonder if it can succeed. His dependence on music is so extravagant—I never met anyone like him."

"Music is his refuge, a fairy-tale country where he is undeniably a king, and where no pain can touch him. Nicholas," said Edward, with a weary contempt, "shows every sign of shaping into the sort of man who spends his life running away from the hardships he is too feeble to conquer."

That week a dumb depression hung over the house. They all missed the sound of Nick's practising. Mary hoped that he was making good use of his time. He sat with his nose glued to the detested pages of Virgil and Cicero, yet he did not give any impression of achievement. Ink-stained and dreary, he had lost his appetite and withdrawn into a shell of self-pity.

"We've had no renewed outcry against his hard lot," said Edward. "He's keeping the rules I set him, and studying diligently."

Mary refrained from saying that Nicholas was far too frightened of his father for any wholehearted defiance.

"I think we'll take him with us on Saturday," pursued her husband. "Poor little wretch, I don't want him to go on feeling he's in disgrace."

They were going to visit one of Edward's colleagues who lived a few miles north of London.

It was a fine February morning; the sky was bright though perhaps a little treacherous. They passed through Newgate into Holborn, crossed the Oxford Road and set a steady course uphill towards the villages of Hampstead and Highgate. Presently they looked back at the white-spired city below them, beautiful in its own special softness of line and colour as it swam in the gauze atmosphere of the Thames Valley. Here on the Heath there was a contrasting sharpness and vigour. It was a wild place, supposed to be haunted by highwaymen, but they had it to themselves this morning, and could enjoy the clean-smelling air, and the first snowdrops, their tiny, immaculate petals delicately veined with green.

Nicholas did not appreciate the treat Edward had arranged for him, slumping along with a slack rein and a gloomy scowl. It was not easy to be kind to Nicholas. Mary refused to let him spoil their day. She talked to Edward, and they soon arrived at Mr. Collard's red-brick house outside Finchley.

All the time they were there Mary was uneasily aware of Nicholas not enjoying himself. He hardly touched his food and somehow managed to isolate himself from the cheerful party round the dinner-table. Which was not only disagreeable but stupid, because Edward would have something to say about it on the way home.

Sure enough he did. As soon as they had parted from the Collards and ridden through the arched gateway his irritation broke out, and he told Nicholas he was an ill-mannered lout, unfit for the company of gentlemen.

Nicholas did not answer. He had assumed that mask of dogged indifference which Edward found so infuriating. Mary decided it was time to intervene.

"Could we travel a little faster? The weather looks like breaking."

The sun had vanished and there were leaden-grey clouds banking in the sky overhead. They began to ride more briskly. One of Mary's gloves was chafing her; the embroidered gauntlet had got tucked at the wrist. She tugged it free, and then, because her fingers were numb, it slid out of her grip and spun into the road. She reined in her horse, and the others drew up a few paces in front of her.

Edward would have dismounted as a matter of course, but she stopped him.

"Don't you trouble. Nick will retrieve it for me."

Nicholas showed none of his father's innate chivalry. He sat there and did nothing.

Edward had to prompt him. "You heard what your stepmother said. Haven't you the common civility to pick up a lady's glove for her?"

For a moment she thought Nicholas was going to
refuse. Then he clambered down, not bothering to
hide his reluctance, and led his mare back, as slow
as a snail, making a most ridiculous labour of everything. Finally he nearly trod on the glove, as though
he didn't know it was there. Granted, the boy was
short-sighted, but you would have to be practically
blind not to see that gay slip of scarlet lying in the
dust. In picking it up Nicholas managed to stumble,
so that he jerked the mare's tender mouth. She
snatched away from him, and frisked off along the
road in a flurry of indignation.

"It only needed that." Edward's voice was
caustic. "Can't you even hold your own horse?" He
went after the truant at a sober jog, cajoling her.
"Come up, Jewel, there's a good lass."

The little chestnut mare had not gone far; she
was standing on the grassy verge, watching his approach. As soon as he was level with her she shied
and dashed away, stirrups jangling. Edward followed her and played the same scene over again.
This time she let him come close enough to lean
across and reach for the reins. Then she plunged
aside so suddenly that he almost landed on the
ground. By the time he had regained his balance
Jewel was kicking up her heels on the Heath.

Edward turned his sturdy bay, cursing all horses
and children impartially. "We'll have the devil of a
job to take her now," he said, as Mary joined him.
"Will you ride round by those bushes and try if you
can to drive her towards me? Nick, you stay on my
other side and head her off."

So they began an absurd game of tag on a corner
of the Heath. Jewel could have streaked off into the
open country whichever way she pleased, but she

had no wish to leave her stable-companions. Jewel
was enjoying herself if no one else was.

She would caper about for a few yards, and then
stand stock still, waiting with interest for her
master's next move. Directly he advanced on her
she would pretend to take fright and flounce into
retreat, teeth bared in something suspiciously like a
grin.

Jewel was a born comedian. Mary's amusement
was stifled by her consciousness of Edward coming
to the limit of his patience, and Nicholas, a
harassed, apologetic figure, floundering about on
foot among the marshy tussocks. Also it was starting to rain.

Perhaps that was a blessing in disguise, for Jewel,
having had her fun, was ready to go home. She
sauntered up to Edward and rubbed her velvet nose
against his knee, quite shameless. She had kept
them dancing round her on the Heath for thirty-five
minutes.

By now Mary was very cold. Nicholas was very
hot, and Edward was in a temper he could control
only by keeping his mouth shut.

Nicholas, reunited with his mount, stammered
out that he was sorry for the delay. Edward did not
reply. Mary had the sense not to ask for her glove;
she realized that Nicholas had dropped it during
the chase.

They resumed their journey. It was raining hard
by now. They were going as fast as they could, brav-
ing the rain, when there was a tremendous roar of
thunder and a volley of hailstones shattered down
on them from a black sky. The horses were terrified,
laying back their ears and jibbing. Jewel sidled into
Mary's barb. Mary's immediate reaction was a cer-

tainty that Nicholas would fall off and lose his horse for the second time. In the saddle, however, Nicholas was fairly competent. He sat firm, and they battled on through the whirling hail. The stones stung their cheeks and spat against their horses' feet, to pile dangerously in the ruts and crevices: slippery balls of ice as large as nuts.

Edward shouted. ". . .The next crossroads, there's an inn." His words were engulfed in the storm.

At last they reached the crossroads and the shelter of the Golden Ram; ostlers came hurrying round, and the door swung open to welcome them. It was a prosperous inn, catering for the gentry; the landlord quickly summed up his customers, in spite of their draggled condition, and made his best bow.

"I can offer your worship a separate parlour, with a fine fire burning. Let me take your cloak, madam—this plaguey weather! Thunder in February! What does your worship desire to be served with? Might I suggest a mazer of mulled ale?"

"That will do very well, landlord. As hot as you can make it. We shall soon thaw out by this great fire."

It was a splendid blaze, the flames leaping high in the hearth and hissing as they swallowed a few lumps of ice that spluttered down the chimney. Mary shook herself like a water-spaniel and took off her hat, lamenting over the broken feathers. Edward stood beside her. They were wrapped in the scent and vapour of steaming wool.

Nicholas was hesitating in the doorway with a forlorn air of being unwanted. It was entirely due to him that the deluge had caught them on the Heath,

and perhaps he felt he had no right to a place by the
fire.

"Come along in, Nick," Mary encouraged him.

Now, like as not, he would trip on the step and
Edward would make some acid comment. Nicholas
didn't trip, but he did something else she had observed before: he pressed his hand against the
doorpost and ran it along the edge of a settle that
was just inside. Why was that gesture so familiar?
she wondered. She considered other gestures and
incidents with a vague discomfort. A stray thought
had brushed through her brain when he was
fetching her glove, just before Jewel got away.
Frowning, Mary traced the memory to its source,
and then rejected it. No, not that. It was impossible,
too dreadful to contemplate. And yet it would explain so much. . . . Nicholas was next to her now,
warming his hands. How pinched and drawn he
had become these last weeks. If her solution was the
right one she had to prove it here and now.

She searched for some sort of key to her dilemma.
The parlour was small and well lighted. The opposite wall was covered by a painted cloth, the
cheap substitute for tapestry, with a picture of the
"Judgement of Paris."

"That's a pretty hanging," she said. "Don't you
think so, Nick?"

Nicholas turned his head obediently. "Yes,
madam. Very pretty."

"The two babes guarded by the wolf." She was
recalling a similar cloth she had seen recently.
"That's some ancient legend, isn't it? I have such a
scanty knowledge of history."

Edward had been half attending to this conversation. Astonished by Mary's last statement he

roused himself to ask her what on earth she was talking about, when Nicholas fell into the trap.

"It's the story of Romulus and Remus, the founders of Rome." He was glad to identify one piece of classical lore that he really knew.

Edward and Mary gaped at him, too shocked to speak. The painted cloth was about ten feet away, the vividly coloured portraits of Paris and Venus were almost life-size. And Nicholas was staring straight at them, his eyes wide open.

The landlord came in with a piping bowl of ale, aromatically spiced. He set out three cups, a dish of apples and a plate of comfits. Mary murmured a word of thanks, willing him to go away.

Nicholas had wandered round to the other side of the table. He touched the hanging and peered at it. As the door closed behind the landlord he burst into a startled protest.

"This isn't what you said—there's no wolf! Why did you play such a trick on me?"

"It wasn't done to tease you, Nick. I wanted to know how far you could see."

"Nick," put in Edward, "since when has your sight been getting weaker? Can you recognize me from where you are now?"

Nicholas blinked, prodding the rushes with his toe. "I can see the colour of your beard, sir," he volunteered, adding helpfully: "I'd know your voice anywhere."

Edward had become very pale. "You can still make out what's near enough to touch," he persisted. "You can read your books."

Nicholas jibbed at the mention of books; this was too sore a subject. But Edward was not the ruthless inquisitor today. He was begging for reassurance. Nicholas gave him none. He stood in front of the garish cloth, pushing that untidy lock of hair back from his forehead; slim, defenseless and very young.

"Oh, my God," whispered Edward. He had just realized the full implications of the struggle he had been having with his son.

"You make shift to read and write," said Mary. "It's a continual strain, isn't it?"

"The letters get blurred," admitted Nicholas. "And they run about so on the paper."

"Run about on the paper?" repeated Edward.

"No, that's not true." Nicholas made a painstaking attempt to be accurate. "It isn't the letters that move, it's something inside my right eye. As though there was a swarm of butterflies flitting about behind the surface of the eye, and I have to look between to see the words. I can only see bits at a time, and that's what makes the lines so hard to follow."

Edward and Mary were silenced, appalled by the idea of this unfortunate child, trying to get some sense into fragments of Virgil as they slid through the ripple of distortion.

Collecting his wits, Edward said, "The damage is in your right eye; what happens if you shut it and rely on the left?"

Nicholas did not want to answer. He shifted his hands and feet in the way that had always maddened them when he was going to launch one of his specious excuses. Then he changed his mind and said, with an extraordinary tremor of guilt, as though he was confessing to a crime, "My left eye went black three weeks ago."

Edward said, "Nick," with a ring of horror and compassion.

Nicholas ran towards him. It was the first spontaneous movement of affection that Mary had ever seen him make. He hurled himself against the broad shoulder, and sobbed, "Father, I'm going blind."

The instinctive appeal met with an equally instinctive response from his natural protector. Edward held him tight, as he would have held the little boy Nick had been ten years ago, gently trying to comfort him.

"You mustn't lose hope—we can't be sure—all may yet be well. There, Nick—don't fret. I'll look after you."

His confident words were meaningless and he knew it.

Nicholas gave in to a thorough bout of weeping. Then he pulled himself together, wiped his nose inelegantly on his sleeve, and muttered that he was ashamed of sniveling like a wench.

Mary realized that Edward and Nicholas were so badly shaken they hardly knew what they were doing. The slightest return to normality would be a help.

"What you need," she said prosaically, "is to drink this posset while there is some heat left in it. Then you'll feel more cheerful. It will serve no purpose to have you both sneezing your heads off."

They all managed to laugh; the effort was worth it, for the nightmare receded a little.

Sitting round the fire, the pungent ale tingling in their throats, they drew some more details from Nicholas and pieced them into a coherent pattern. His sight had been deteriorating for about a year, so slowly that he only noticed gradually what was happening. It was then that he found it hard to focus on a printed page that the real trouble started. Of course he was still able to read and write; a total breakdown would have been impossible to hide. But his hazy progress faltered and dragged until it was beyond him to cope with the work that was heaped on a scholar in his last year at Paul's. As a result, he was given extra tasks and impositions, and he was worse off than ever. He hated his lessons for the drudgery they entailed, for the scoldings and punishments they brought in their wake, and most of all because they reminded him, each time he opened a book, of his dwindling sight and the terrors that loomed ahead. In the end his mind was so bludgeoned that he was too stupid to learn anything.

It was an agonizing picture—the fourteen-year-old-boy blundering on alone in the growing darkness, and getting nothing from those who should have strengthened him but misunderstanding and abuse. I ought to have guessed, Mary reproached herself. I ought to have watched him more carefully, and persevered in trying to win his love. How miserably I've failed him. The chief failure was Edward's, and he was perfectly conscious of it. He looked quite haggard.

Nicholas did not complain; he merely stated the facts. The one solace had been his music. Though he could no longer read a score, this had not stopped him, because there was a fine collection of printed and hand-copied pieces at Warwick Lane, which he had been browsing through since he first mastered the recorder. He had taken an ambitious fling at most of them, and now, owing to his extraordinary musical memory, he had plenty to choose from until Edward stopped him playing.

Poor Nick—and poor Edward, who was now appalled by what he had done.

"If I had known the other evening—if only you had told me, instead of letting me add to your intolerable load."

"It doesn't matter, sir," said Nicholas awkwardly.

"It matters a great deal. For months I've been driving you beyond endurance, and allowing your schoolmasters to do the same, without taking any steps to get at the truth. I shall never forgive myself."

It was dawning on Nicholas that his position had changed completely in the last half-hour. Going straight to essentials, he asked, "Can I have my lute back when we get home?"

"Indeed, you shall have your lute. You shall play it whenever you like. Well, not at night," amended Edward, salvaging some shreds of discipline. "My dear Nick, I've treated you very unjustly, and I am most truly sorry for it. I can't escape the greater share of the blame, but you must admit that it was partly your own doing. You could have spoken out months ago. What can have induced you to suffer in secret for so long? In heaven's name why didn't you tell me what was wrong?"

And then unwittingly and without any trace of malice, Nicholas exacted his revenge for Edward's past mistakes.

"I thought you'd be so angry," he said. "I thought you would accuse me of lying."

9

"Am I a monster?" Edward asked Mary, pacing up and down the great chamber at Warwick Lane.

They had ridden home as soon as the weather cleared. The other children had sensed a crisis immediately, and the explanations had been an added strain. None of them, not even Susan, had been in Nick's confidence; they were distressed and bewildered, and there were a good many tears. But Nicholas had been reunited with his lute; he had eaten his supper and gone early to bed, exhausted by so much emotion. In ten minutes he was sleeping soundly, as though he hadn't a care in the world. The cares were left to Edward.

"Am I a monster, that my children dare not come to me with their troubles? Do I treat them so harshly? That poor little devil, hugging his secret, expecting nothing from me but anger and disbelief —it doesn't bear thinking of. How can I have misled him to such a degree? God knows I tried to stop him hiding behind a cloud of daydreams and pretence. It now turns out that I was wrong and all I did was to drive him away from me, just when he needed me most. But surely he was old enough to know that I was acting out of love. Have I seemed more of a tyrant than any other watchful father?"

The answer to this question was, unfortunately,

yes. It would be impossible to convey to Edward the effect of his compelling character and steely integrity on those who felt inadequate beside him. He simply could not recognize the insidious claims of fear and weakness, because he had never given way to them himself. He was the last person to trade on his reputation as a hero, but it was an unforgettable part of him, somehow implicit in his self-assurance and in the slightly austere splendour of his physical presence. No one could become a legend in his own lifetime without running the risk of being isolated on a pedestal. Which was not the right place for the father of a delicate and vulnerable child.

Mary did not say any of this. She tried to reassure him, but Edward was not to be consoled. "It's all my fault."

"Dear heart, I'm sure that isn't so. His work at school may have hastened the disease a little; it cannot have been the cause."

"If Nicholas goes blind it will be a judgment on me."

She stared at him, baffled. "This is the wildest notion I ever heard. For what are you to be so sternly judged?"

"For my sins," he said quietly.

Mary, who had been considering his rather overwhelming virtues, was not impressed. She had a clearer picture of Edward's sins than he probably imagined. There had undoubtedly been some amorous adventures, now repented and done with; there was also his ingrained hatred of the Catholics, though that, he insisted, was perfectly justified. It was not such a terrible reckoning. Here, of course, you had the defects of an exceptionally learned and over-scrupulous Protestant: he had wandered so far into the maze of guilt-ridden theology that he had lost the true perspective of his religion. The God Mary worshipped did not send children blind to punish their fathers. Edward might think she was indulging in a heresy, but she didn't care. That was one advantage of not being very clever. You simply read the Gospels and believed what they said.

Though this did not make it any easier to accept what was happening to Nicholas.

Next day Edward called in Dr. Vaughan, a Fellow of the College of Physicians at Amen Corner, fifty yards from their own door.

He came and examined Nicholas and prescribed some lotions and ointments, but his diagnosis was depressing. He had come across similar cases, though never in anyone so young; the cause was unknown and there was no cure. He was afraid that the sight of the left eye had gone for good; there was a faint chance of saving what remained in the right, provided Nicholas was never allowed to tax it in any way.

Edward went off to tell the high master why Nicholas would not be returning to Paul's. In fact, Harry and Roger had already spread the news round the school, and during the next few evenings there was a stream of schoolboy visitors at Warwick Lane. Quite unable to express the feelings that had prompted them to come, there was something very touching in their awkward friendliness and the presents they brought to cheer Nicholas in his affliction: sticky sweetmeats, oranges and an odd assortment of "personal" treasures, including the broken model of a ship, several foreign coins and an incantation for charming warts.

"Though I don't know anyone with warts," commented Nicholas later. "I wish I did; I'd like to find out if it works."

He was surprised and rather pleased by his sudden popularity. He realized that these tough, healthy boys were sorry for him, but did not seem to mind. He had grown used to the idea that he was less effective than other people, and had acquired an undemanding humility which protected him from the agonies of resentment.

They were sitting down to dinner several days later when Edward said: "I've found a new occupation for you, Nick. Or, rather, a new way of pursuing your favorite occupation. How would you like to study music under Mr. Verney?"

Nicholas did not need to answer. The virginal-maker's house in Paternoster Row was his idea of paradise. He flushed with excitement. "Would you let me do that, sir? Go and work in the shop? But he'd never take me as an apprentice—you have to be a joiner too, and I couldn't follow that trade."

"No, you could not qualify for an apprenticeship," said Edward gently. "That's not what I had in mind. You are to be his pupil: it's all settled, and you start on Monday. Mr. Verney thinks highly of your gifts; he will teach you to cultivate them. If he finds other employment for you around the shop of course you will make yourself useful."

A week ago he would have considered this a most unsuitable arrangement. Verney was an educated man and a fine musician, but Edward had always maintained that music was no profession for a gentleman; it was chancy and ill-paid, and carried little prestige. Now he had got to grasp at it as the only future open to Nicholas. Whether the boy would ever be able to earn his living was a question they dared not consider. It was some reward to see him looking so happy.

"Does Mr. Verney know that I can't read a score?" he asked, a twinge of doubt creeping in.

"We discussed that. He says that you can enlarge your scope by having new pieces played over to you and getting them by heart. It will make the process more laborious, but your ear and memory are both so acute that he is certain you can succeed, and so am I."

Nicholas ruminated over this, and then said diffidently, "I've always known what I wanted to do in the end." They waited while he helped himself to salt, spilling most of it; nobody scolded him, though Mary was sure this particular lapse was due to sheer inattention.

"I want to write my own music. I can compose the melodies in my head, and then shape and polish them on the keyboard, provided someone else will prick them out on paper."

"Well, that may be your true calling: all the more reason to study as widely as you can. Everyone who aspires to build must begin by first climbing on the other men's shoulders."

"Do you mean you are going to write real music that gets published?" asked Jane. "Oh, Nick—will you make up a tune for me? With my name on it, so that everyone will know?"

"Yes, if I can," said Nick. "What will you have? A dance measure, very lively, I think. Mistress Jane Dacre's Galliard."

Clemency piped up: "One for me, too. For Mistress Clemency Dacre, as if I was a proper lady."

The other children joined in with suggestions. "Mistress Susan Garnham's Air . . . Mr. Roger

Dacre's Fancy . . . Mr. Henry Garnham's March."

"And Mr. Greville Dacre's Brawl," concluded
Edward, removing the spoon with which his
younger stepson was cheerfully hammering on the
table.

On Monday morning Nicholas went round to Paternoster Row; it was luckily such a short and familiar journey that he could go by himself, like any
ordinary boy. He was bursting with expectation; as
soon as he got back that evening they knew his
hopes had been fulfilled. He had spent nine hours
soaking in music, surrounded by the apparatus of
musicmaking, and he could think of nothing else.
There was no space left in his brain for worrying
over his defective sight.

Edward and Mary restrained themselves for a
week before their curiosity drove them to Verney's
shop.

The front part opened on the street: a soberly
panelled room in which the stock was displayed.
Miles Verney was a member of the Joiners' Company and a craftsman in everything he made; his
organs, virginals, clavichords and regals looked as
entrancing as they sounded. Some were mounted in
polished boxwood, some in gilded leather. Glittering copper pipes, like the towers of a fairy castle,
rose above a splendid church organ; next to it, the
smallest of the same tribe, a portable regal with
pipes of painted reed, destined for some rich man's
study. Mary was particularly intrigued by the ivory
virginals, decorated in velvet, with a looking-glass
inset; here a Court beauty could admire herself
while she played it; it would be a charming tribute
from a lover.

The virginal-maker was a quiet man of fifty

whose silver hair and beard gave him a deceptive
look of gravity. He was talking to some customers,
and broke off to greet his visitors, ushering them
towards the rear of the shop.

"You've come to see your young Orpheus. I'll be
with you shortly; in the meantime my wife will take
care of you. . . . Meg! Show Mr. and Mrs. Garnham to the gallery."

Mrs. Verney appeared in a doorway, a deep-
breasted prodigal creature and a complete contrast
to her husband. She was about Mary's age and already had eleven children, about half of them
clustering round her skirts.

"You are very welcome," she said, smiling. "You
will find Nick quite settled with us now; it's a delight to my husband to have him. Along here, if you
please; Margery, let the gentleman pass. . . . Mind
how you go, madam, there is a step. . . . Simon,
pick up your top. The brats will leave their toys
lying around for us to break our legs. . . . No, Frank
—don't plague your sister!"

"What fine children they are," said Mary, in
genuine admiration. The little Verneys were rather
grubby and ungroomed, as large families were apt
to be, and they all inherited each other's clothes,
but they looked wonderfully healthy.

"They are a pack of ruffians," said their mother
in a placid, loving voice. She was bouncing the
latest baby on her hip, and there was another on the
way. A tiny boy, still in long coats, tripped and
tumbled on his nose. There was a deafening wail.
Mrs. Verney scooped him up with her free arm.
"There, my poppet, you didn't hurt yourself. . . .
I'm sorry for this outcry. It's the door at the far end,
if you will just walk in."

The gallery ran across the back of the house, its three high windows facing north. Drifting motes of sawdust hung in the hard winter light, for this was the workroom where the instruments were built and put into their cases. Naked as skeletons they stood, the attentuated wires stretching across their frames like threads on a loom. A group of men and boys were heaving one of these delicate contraptions on to its painted stand; another man was beating a thin sheet of metal into a cylinder, while a young 'prentice was applying gold leaf to a strip of embossed leather, and getting himself pretty well dusted in the process, so that he shone like an ornamental cherub. Everyone seemed too busy to notice the strangers. There was a strong smell of fishglue, and also a feeling of mental and physical concentration which permeated the whole scene.

Gazing round they saw Nicholas. He was tuning a clavichord, tapping each note in turn, listening to the plucked "plang-plang," and sometimes adjusting a peg with infinite precision. It was all done by touch.

"That's a skill worth having," said Edward, coming up behind him.

Nicholas looked round vaguely. "I didn't hear you come in, sir." He slid off his stool. "She's a pretty little piece, isn't she?" He stroked the clavichord as though it was a live animal. "And this chamber organ here—there's a real beauty for you, with a nightingale pipe and all."

"What's a nightingale pipe?" asked Mary.

"You pour water into it, and it gives the most glorious, vibrating trill. I suppose you wouldn't like to buy a chamber organ, sir? I'm sure I could arrange it for you."

"Very civil of you," said Edward, amused.

Nicholas took them on a tour of the gallery, and presented his various friends. The apprentices were tradesmen's sons with an aptitude for music; one of them had been at the Chapel Royal until his voice broke. They treated Nicholas as a member of the same fraternity, and he was already more at home with them than he had ever been among his contemporaries at Paul's.

Walking home later Edward said, "He is in his element."

"Yes. I hope you don't mind that it is so unlike what you planned for him?"

"My plans have suffered some shrewd knocks lately. I'm only thankful he can find his level among those who can do more for him than I can. He can't remain there for ever, but I think this is a case where we must take no thought for the morrow."

So Nicholas went off every day, eager and punctual, and came home in the evening whistling gaily. If he was afraid of the threatening darkness—and of course he must be—he had gained the strength to control his fear. Fortunately, he still had the child's gift for living very much in the present, as well as the single-minded passion which absorbed all his energy. He was probably less unhappy than he had ever been before.

10

During the next few months Mary felt that her second marriage was settling into its stride. The jarring of early differences and surprises had smoothed down, and now that Edward was no longer at cross-purposes with Nicholas they were both easier to live with, and the house was altogether more peaceful.

Spring merged into summer, and the Garnhams went down to Maringale Bois. They had not been there once in the eight months since their wedding visit, which was astonishing, considering it was only a day's journey. Edward could never spare the time, insisting that he had much work to do.

It was July; the sheep-shearing was over, but there was still some hay to toss and dry, and all the fruit to pick. The bristling, green heads of the standing corn grew fat and glossy with a ripe, golden burnish. It would be a good crop, so long as the deer from the forest did not break into the enclosure and trample it down. Every night their horns battered the fence, and every morning the men repaired the damage, Edward and the boys working with them in their shirt-sleeves. It was like building a sea-wall against the tide—only this tide was the wild element of nature, always ready to sweep away the puny achievements of man.

Edward was happily engrossed all day, generally

with several children in tow. In London he was so often preoccupied and remote; down here he was a perfect father. Retracing his own youth, he knew exactly what boys wanted. The iron discipline was forgotten; he did not seem to mind when they were noisy or late for meals—if anything, he incited them. Once he kept Harry and Roger out half the night, looking for a badger.

Jane had a new enthusiasm: Susan taught her to take honey from the hives. Susan had a magic touch with bees and all small creatures; one day she would make a good mother. Perhaps that day was not so far off, for she was getting remarkably pretty. The thick, fair hair drifted over her shoulders, bleached fairer than ever by the sun; the constricted lines of her face and body had melted into a new, peachlike softness. She was coming out of her chrysalis. Mary was almost sorry there were no young men to admire her, but that could wait till the autumn. It was probably better for such a timid creature to mature unconsciously among people she knew and loved.

Clemency and Greville spent hours fishing in the moat. They never caught anything; the main object was to get gloriously wet and dirty.

One broiling afternoon the whole family wandered far into the forest. Here the burgeoning summer world had the strangeness of another continent. The sturdy beech trees were so tall and widely spaced that there was no sense of being shut in. There were acres of airy space under the branches; the light, cool as it was, had a radiance from the invisible sun above the trees, and everywhere the ultimate colour was green; the infinitely varied, lively and refreshing green of a million growing leaves.

Presently Edward and Mary sat down on the
mossy ground, luxuriously at ease. They could hear
Harry and Roger shouting and rushing about in
some energetic game. Clemency and Greville were
furnishing a make-believe house, busy as a pair of
squirrels. The older quartet—Tom, Susan, Nicholas and Jane—were sauntering along together.
Nicholas was singing a popular ballad. His voice
had broken at last into a firm and effortless tenor.

> "I say not nay, but that all day
> It is both writ and said
> That woman's faith is, as who saith,
> All utterly decayed.
> But nevertheless, right good witness
> In this case might be laid,
> That they love true and continue,
> Record the Nut Brown Maid . . ."

Snatches of verse floated back as they came and
went between the wooden columns of the tree-
trunks.

> "I am the knight, I come by night,
> As secret as I can,
> Saying, 'Alas, as standeth the case,
> I am a banished man. . . .
> Wherefore adieu, mine own heart true,
> None other rede I can,
> For I must to the greenwood go,
> Alone, a banished man.'"

Tom joined in. Jane, beside him, seemed to be
living intensely in the touching story of the outlaw
and his faithful love. Possibly she cast herself as the

Nut Brown Maid; she was certainly a brown girl.
There was a topaz gleam in her curls, and her skin
was vivid and glowing. Her eyes, much darker than
Mary's, still had the surface sheen of healthy childhood. She piped up boldly:

> " 'Why say you so? Whither will you go?
> Alas, what have you done?
> All my welfare to sorrow and care
> Should change, if you were gone,
> For in my mind, of all mankind,
> I love but you alone.' "

Acting out the song, she flung herself on Tom
and embraced him with great enthusiasm.

Tom gave her a smacking kiss on the forehead,
and said, "You little Amazon, you nearly knocked
me flat."

Nicholas grinned. Susan was not amused.

"For pity's sake, Jane—can't you ever stop
plaguing Tom? It makes you look a proper fool, I
can tell you—a girl of your age. And it's most unseemly."

She stalked on, her fastidious mouth primly set.
Tom caught up with her; they could hear him scolding her, but too gently to hurt.

"Sue, that was a little harsh. You mustn't be unkind to Jane. It was all done in play."

Jane, very flushed, was midway between sulks
and tears. She followed them, muttering angrily to
Nicholas, who went on humming "The Nut Brown
Maid."

Edward and Mary looked at each other and
laughed.

"That was a sudden storm," said Edward. "Poor Susan. Did you ever meet such a champion of propriety?"

"She is too much disturbed by any display of feeling, I've said so all along. Though she may be partly justified," added Mary honestly. "Jane is too old to go kissing young men as the fancy takes her. I ought to be more strict with her, or we shall have trouble later on."

"Oh, Jane is bound to give us more headaches than my sober Susan, that's plain enough. But she's as good as gold, and as for kissing Tom, she simply treats him as a brother by adoption. We've been lucky with our two families, Mary; they've shaken down as though they were all born under the same roof. And a handsome set they make. I feel like a patriarch."

Something was needed to extend the patriarchal design, thought Mary. A child of their own. She had been faintly disappointed that there was no prospect of a baby yet. On the other hand, she had so much to do, and was so absorbed by the delight of being in love; perhaps the delay was all for the best.

"Yes," he said, watching her. "We can afford to wait."

"Just what I was thinking—Edward, you knew! It's the first time you've done that."

"Done what?"

"Answered what I said inside my brain." Her meditations must have been pretty transparent, but she was irrationally pleased. "Soon we'll be talking in cipher. You know, half the sentences left out because there's no need to speak them aloud."

"Shall we?" he hesitated. "Is that how it was with you and Jack?"

"Why, yes. Surely most people learn that language when they are happy?"

She saw that he was mystified, and there was another emotion too. She wondered for a moment if he was jealous of Jack, and then realized that it was not jealousy but a rather wistful envy of an experience that had never come his way.

She was astonished. Conscious from the start that he knew more about love-making than she did, she was slowly grasping the fact that he knew practically nothing about love. The frank, instinctive give-and-take of initimate companionship was quite alien to him. In spite of his undoubted attraction, he was a very lonely person.

She studied him as he leant back on his elbow, crumbling a tuft of moss between his fingers and frowning, his grey eyes masked by those curiously protective lids. His features had the rare quality of an entirely masculine beauty: decisive, intelligent and strong. The strength of a locked door. She remembered Etienne d'Aubais saying, "In effect he is still a prisoner." That could be true in more ways than one.

She said softly: "When two people live together in a true marriage, I believe that over the years they come to know each other right through to the heart. That's the answer to this trick of thought-reading. You can't get it by force, or hurry the pace; it grows of its own accord. I'm certain it can grow for us—if that is what you wish."

He shifted a little, gazing absently across the grove. Far away, through a gap in the trees, the brindled body of a leaping hind splashed between the shadows and was gone.

"You will have to be patient with me," he said. "I haven't your gift of a confiding nature. I've been a solitary half my lifetime. When I was young," he paused, selecting the words, "I found it—expedient —to guard my tongue and trust no one. And that's how it has been ever since. I laid the foundations of my future; it was a deliberate choice, though nothing else seemed possible at the time. I didn't forsee what it would make of me. As it is, I am trapped, for I can neither speak of the past nor escape from it. There are times when I must be unbearable for any woman to put up with. I'm well aware of my failings. You don't know how often I've longed to cut the strangling knots I've tied for myself. Especially since I met you."

Mary sat very still, weighing every phrase and implication. He was spiritually paralysed by what he had suffered in prison as a boy of twenty-two. She knew that already, but today she detected a change in his outlook. She thought that he both wanted and dreaded to bring his memories out into the open, and that it depended on her which factor won, the dread or the desire.

And at that crucial point Harry had to come bounding towards them, hot and excitable.

In the past few minutes they had noticed a good deal of noise, which they had both ignored. Now it transpired that Roger had fallen out of a tree and cut his head. "He's pouring blood," announced Harry importantly.

"He would be," said Roger's mother, resigned to this sort of calamity. She got up, controlling her ir-

ritation. Here was a real snag about being in love
for the second time at the age of twenty-eight; your
most vital and fascinating exchanges were liable to
be interrupted by the children of your first love,
clamouring for attention. Selfishly affectionate as
puppies, having to be clothed, fed and comforted,
asking endless questions and continually falling out
of trees.

It didn't matter, she thought, as she staunched
Roger's wounds and told him briskly that he wasn't
dead yet. There were plenty of opportunities, down
here in the country, for her and Edward to cultivate
their private relationship. Weeks of summer
stretched ahead of them.

But when they returned to the Manor there was
a strange horse in the stableyard. A Crown Messenger had just ridden in with a letter from the Secretary of State. There were rumours of a new Catholic
plot which had to be investigated, and Edward was
ordered back to London immediately.

11

Right through August Edward was kept in London, trying to unravel the tenuous threads of a suspected conspiracy against the Crown. There had been a drift of alehouse gossip about a stranger who appeared in the criminal district of Alsatia, offering mysterious bribes. . . . A discharged soldier, dying in St. Bartholomew's Hospital, had made a muddled confession and mentioned a certain name. . . . That was all Edward had to start from, and he was patiently hunting for evidence in the usual unsavoury haunts of intrigue and rumour. They were also the hotbeds of infection, and Mary hated to think of him running the gauntlet of plague and fever as he questioned endless witnesses in the taverns, brothels and prisons.

He wrote to her; long letters at first, and then sparse, unsatisfactory scribbles, because he had no energy to spare from his chase. Tom acted as his messenger, riding down to Essex and staying the night.

On one of these trips Tom told her that Mr. Garnham had achieved his first object. By concentrating on the recognized mercenaries, the prodigals and black sheep who could be hired for any villainy, and by dovetailing many fragments of information, he had identified the group he was really

after: the gentlemen of birth and reputation who
were preparing to betray their country in the name
of religion. It was a matter of shrewd and ex-
perienced deduction—now he had to get proof.

Mary did not feel any softening of pity for
Edward's quarry. These men were too dangerous,
both to the State and to her husband personally.
Catching traitors could be a bloody business. She
lay awake that night, wishing it was all over.

It was very late. There was nothing stirring in the
passive darkness except the too vivid pictures inside
her brain. She was wearily pushing them away
when a sharp sound banged through the silence,
making her nerves jump. In a moment of confusion
she thought this noise was part of her own alarming
fancies; then it was repeated, and she realized that
the sequence of short raps was definite and ex-
ternal. Someone was knocking on the front door.

Mary hesitated, but not for long. Groping for a
flint, she lit a candle and got out of bed, shrugged
on her loose velvet gown and fumbled for her
slippers. No one else seemed to have heard; the servants slept at the back. As she reached the foot of
the stairs there was a low growl, and Edward's old
spaniel Trojan came lumbering through from his
basket in the kitchen passage. Fat and lazy as he
was, Trojan was standing no nonsense from in-
truders. He growled again, the crest of hair on his
neck stiffening with indignation.

"Good boy," said Mary, rather glad to have a
bodyguard.

The unknown visitor called out something that
was muffled by the thick oak door. Trojan picked
up the intonation quicker than Mary. His growls
changed into a high-pitched ecstasy, his tail wagged

madly, and he bounded at the door in a flurry of delight.

Then Mary ran forward. "Edward!" She wrestled with the iron bolts, much impeded by Trojan. "I'll soon have it open. Do get down, you imbecile dog! My love, how happy I am to see you. I never thought—Tom didn't say you were coming."

"Tom didn't know. It was a sudden decision." He gave her a brief kiss and said urgently: "Mary, what's happening here? Haven't you been disturbed? There's a ladder propped up against the side of the house."

"No," she said. "We've had no trouble, not a sound until you started knocking. Where is this ladder?"

"Under Susan's window." He had seen it in the moonlight while he was crossing the green, and had left his groom with the horses so that he could approach the house unnoticed.

"Susan's window? But that's impossible. No thief could have come through that way without my knowing."

They made for the stairs. Mary hardly knew what she expected to find. Her mind was still full of plots and ambuscade. She stuck close beside Edward, wishing he would draw his sword.

The great bedchamber was just as she had left it. Or was there a sinister bulge behind the arras? The light was so dim, you could not be sure. Susan's room lay immediately beyond, through a narrow door in the corner. Edward moved quietly forward.

"Take care," whispered Mary.

Edward flicked the latch and stood in the doorway, holding the candle high. Its anaemic flame was quenched by the rush of moonlight, for the curtains were pulled wide, revealing the empty room and the flat, neat surface of the bed that Susan had not slept in.

Mary gasped. "Where can she be? Even if a robber got in——"

"No one got in." Edward's mouth was very grim. "Susan got out."

Mary's glance travelled across the smooth expanse of sheet to the open window, with the top rung of the ladder projecting above it. She forgot her fantasy of lurking cutthroats in the grip of a crisis that was purely domestic.

"Surely you don't think——"

"I don't suppose she was carried off by gypsies." He was surveying his daughter's dressing-chest. "At least she hasn't gone for good. All her stuff is still here."

"Run away? Of course she hasn't. I don't understand any of this, but there must be some reason for it. Susan isn't the kind of girl . . ." She faltered, unable to get round the facts.

He turned impatiently. "My dear Mary, she's slipped out to meet a man, and you know it as well as I do. However unlikely it may seem. The question is, who? You must have some idea."

"But I haven't. Susan never looks twice at any man. And there's no one down here."

"The Foyles are at Ravestock. Could it be one of Blanche's sons?"

"Those young courtiers? She's afraid to speak to them."

Ravestock Hall, five miles away, belonged to the heiress, Lady Foyle; it was generally filled with the fashionable guests whom she found more entertaining than her country neighbours. Certainly the

Foyles' rare invitations were no treat to Susan, yet she was too fastidious for village boys. Susan, so timid and decorous, climbing out of her window on a midnight escapade—the whole thing was incredible.

They retraced their steps, softly, because Jane and Clemency slept in another small chamber that led out of their own.

"What are we going to do?" Mary asked.

"I shall have to search for her. I can't use the servants on such an errand. But I might take Tom——" He stopped short. "Good heavens, Tom! Is that the answer?"

"Oh no! I don't believe it." And then, in spite of her automatic rejection, she began to believe it, because however ugly the suggestion might be, Tom was the one man who had got close to Susan within the family circle; close enough to overcome her natural reserve and lead her into mischief. If anyone had brought off this feat it must surely be Tom. Edward had gone to look in his room.

He was soon back. "So much for my honest secretary." He made no further comment, and his voice was arctic. Mary had never seen him so angry.

She followed him downstairs, thinking: Tom and Susan, what a precious comedy of deceit they've been acting for our benefit. Their shabby hypocrisy disgusted her. Certainly Tom was no puritan; she remembered, a few weeks ago, his setting off after dinner with a jaunty, all-conquering air which had made her wonder vaguely if he was pursuing some rustic wanton. Yes, and wasn't that the day Susan took a gift of eggs to the old woodcutter's wife, and came home late with a rather lame excuse? A fine fool they've made of me, thought Mary bitterly.

They left the house, turned along the edge of the
forecourt and into the garden. All round them the
breathless silver night was their enemy. This was an
element for young lovers, not for anxious parents;
you could feel beauty tugging at your heartstrings,
and that rebellious surge in the blood. The magical-
ly white grass and the amorous-scented lilies glowing pale against the sculptured ebony of the dense
yew hedge. The harvest moon swimming low in the
galaxy. And outside the clearing the eternal forest,
no more than a subtle imprint of dark trees blurring
the fringe of the stars.

They were casting about at random. Tom and
Susan might be anywhere; probably a mile away in
one of those hidden groves. At an angle of the brick
terrace, Mary felt Edward's warning pressure on
her arm. They stood still. The ground below them
curved away in a gradual dip toward the moat, and
there, under the full sweep of the moon, the boy and
girl were stretched in each other's arms.

She gaped at them stupidly; the sheer, brazen
impudence of lying there, a hundred yards from the
house—it was outrageous. Trojan was padding
down to the water for a drink. Tom must have
heard him; he sat up, curious rather than alarmed.
Mary was thankful to note that he and Susan were
completely dressed. She saw Susan's upturned face,
and it was like looking at a stranger. Pleasure-
drugged, her lips parted and coaxing, this was a
siren out of a pagan legend. Or any silly child of
sixteen, breaking every rule she had been taught,
and too besotted to care.

Edward started down the bank at full tilt. As he
came out of the shadows, the culprits jumped to

their feet, jerked up like puppets, and Susan gave a little scream of panic. Mary was not equipped for running. Her slipper flew off; she retrieved it, painfully, from a patch of nettles, her long, loose hair cascading round her. She got a glimpse of Edward seizing hold of Tom and flinging him backwards so violently that he nearly fell in the moat.

By the time she reached them they were all talking at once.

". . .A precious couple of cheats I've reared. Susan, you must be proud of your accomplishments. Setting up as a model of sanctity, too high-minded for the simple pleasures the rest of us enjoy, and all the while you were creeping off to wallow in your furtive lust like a dirty little kitchenmaid."

"I didn't—it wasn't—Father, don't be too hard on me. We haven't done anything wrong."

"You mustn't blame Susan, sir. The fault is entirely mine; I prevailed on her to come out here—"

"We haven't done anything wrong," repeated Susan in a despairing wail.

"I might have guessed what you would grow into. You come of tainted stock, after all. Stop snivelling, my girl, and look at me." Edward's voice was low and regulated, every syllable forced home his indictment. A hand on each shoulder, he slewed her round into the pitiless ray of the moon, tousled and trembling, the tears crusted on her cheeks. He stared down at his daughter, as though he could deduce some hidden facts from her particular degree of fear and evasion. Perhaps he could. This was Walsingham's principal agent, examining a dubious witness. "So you haven't done anything wrong?" he remarked at last. "Small thanks to

Master Tom. I should say we've preserved your virginity by a matter of ten minutes. You can count yourself lucky."

"That's not true," protested Tom. "I swear to you, sir, I wasn't trying to seduce her."

"Then what precisely were you doing?" Edward pushed the weeping girl aside and concentrated his caustic fury on Tom. "What other end could there be to such a beginning? Susan may be ignorant—though hardly innocent. You are neither. You've played this game before. Given such a willing accomplice you weren't the man to refuse a golden opportunity."

"Indeed, you are mistaken," Tom persisted. "She was in no danger from me. I wouldn't have hurt her for the world."

"You'll be telling me next that you wanted to marry her. Perhaps this is your idea of how to conduct a courtship?"

Tom muttered that he knew he would not be an acceptable suitor.

"Acceptable—my God! An unwanted brat from a mean street, without a penny to your name. Though if you dug up half the gold in the Indies it wouldn't take you far from your native gutter. The mistake I made was in trying to turn you into a gentleman; in thinking I could teach you some rudiments of honour. I trusted you to keep your greedy hands off my daughter—how else could I have let you live in the same house with her, all these years? I should have left you where you belonged. For you're a peasant still, Tom, and that's all you ever will be. No more able to subdue your appetites than a rooster crowing on a dunghill."

It was a cruel attack, not least because it was partly justified. Tom, caught out and thoroughly ashamed of himself, had lost his graceful assurance. His forehead was clammy with sweat, and as he plucked nervously at his belt he exposed what now seemed to be the stubby, broad fingers of a manual labourer. Shifting, dumb and wretched, he was reduced in status: a splendidly built young animal and nothing more. He had no carefully nourished pride of race to sustain him; his confidence was simply what his master had given him and was brutally taking away.

Susan had been crying drearily in a kind of daze. She rubbed her puffy eyelids and blinked at Tom, becoming conscious of this alteration. It was possibly the most disturbing shock of all: seeing him humiliated, stripped of all the gaiety and strength that had dazzled her and made their secret meetings into a glorious adventure. Now the glory was gone.

She burst out, on a shrill note of hysteria: "Why did you drag me into this? I wish you'd never come near me. I wish I was dead."

Poor Tom looked more stricken than ever. "I'm sorry, Sue." The words were scarcely audible.

Mary put an arm round Susan, who was working herself into a frenzy. "Edward, I'm going to take her indoors. You can talk to her again when she is calmer."

"Yes, she can go. But I've not finished with Tom."

He waited, poised in a threatening silence, while Mary and Susan climbed the grassy bank. Glancing back, Mary saw the two figures outlined against the shimmer of the moat. The moonlight crossed it with a stroke of crystal. There was not the faintest sigh of wind to break the untroubled water.

Susan clung to Mary; she could not stop crying. "My father will never forgive me," she sobbed, stumbling along the brick path. "He hates me now, he despises me for being a slut—I never had a chance, I might have known how it would be."

There was no mention of Tom, left alone to meet the worst of her father's anger. Susan was so overwhelmed by terror and self-pity that she could not think about anyone else. The reckless pagan had vanished: this was merely an aspect of the old Susan, plunged into difficulties she wasn't brave enough to tackle. Well, she deserved to be thoroughly chastened, and so did Tom. They had both behaved disgracefully, thought Mary, resenting the fact that she had been their dupe. Yet in an unregenerate corner of her mind she was judging Susan by other standards. What a poor thing the girl is, she told herself contemptuously. If I'd been placed as she is I think I might have had the guts to stand by my partner and take the consequences without bleating. Anyone so feeble had no business to dabble in love, she thought irritably.

She shook off these unsuitable ideas, conscious of her duty as a stepmother. She ought to be preaching a sermon on chastity, making Susan believe that she was irretrievably corrupted and that her soul was in danger. She could not do it. Susan was in no state to attend to sermons. The dry, hiccoughing sobs of exhaustion shook her whole body, she was dreadfully cold and she said she felt sick.

Mary could not be unkind to her. She got her to bed, brought her some warm milk and coaxed her to swallow a little, even kissed her good night. Susan winced away from the kiss and huddled under her blankets. She seemed so crushed and guilty that surely no moralizing was necessary.

It was nearly dawn, but the curtained house was like a tomb. The front door was bolted, so the men had come in. She discovered Edward in the parlour, sipping a cup of canary and contemplating the bare table, his expression schooled to indifference. A flash of insight reminded her how Nicholas had looked all those months when he was hugging his private tragedy. And Susan—it now turned out that she too was an expert at masking her feelings. Mary was disconcerted by the oddly secretive character of this family she had married into. She did not understand any of them.

Trying to sound easy, she said: "My poor love, what a home-coming you've had. You must be worn out. I'll fetch you some meat."

"I don't want any food."

She knew from his tone that he would not be persuaded, so she sat down and gave vent to her indignation. "Those two brats, creeping off to make love on the sly, and laughing at us, I suppose, behind our backs! I wouldn't have believed it possible. Susan was always so good, and as for Tom, how he can have allowed himself—still, it might be worse: There's no harm done, and this will be a lesson to them. Susan has had such a fright that I doubt if she'll ever go astray again, nor Tom either, I dare say, after the slashing you gave him. Where is he, by the way?"

"Gone," said Edward, reaching for the wine bottle.

"Gone where?"

"How should I know? London, I imagine. It will take him some time to walk there."

Mary felt a cramp of apprehension in her stomach. She did not want Edward to let Tom off lightly —in any case the things he had said in the garden were a pretty severe punishment in themselves. What he was implying now seemed altogether too drastic and final. "Edward, you can't mean that you've sent him away for good?"

"What did you expect me to do? Keep him in my house so that he could make a strumpet of my daughter? And yours too, in a year or so, if they pleased his fancy?"

"That's nonsense. Tom isn't vicious; he's a lively young man who's let himself get too fond of a pretty girl. I don't think he meant to seduce her; it was just a harebrained folly. Surely this is too stern a retribution for one lapse. . . . Has he any money?"

"I didn't ask. I dealt with him as most men deal with a dishonest servant."

"But, Edward—Tom isn't simply your secretary. He has a far greater claim on your forbearance than an ordinary servant. You've been his patron and protector since he was a child, you've inspired all his loving devotion. If you cast him off he'll be lost. He has no family, nowhere to go. Your house is his home."

"Which makes his treachery ten times worse," retorted Edward. "With all his vaunted gratitude he was willing to pervert the innocent affection which started when Susan was in the nursery, an affinity that should have prevented any tinge of desire—it comes near to incest!"

Mary frowned. There was a fallacy here. "There was nothing unnatural in their change of feeling. You didn't teach Susan to regard him as her brother, for if you had he must have been her equal also. Yet tonight your first instinct was to taunt him with his humble birth. No, it won't wash. You can call Tom either presumptuous or incestuous, but you can't have it both ways."

Edward did not like having his logic corrected by a woman. He changed the subject, saying in a hard voice: "You would do better to leave my judgment alone and examine your own conscience. I hold you very much to blame for the whole business. If you'd looked after Susan properly none of this would have happened."

He took her completely by surprise. Stung by the injustice, she got ready to retaliate: no one had said that Susan needed a gaoler. If she and Tom were unable to behave properly to people who trusted them they must have been very badly brought up. Then she realized that Edward had reached the limit of nervous exhaustion.

And no wonder—after a full day's work in London, half the night in the saddle and a distressing family upheaval at the end of it. This was not the time to pick a quarrel. Besides, she did feel partly responsible, so she throttled her grievance and said meekly: "I'm sorry, Edward. I don't think I neglected Susan, but it was stupid of me not to observe her more closely. You are right, I have been very dull-witted."

She hoped this apology would touch off some generosity in return. He did not respond. She tried again.

"I am so glad to have you home, my love; you need a spell of peace in the country. None of this will seem so black once you are rested."

"I'm not here to rest; I came only to collect some documents that are locked up in my study. And I don't foresee any particular cause for rejoicing."

Mary had never been so ruthlessly snubbed.

12

Next morning Edward retired into his study to sort through those important papers—so he said. Mary had a shrewd idea that he wanted to avoid any further family scenes. Typically, he left his wife to deal with the aftermath.

The children were bursting with curiosity. Edward had reappeared, Tom had vanished, Susan was shut in her room; naturally they wanted to know what was going on. Mary gave them a modified account, skipping the details and suggesting that Tom's absence was only temporary. (In fact she hoped this was true. Edward was so fond of the boy; surely he would relent, once he had recovered his temper.)

Harry and Roger received the news with scoffing incredulity. A tremendous fellow like Tom, a paragon in all the skills that mattered, wrestling and sword-play and archery; why should he waste his time mooning round a silly girl? And of all girls to choose Susan! He must have lost his wits. Mary found their schoolboy jokes particularly trying. Nicholas was old enough to appreciate the real dangers of the situation. He said very little, and wandered upstairs to the gallery. Presently they heard a muted and poignant air on the virginals which expressed, better than words, Nick's sadness for his sister and Tom, and perhaps for something they had destroyed, a close-knit pattern of unquestioning childhood relationships that could never be quite the same again.

But it was Jane who was most upset. Pink with indignation, she stamped up and down, saying that it was a wicked shame; why should Tom be punished because Susan would hang round his neck, making gooseberry eyes and leading him on? Jane took the original view that Tom was an injured innocent and it was all Susan's fault.

"Poor Tom, there's no justice in it." She struck a tragic attitude and declaimed: "For he must to the greenwood go, alone, a banished man."

"He's more likely gone to London," snapped her mother. "And we don't want to hear that silly ballad. Nick's dirge is bad enough; you'll get short shrift from your stepfather if you disturb him."

Mary dawdled over the chores, putting off the evil hour when she must have a solemn interview with Susan. Edward had made it plain that this was her job. At last she went reluctantly to confront her stepdaughter; a dejected little figure, all the colour washed out of her by so much crying. Now her eyes were dry and dull, her mouth sagged in a line of defeat.

She stood up as Mary came in. Her mane of fair hair hung raggedly forward; she had not bothered to brush it. They surveyed each other for an instant, both awkward and tongue-tied. Then Susan whispered, "Do I have to see my father?"

"Not now. He has too much work to do this morning."

Susan was plainly relieved. Mary began her well-rehearsed lecture, teased by a mental echo of some

of the scoldings she had received when she was a
resentful fifteen. It was disconcerting to find oneself
on the side of venerable authority. Susan stood
there like a block of wood, though she did show
some distress when she heard that Tom had been
sent away.

"You mean my father has dismissed him? Oh, I
am sorry. He's so attached to Tom, I never thought
for a minute——"

"It's unlucky that you didn't think, Susan. Tom
has done something which your father considers
unpardonable, but your conscience must tell you
how far you encouraged him. And it is Tom who
has to pay."

Susan sucked in her lip. "My father would prefer
to be rid of me. I suppose it's more difficult to turn
your daughter out of doors."

She sounded so forlorn that Mary's tone sof-
tened. "That's not true," she said quickly. "My
dear Sue, you cannot believe that we should ever
wish to disown you. Your father is angry, yes—but
he's well aware that you are hardly more than a
child, and that Tom traded on your youth and led
you into this stupid escapade. Even so, you must
have known that it was stupid." She paused. "What
did you think was going to come of it in the end?
Were you hoping that you would be able to marry
him?"

"No, I wasn't!" Susan flung up her head in a
clumsy, violent gesture, like the shying of a nervous
colt. "Whatever I wanted with Tom it had nothing
to do with marriage."

"You aren't in love with him?" Mary persisted.

Susan shrugged. "Love? That's a pretty title for
it. How can I tell you what I felt? You don't under-

stand the first thing about a girl like me."

"I'm not so thin-blooded as you think," retorted Mary, very much put out by this remark. "Nor am I a hundred years old. I understand exactly what you felt. You are not unique. We are all given these passions, for a definite purpose; they are not meant to be carelessly abused. The plain fact is, you are now ready to marry. If you had fallen truly in love with Tom I should be very sorry for you. As it is, you have been wanton, rash and senseless. Couldn't you let your father choose you a husband? You wouldn't have had long to wait."

"I shan't ever marry. I haven't any suitors." Susan began to cry again. "A fine chance I've got of being happy."

"What on earth is the matter with you?" demanded Mary. "Why shouldn't you be happy? You may not have any very ardent suitors as yet, and whose fault is that? If you want to be courted for your own sake, and not merely for your dowry, then you must try to be more lively and less ungracious; talk pleasantly and take some interest in the men you meet, the way other girls do."

"Yes, and if I tried that what would happen? If I fluttered my eyelashes or held hands in corners—the way other girls do—what would my father say when he caught me at it? What do you suppose he is waiting and watching me for all the time?"

Mary was completely baffled.

Susan had her hand up to her mouth; she was biting her thumbnail, and she stumbled over the words. "He'd say I was a whore like my mother."

There was a stupefied silence. The impartial sunlight streamed across the floor and cut shadows round the darkly solid furniture; a fly drummed against the windowpane, and Mary's mind staggered under the name Susan had just used about her mother. Edward's first marriage was one of those things he never mentioned, and Mary had been too fastidious to probe for details from Cousin Eulalia or any of their friends. Privately, she had suspected that he might have been unfaithful to Elizabeth. It was the other way round—staunchly partisan, she thought it ridiculous. Why should a woman take lovers when she was lucky enough to be married to Edward?

Susan was watching her. "You didn't know," she muttered. "So he never told you."

"No. Susan, I wonder if you grasp the full import of what you are saying. You were nine years old when your mother died, you can have no positive recollection to go on—you heard a spiteful rumour, the servants gossiping perhaps, and you have let it grow out of all proportion."

"This wasn't servants' gossip. I heard it from my father himself. He called my mother a whore, and he said I should go the same way, like as not."

"He said that to you? I don't believe it."

"No, he said it to her, to my mother. They were in their bedchamber and I was in here, listening through that crack in the door. Eavesdropping. I used to wake in the night and hear them quarrelling —it was the same in London, too—and I would get out of bed and creep to the door. Oh, I know it was wrong, and I hated doing it, but I couldn't drag myself away. I shall never forget how he spoke to her in his terrible, quiet voice—he never shouts, you know; it might be easier if he did. And when she tried to convince him that she was sorry he'd tear her excuses into shreds, the way he always does, half mocking and half cruel. Then he'd go away to sleep in another room, and leave her to cry. That was the worst part: to hear my mother crying. I felt as if I was lost. I suppose you think it serves me right for listening."

"My poor Susan, of course you listened—what child wouldn't? And there was no one you dared confide in, so you've gone on brooding all these years alone?"

Susan nodded. Drawn by the warmth of compassion, she edged forward to sit beside Mary on the bed, fragments of memory tumbling out compulsively.

Her heart flooded with pity, Mary could visualize the little girl, about the same age as Clemency, shivering in her nightgown as she cowered behind the door, while her parents dragged out their quarrels, too obsessed by their own wretchedness to guess what they were doing to their daughter. And some of their bitter exchanges were scarred on Susan's brain for life; one savage prophecy of Edward's in particular: that Elizabeth's example might lead to the corruption of her own children— it was just the kind of taunt that a jealous husband flung out on these occasions, without even considering it seriously. But Susan had been too young to know that. She had taken the threat quite literally.

Mary tried to explain this to her, but Susan would not be reassured.

"He did mean it. He still does. He said last night that I came of tainted stock. And, anyway, it's true," added Susan, plucking at the braid on her skirt.

"My dear, you mustn't dwell too much on this adventure with Tom."

"I wasn't thinking of Tom. You see, I've known all along that I was the same kind as my mother. She was a bad woman; I heard her admit that she had done those things my father accused her of, but I never cared a straw how wicked she was. I was on her side always. I loved her far more than I love my father.

"I missed her so when she died. You don't know what it was like, being left alone with the servants. And when Cousin Eulalia arrived, so bumbling and tedious. *He* hardly came near us, and when he did we were sure to be in disgrace, for one cause or another. Nick and I were afraid of him, and he knew it and despised us. It was harder for Nick, being a boy; besides, he worships my father, only he says it's hateful being the son of a hero. Everyone is bound to be disappointed in you. Tom was up at Cambridge and Harry was too young to count, so Nick and I used to wander round those empty rooms in Warwick Lane and pretend we lived in a proper family where everyone was happy." Susan stopped. "I shouldn't be saying this to you, madam. You see my father in such a different light."

"Never mind that. Though I think you are unjust to him, he does love you dearly——"

"He loves you," interrupted Susan. "He's changed out of all knowledge since you married him. It still amazes me to see how he looks at you. Of course it wouldn't seem strange to you; as lovely and talented as you are, you must have had dozens of men at your feet. Only I didn't know my father could fall in love."

Mary could not help being touched by this ingenuous tribute, though she was also appalled by the distorted image that Edward had presented to his daughter. He had certainly failed disastrously in handling his children. Yet you could not wonder that life had soured him. After his torments in prison there had come the sordid betrayals, the humiliation of being tied to that slut. Mary would not say a word to Susan against her dead mother; she was deeply sorry for the child, and for Edward. She had no pity to spare for Elizabeth.

As she went on talking to Susan, she uncovered the legacy that Elizabeth had left behind her. Susan had identified herself with her mother, she was haunted by that one random jibe of Edward's, and she grew up believing that she had inherited an incurably vicious strain. The ugly memory of her parents quarrelling, combined with her own sense of complicity and guilt, had poisoned her view of love. It could bring her nothing but misery; she could not bear the thought of a man touching her.

Any man except one. Even Susan could not be frightened of Tom Fletcher, her casual contacts with him went back too far. Tom had lifted her on to her pony, held her hand when they were sliding on the ice, leant over her shoulder to share the same song-book.

"I felt safe with Tom," said Susan.

And because she was so guarded with everyone else that safety had become a trap for them both, so that one day Tom sprang it, probably without meaning to. It must have been so easy to kiss her in a moment of casual affection—and enchanting to discover how much they both enjoyed it.

After that Susan hardly knew what she was doing. Her human nature, that thirsty, ill-treated drudge, took its revenge; having thought too much and felt too little, she reversed the process and

stopped thinking at all. She was not fully in love
with Tom; the old aversion to marriage was still
strong. She did not want a husband. She simply
wanted to drift along on this glorious tide of sensation, trusting Tom to look after her, without apparently realizing that he was not invincible.

When Mary finally left Susan's room her head
was throbbing and her biggest worry was not knowing what she ought to say to Edward. He should be
told the truth in justice to Susan, and also to Tom,
who had drifted into a situation he did not properly
understand. Yet how could she say, in effect: I have
uncovered one of those secrets that you keep so
carefully locked away. I know that Elizabeth made
you a cuckold, and what's more, your daughter
knows it too, and always has known, entirely
through your own negligence—fighting out your
battles with her mother, night after night, without
even pausing to wonder whether the child in the
next room could hear what you said. Now you see
the result of your stupidity.

She went into the garden. Harry and Roger were
fencing; their idea of the Noble Science was to lunge
about untidily, making a great deal of noise, and
each claiming a bloody victory with every thrust.
Harry volunteered that he had a message for her
from his father.

"He set off into the forest on foot, and said he
might not be back till after dinner."

So Edward was in one of his moods. Mary was
still standing in the sun, absently watching the ex-
cited little boys, when she caught the sound of hoof-
beats from the far side of the village green. A
gorgeously painted coach emerged from the narrow
chase between the trees. Mary swore under her

breath. There was only one person in the neighbourhood who travelled with such a flourish, and she did
not feel equal to a visit from Lady Foyle.

However, there was no escape. Mary knew that
she must be plainly visible on the rising ground in
front of the Manor. Feeling untidy and plain, she
went forward, as the coach crossed the bridge, to
receive her unwelcome guest.

She always thought of Blanche Foyle as she had
seen her first, the heroine of her son's christening
party in her satin-hung bed, laughing with her
cronies at Edward Garnham's failings as a bridegroom. The dazzling vision who stepped down from
the coach had the same gleam of lazy amusement in
her eyes. She wouldn't be seen dead in Mary's old,
narrow farthingale, and her polished nails never got
broken fruit-picking.

The two women greeted each other formally,
Mary saying insincerely that she was delighted to
see her ladyship. "Will you be pleased to come into
the house—unless you would rather take the air?"

"By all means let us profit by the summer while
we have it. You must forgive me for this visitation,
madam. I can so seldom lure you over to Ravestock,
and this morning I was seized by a whim that I
should like to see my godchild."

"How unlucky that you should have chosen today. Susan has a severe headache, she's lying down
in her room."

Lady Foyle murmured her regret and made polite enquiries about Edward and the other children.
They strolled along the grass alley in a thick chunk
of shade from the clipped yews; it was cool and refreshing. Mary inspected her companion critically.
What a ridiculous hat to wear in the country, and

all those pearls—she was only a jumped-up alderman's daughter aping the fashions of a great lady.

As they reached the end of the path, Jane came round the corner at full speed and nearly knocked them over. Absorbed in her own affairs, she seized on her mother without apparently noticing the visitor.

"I've been looking for you everywhere, madam. How long is Susan going to be locked up like a prisoner? We've got to take the last lot of honey from the hives, and if I do it by myself I shall probably be stung to death. Surely you can let her out now?"

Mary could have shaken her. Instead, she asked on a very sharp note: "Has the devil run away with your manners? You can see that I am engaged with Lady Foyle. You had better make your curtsey properly and leave us in peace. I hope you will excuse Jane, madam. She goes about with her head in a beehive."

Jane curtseyed with a sunny smile, saying, "I didn't mean to be rude." She was quite unabashed.

Lady Foyle laughed. "You have more important matters on hand, and you are braver than my girls, they show no aptitude for bee-keeping. Will you come over to Ravestock and give them a lesson?"

"Oh yes, my lady. Whenever you wish."

Jane liked Ravestock and Lady Foyle's pack of good-looking assertive children. But, then, Jane liked everyone.

When she had gone, Lady Foyle said: "How pretty she is. She does you credit, madam." And then, without a break: "So Susan has to be locked up for having a headache. It must be a grave disorder."

Mary resented the satirical twist, and her own appearance as a harsh stepmother. "The fact is," she said stiffly, "Susan has behaved stupidly and has had to bear the consequences. She is not locked up—but I need not weary your ladyship with the details. They are very trivial."

"She is rather beyond the age of childish punishments, isn't she? Unless—don't tell me Susan has been star-gazing with some enterprising young man!" This was so near the literal truth that a brief glance at Mary gave her the answer. "Well, I am devoutly thankful to hear it. I had begun to fear she was made of pure marble."

"It was a most harmless indiscretion." Why did I have to let her guess? thought Mary, furious. We don't want Susan's reputation chewed to pieces by half the gossips in London. "I must ask your ladyship not to speak of it. Susan may be a little fool, but she is entirely innocent."

"I can believe that. Meanwhile, I suppose Edward is going round with a brow of thunder, saying that she is headed for damnation, like her mother."

"He hasn't said anything of the sort! I don't know what poor Edward's done that you should all put such monstrous words into his mouth." She pulled herself up. There was no point in losing her temper. Then, with a cold assumption of dignity: "Edward is more loyal than you seem to imagine. He never discussed his first marriage, and I don't consider it my place to go ferreting out ancient rumours."

"That's a very lofty sentiment. If I were you I should try to discard it. You will never be much use to your stepchildren until you do."

Mary was coming to the same conclusion. There

was a temptation to ask questions. And why not? Blanche Foyle had been Elizabeth's intimate friend. Her opinion of the past might be biased; it must obviously be more complete than Susan's.

"In that case—perhaps your ladyship will enlighten me. Was Elizabeth—did she have many lovers?"

"Only one."

Only one. To be dismissed in a light drawl, as a minor deviation that hardly mattered. Lady Foyle presumably took lovers as a matter of course. I expect she's had a good few, thought Mary with a flash of contempt.

Lady Foyle said, "If Elizabeth was unfaithful it was because Edward drove her to it."

"So he must accept the blame as well as the injury? I call that a most pernicious doctrine. Come, madam—how can any grown woman be driven to sin against her will? What was she, a misunderstood saint?"

"She was a lonely and unhappy girl with a husband who didn't care a straw for her and couldn't be bothered to dissemble. Elizabeth was sixteen when she married him. He was twenty-four, a popular hero, handsome as the noonday—but I need not list his qualities for you. She found from the start that her Adonis was the outward shell of a man who had nothing to share with her. He was totally indifferent to her wishes, wouldn't take any steps to entertain her himself, and when they were invited out he generally cried off at the eleventh hour. She was left to sit at home and mope, while he ran errands for the Secretary of State."

"He had his way to make, and an overwhelming sense of duty——"

"Not towards his wife," said Lady Foyle acidly.

They had reached the end of the path again. By common consent they sat down on a stone bench, facing into the sun. Lady Foyle went on talking.

"As he ignored her more and more, she came to spend most of her time at our house. Edward did not approve."

Probably not. Blanche must have been in her early twenties, Mary calculated, and married to the second of her three husbands, a courtier named Walter Trencham, who had later been killed in a riding accident. The pampered, extravagant Trenchams could scarcely have been ideal companions for the discontented wife of a hardworking under-secretary.

"I don't know if he expected Elizabeth to shut herself up like an anchoress. Oh, I grant you he gave her three children; even that was a condescension. Do you know there were months on end when he would not sleep in the same bed with her?"

"That was after this other man——"

"No, it was long before. Elizabeth never knew what she had done to displease him. That was what defeated her. Finally, after eight years, she turned to a man who was frank and gay, and who knew very well how to make a woman the centre of his world. And I maintain she had the greatest provocation."

And I dare say you encouraged her, thought Mary.

"I admit that Elizabeth put herself in the wrong," continued Blanche, "but there was no cause for Edward to condemn her so unmercifully. He wouldn't acknowledge that she had any defense, and he brushed aside all her tears and entreaties.

He said that no amount of belated remorse could alter the facts. That's the worse of these paragons of virtue; they stake their souls on the Ten Commandments and they can't make allowances. I often wonder how they define Christian charity."

"It's easy for an onlooker to be charitable. If you had been her victim, instead of Edward, you might not be so magnanimous."

"An interesting premise, Mrs. Garnham." Blanche flipped back the lawn ruffle at her wrist in a gesture of casual grace, and her rings sparked with light. "Strange as it may seem, I was her victim. Edward and I were both in the same boat. I should have told you that Elizabeth's lover was my husband."

"Oh," said Mary, nonplussed. "I'm sorry, I hadn't the faintest notion. . . ." She glanced doubtfully at the woman beside her, and saw the beautiful, sensuous face suddenly naked to the onslaught of pain. She looked away, repeating: "I'm sorry. You are the last person I ought to have troubled with my questions. I had no intention of trespassing among your private concerns."

"It doesn't matter." Blanche sounded perfectly composed. After a few seconds she said: "My lot has fallen in pleasant places. Now, with Gilbert, I am devoted to him; he is an angel, far too good for me. But every marriage is different, you know that. And Walter was different from anyone else. Walter was the love of my life. We were marvellously suited, and I didn't expect any rivals. When I discovered his intrigue with Elizabeth I was so angry I could have murdered him. I raged and screamed and threw plates at his head—a proper shrew I was, for three whole days. And then Walter was so con-

trite—he was my husband and she was my friend,
and I couldn't go on hating them to order. So I took
him back, and together we managed to mend everything we had broken (except for the plates). Even
my old affection for Elizabeth. I had no means of
guessing that within five years they would both be
dead. But I've been so thankful ever since that I
forgave them.''

"Yes, indeed," said Mary, sobered by this revelation of the real Blanche. This was no selfish
hedonist. Behind the frivolous façade there were
strong feelings and strong principles. The spoilt
heiress, who screamed and threw plates at her
philandering husband, was, at heart, amazingly
generous. With this reassessment came the disturbing idea that her description of her friend's marriage was probably honest and intelligent. Mary
could no longer refuse to take it seriously.

Blanche said: "You will see why I haven't much
patience with Edward. If he had been more loving
to his wife in the first place—however, I won't ride
my hobby-horse, I am too ready to talk out of turn.
Which reminds me, I owe you an apology. I was
odiously uncivil when we met at Rob's christening,
though I didn't mean you to hear what I said. It
may console you to know that I got the rough edge
of Gilbert's tongue afterwards. He reduced me to
sackcloth and ashes.''

"Oh, there was no need! You may tell Sir Gilbert
I never gave it another thought." Which was not
strictly true, but all the rancour had been washed
away, as dislike changed to admiration. Mary was
now ashamed of her rather stodgy antagonism, having a shrewd suspicion that it was due to pique.

The two women went on talking for some time

and when Lady Foyle drove away in her coach
Mary was actually sorry to see her go. There was
certainly no pleasure in being left to contemplate
the new and ugly ideas that had been forced on her
in the past few hours: the portrait Blanche and Susan had drawn of a cold egotist, indifferent yet unforgiving, whose continual neglect of his wife and
children had hurt them all so desperately.

Edward isn't like that, she insisted. I know him
better. He can be wonderfully gentle and chivalrous. Right at the start, before we fell in love,
that day I made a fool of myself and said I wouldn't
marry him, could any man have been more considerate? Or after the wedding, when he knew I was
still thinking of Jack, how patient he was with me
then. He does care for the children, and they know
it, too; look how the boys have dogged his footsteps
all the summer. Yet she was not entirely reassured,
for against her will she recognized something familiar about the man who rejected his wife without
pity, in the depth of her guilt and despair; who left
his little son and daughter alone to grieve for their
mother. A man with a strange and ruthless capacity
for shutting his eyes to the needs of people who depended on him to protect them against their own
weakness. For that was exactly what Edward had
done last night, when he repudiated Tom's claim
on him, and threw him out of the house which had
been his haven for eleven years.

It was nearly six when Edward returned from his
solitary walk in the forest. Mary met him with a
slight constraint, embarrassed by the knowledge
that she wanted to conceal; she also had an odd
feeling that she might see him differently now; as
though cuckolds really worn horns. But there was

only one noticeable fact about Edward this evening:
he was physically exhausted, so tired he could hardly speak.

They went to bed directly after supper. Several
hours later, through an immense, blank stupor of
sleep, Mary heard someone shouting, a senseless
jumble and then the terrifying word: "Fire!" Her
heavy brain rebelled. No, this is too much. I can't
stand any more. There was a longing to plunge
deeper into the blissful feather-bed, followed instantly by a fiercer necessity: the children. She must
get to the children, to Greville, her baby. She was
sitting up, grappling with the sheets, while she was
still three parts asleep, muscles flabby and eyelids
gummed down tight.

She blinked herself fully awake. The curtains
were drawn round the bed, and it was quite dark.
Edward had moved already; his weight shifted
somewhere near her feet. There was still this urgent
voice talking about the fire, but nothing else.

"Where is it?" she asked. "I can't smell any
smoke. We must make haste."

"The flames are like wolves, they lick your skin,
they eat your flesh. There's nothing left but the fire.
The fire and the pain."

She realized with a shock that the voice belonged
to Edward, though she had never heard anything
like it before, taut and high-pitched; the agonizing
phrases poured out, slurred and ran into each other. He was talking in his sleep.

"My fingers crumbling into dust. And I didn't
want to die. . . ."

She had got her bearings now. This was one of
those nightmares he had warned her about, when
he dreamed he was being burnt alive at Smithfield.

It was unbelievably horrible, and she did not know what she ought to do. Was it safe to wake him?

The sharp cry dropped into a sob, and he was praying. "Have mercy on me, O Lord, according to Thy great mercies. Enter not into judgment with Thy servant, for in Thy sight can no living man be justified. No man living—O God, release me from this living death."

Whatever the risk, she could not leave him in this state of distress. She knelt beside him and put a hand on his shoulder, which was slippery with sweat, saying firmly, "Wake up, Edward."

She felt the check in his breathing, the nerves quickening to consciousness under the bare skin. He caught hold of the bedpost, and asked: "Who is it? Mary?"

"Yes, love—it's Mary. You've been dreaming, but all's well now."

"What did I say?"

"You spoke of—of the fire. And then you quoted from the Book of Psalms."

"Was that all?"

"Yes. Lie down again, sweetheart, or you'll catch a chill."

She tucked in the quilt, and lay close to him, holding his hand. She dared not embark on the subject of the dream, since he gave her no lead. Presently she asked, "Could you sleep more peacefully now?"

"No," he said. "No, I'll not sleep."

In the morning he got up and tackled the day with the grim resignation of a man who had often gone without rest. He toyed with his bread and meat, swallowed a cup of ale, and then rode back to London.

13

Late in September, Mary and the children returned to Warwick Lane. It was not the most cheerful of homecomings; Edward was engrossed in his work and did not seem particularly pleased to see any of them.

He must be near his quarry now, she thought, remembering the few facts Tom had been able to explain to her. Soon the State would pounce, and one more conspiracy would become public property, a nine days' wonder. There would be outbursts of anger and alarm, and everyone would talk as though the danger had suddenly arisen and been crushed in a matter of hours; few people realized the months of patient hunting that went before the kill. Months in which there were two parallel conspiracies. The traitors unaware that they were being gradually out-manoeuvred by that other group of Government agents, as subtle and determined as themselves. You could only be grateful that there were men like Edward, capable of fighting for England in these invisible battles, and perhaps it was not surprising that his family had to share the cost of his devotion.

Edward's new secretary was not living in the house, and Mary did not see much of him. However, there was one frequent visitor who was very welcome: Etienne d'Aubais.

The Frenchman had given up his post as a tutor in Chelsea. His wife's rudeness and stupidity had put an end to that. Luckily Edward had managed to find him a niche among the collection of useful followers employed by the Secretary of State. D'Aubais's experience of Continental politics and Catholic machinations made him a valuable recruit, and he seemed to be working closely with Edward.

One afternoon when they had arranged to meet, d'Aubais arrived early, and came upstairs to gossip with Mary. They soon got on to the subject of Tom.

"I was astounded to hear that your husband had been obliged to send him away. A charming boy, I should not have cast him for a villain."

She thought that Edward must have confided in him. "Do you think Tom's conduct was so infamous?"

The little man spread his expressive hands. "Madam, I don't know what he has done. I know there must have been some grave reason why Edward should be so implacable. Of course Tom has a roving eye—*bon Dieu*! Is it possible? That the young devil was so impudent, and with no chance of success?"

Mary was puzzled, then she smiled. "He wasn't in love with me, though I thank you for the compliment. I may as well tell you the true story."

She told it, adding at the end:

"He has done no lasting harm. They were both thoroughly ashamed, and I'm sure they have learnt their lesson. Give me your frank opinion, monsieur; do you think Edward was justified in being so hard on Tom?"

D'Aubais frowned; his reply was slow and considered. "I should say he was too extreme. It may be wiser to separate these two young creatures, after what has happened, yet he might have made the break more mercifully, found the boy somewhere to go and a new master to serve. He is an admirable secretary, and he hasn't failed in his duty there."

"No, and that is what troubles me most, for who will believe it now? People are bound to imagine some black disgrace. They'll say that he must be very vicious for Edward to treat him in such a manner. We can't bandy Susan's name abroad, and, anyway, it would do no good. This summary dismissal is so damning. The truth would be twisted and exaggerated into something too ugly to condone."

"It is unfortunate that Edward acted in haste. No doubt he was exceedingly angry at the time; may he not have second thoughts? Have you tried to plead for Tom's return?"

"I embarked on the subject yesterday, and was sharply put in my place." Edward had been at his most caustic; the snub still smarted in her mind. "There's no more I can say. He's too preoccupied to listen, and he insists that Tom's future is no concern of mine. That might be so, if Tom were the usual sort of secretary: a gentleman's son, with a family to rally round and give him a fresh start. But he has no one. You know his origins. Edward sent him up to Cambridge and taught him his profession, and what use is that to him now? How can a man with a smeared reputation and no influence find work as a confidential secretary?"

"He was a child when Edward took him in?"

"Eleven years old, too young to have learnt a

trade. And he couldn't go back to the common people. They wouldn't have him. He talks and moves and thinks differently, and they would see him as an intruder. Between us and them there is a great gulf fixed."

"You need not tell me that, madam. I proved the distance last year, when I was living here on your generosity, and struggling to make myself independent. Being a foreign exile, I had no claim to special favours, so I thought I might teach dancing, or go as a clerk to some merchant—heaven knows what Margot would have said! However, she was spared such indignities. No one wanted me. My breeding, you see, had become a disadvantage. A man who kept a fencing-school told me: 'My clients are too rough for the likes of you. It wouldn't be fitting. You are a gentleman.' As though I had three legs or a tail! Once a gentleman is destitute, there's no honest road that he can take. Though there are certain devious byways; I counted five, all fairly well trodden."

"And what are they?"

"A gentleman," said d'Aubais, putting an ironic stress on the word, "can still use his superior talents to defraud simple people of their savings. He can set up as a gambler if he has the skill to handle the cards. He can become a hired bravo, a pander or a spy."

"But that is horrible," said Mary, rather faintly. "I didn't know it was so bad. And haven't you forgotten the Army, or these privateering ventures to the New World? They'd be open to a young bachelor like Tom."

"There again, he is the sort that has to enlist as an officer, and even that takes some money."

"Then what can he be doing? How can he have
lived, all these weeks? I never imagined—it was
foolish of me, having always been so sheltered; I
didn't understand what it was like for a penniless
young man adrift in London. If only I knew how to
reach him!"

"Shall I try to find him for you?"

"Would you? I should be eternally grateful. I
could help him a little; my fortune is all in trust, but
there are the jewels Jack gave me, nothing to do
with Edward. . . ."

It was an immense relief to feel that something
might be done. They made plans and Mary told
d'Aubais all she knew about Tom's acquaintances
and his favourite haunts.

D'Aubais took the search very seriously, though
at first he had no success. After all, London was a
big place.

They had still heard nothing several days later
when Mary went to call on Margot d'Aubais, who
was now the discontented chatelaine of three rooms
over an apothecary's shop in Bucklersbury.

"This is a wretched neighbourhood, madam.
Nothing but shopkeepers, and they are far from respectful. There is no pleasure in walking abroad. So
I am forced to sit here alone and breathe the stench
of boiling poultices till it makes me sick. And
Etienne only says we should be worse off at a
fishmonger's."

Mary condoled, and added truthfully, "You
must be well satisfied with your furnishings;
they are quite out of the common." For the
Frenchwoman had somehow achieved, with very
little outlay, an air of formal grandeur that was

rather pathetic. "I envy you those elegant hangings."

"Painted cloths—paltry stuff. Once I had acres of Flemish tapestry. Ah well, we must thank God for small mercies. There are many worse off than I am."

Mary was astonished to hear her say so. She then learnt that Margot had discovered another Huguenot lady she could patronize, and this was a great source of comfort to her.

"Poor Madame de Brivard, she thought their troubles were over, because her Jean-Marie has been taken up by some rich lord, but I told her: 'These private appointments lead nowhere. *My* husband works for the Government; he is under the protection of Queen Elizabeth.' And now we are bidden to dine with Monsieur Walsingham, which Etienne considers a great honour, though I hear he is not at all well born. A jumped-up sprig of the bourgeoisie, it seems."

"You will not notice that when you meet him: he was the English Ambassador in Paris for some years. Edward says the Queen is much attached to him; she calls him her Moor, on account of his dark complexion."

"Surely he is not an African?"

"No, madam—it is a pleasantry."

Margot looked unconvinced. Perhaps she'll ask him if he has a hundred wives, thought Mary. I wish Edward was here; how diverted he would be.

There was a creak on the stair, and Etienne came in, neat and spruce. He greeted Mary ceremoniously, before saying to his wife: "I thought it was agreed that the Harbottles should not hang their

washing in front of our windows. How is it that all
Obediah's shirts are dangling in the yard?"

"No—not again! They must come down instantly. Wait till I deal with that old trollop."

Margot flew out of her chair like an infuriated
cat, and a few seconds later they could hear her, on
the floor below, scarifying the nearest bourgeoise.

"That was wicked of you," said Mary.

"The good Harbottles are well able to defend
themselves. I had to speak with you alone."

"You have some news?"

"Of a kind, yes. I am afraid it is not good. As you
know, I have been asking round the taverns if anyone there is acquainted with Tom Fletcher. Today
I came across a law student named Tony Vincent
who was up at Cambridge with him, and who has
seen him since he left Maringale."

"How long ago?"

"About three weeks. That would be ten days or
so after Edward turned him out. Young Vincent
was at the Angel one evening when Tom wandered
in, very shabby and downcast. Vincent offered him
a cup of sack, and soon Tom was half drunk."

"He'd been drinking already?"

"No. Vincent, who is not a fool, said that the
wine went to his head because he was hungry. In
fact, Tom admitted that he had not eaten that
day."

"Oh God," said Mary softly.

"Vincent knew that Tom was your husband's
secretary; he asked what calamity had brought him
to such a pass. Tom said he had been discharged
and would give no reason, except that it was entirely his own fault. He said, "I have lost the best friend
I ever had, and earned the contempt of the man I
admire most in the world.""

"Poor Tom. Surely if Edward heard that he would be moved to compassion. What else did Vincent say? Does he know where Tom is now?"

"Unhappily, no. They had a hot meal, which he paid for, and he forced a few shillings on Tom, as a loan. This boy Vincent is not wealthy: a younger son, scraping through his studies on a small allowance. He could do no more. He engaged Tom to meet him again, later in the week. He went to the inn, but Tom never arrived, and he has not seen him since."

"Where can he be?" Mary was almost in tears. "I can't bear to think of him in such a pitiful state. You don't suppose he would take his own life?"

"No, I don't. Believe me, madam, I have seen a great deal of mortal wretchedness, and healthy young men of Tom's quality do not easily sink to suicide. The human animal is far tougher than you imagine. There are always other ways, even when you are nearly starving. It is these other ways that disturb me. I wish I could be certain what Tom is doing now."

14

I shall have to tell Edward, Mary was thinking when she reached Warwick Lane. I shall tell him that Tom has been roaming the streets without enough money to buy food, and what he said about losing the best friend he ever had.

She went down the short passage to the study, shaping tactful sentences in her brain, when the door swung open and Nicholas came out in a rush, nearly knocking her down.

"Catholics!" he exclaimed. "Always seeing bogeys under every bush and insisting they are Catholics. I'm sick of this endless nagging over religion."

"So you may be," said Mary, rubbing her elbow, "but there is no need to wreak your vengeance on me."

He gave her his vague, half-blind stare. "Did I hurt you, madam? I'm sorry. Do you think that a man who says his prayers in Latin has venom in his blood?"

"I don't know what's happened, nor why you are in such a fatigue. Nick, do stop scowling and try to give me the facts."

Edward's cool voice behind them said: "Nick is not concerned with facts at present. He is indulging in a frenzy of distortion."

"Oh, am I?" retorted Nicholas with a surprising lack of respect. "Let me tell you, sir, there's one ugly fact that I have mastered. I know how you plant spies among decent people, you violate their privacy and worm out their secrets——"

"I've told you a dozen times, I didn't invent these methods, I am a servant of the Council. If a man chooses to break the law I can't help that. It gave me no pleasure to find his name on that list."

"Then why can't you ignore it? You said yourself you weren't going to arrest the small fry. What does it matter if he goes to Mass? I dare say he likes to hear the music. It's more beautiful than anything we have."

"Music has nothing to do with theology."

"It is theology to a musician. When I play the virginals I am praying as hard as any canting preacher. And perhaps my prayers may be more acceptable; at least they aren't so damnably contentious."

"There's no call to be blasphemous."

Mary glanced from one to the other as their exchanges ripped like sabre-cuts. They were extraordinarily alike, for there was none of the old, slouching timidity about Nicholas. He stood up straight and contradicted his father in Edward's own astringent vein.

"Do, for pity's sake, enlighten me," she said. "Who has been going to Mass?"

"My father says that Mr. Verney——"

"It seems that Miles Verney is a practising papist——"

"Which doesn't prevent him from being the best virginal-maker in London."

"Hold your tongue. I am talking to your stepmother." Edward turned to Mary. "Miles Verney has been attending these illegal services that are held secretly in certain Catholic houses. I wish it was not so, for there's no other charge against him; his name was simply noted as a member of their congregation. However, in the circumstances, Nicholas cannot continue as his pupil."

So the gentle and talented Mr. Verney was one of the backsliders. Nicholas was right: there were bogeys under every bush. That was the trouble: England was still riddled with the old faith, and you met it everywhere. But why did it have to crop up in the one place where Nick had found happiness and a hope for the future?

He was not prepared to be shut out of his Eden. "Do you think I'm going to desert a friend because his reputation is in danger? That's a fine sort of honour for a Christian gentleman. Besides, I can't break off my studies——"

"I've promised I'll get you another teacher."

"I don't want another teacher, I want Mr. Verney. I shall go to the shop tomorrow as usual, and if you wish to get me back you'd better send the constable and a couple of Walsingham's vultures and have me dragged through the streets to make a public spectacle, for I shan't come willingly."

"You are a little too ambitious." Edward's grey eyes were stormy. "We don't send constables after disobedient children. I can provide all the discipline you need, so don't try my patience any further. You have had too much licence already. If it were not for your affliction——"

"The devil take my affliction! Do you think I'm counting on my weak sight to protect me? I may be as blind as a bat, but I'm not a cripple; you can beat me with impunity. But you won't change my mind at the stroke of a whip, and you ought to know that, sir."

Edward was not accustomed to being told what he could or could not do to his dependents, least of all by Nicholas. Almost too incredulous to be angry, it was several seconds before he could allow himself to speak.

"Very well," he said, regaining command of the situation. "Your point is taken. Your mind is unchangeable, your manners are deplorable and you have aired them both sufficiently for one evening. Go to your room and stay there."

"Sir." Nicholas bowed with a deliberate formality, and marched off, his cheeks flushed and his chin aggressively high.

The transformation was complete. Six months of doing something he really enjoyed, and doing it supremely well, had cancelled every feeling of inadequacy. This was the essential Nicholas: raw and unreasonable as any boy of fifteen, yet true to a fiercely individual nature, a personal set of values. And, just like his father, obstinately brave in his refusal to compromise. His exit was superb, and the minor matter of his tripping over a step did nothing to spoil a remarkable performance.

Mary said: "You can be proud of your son. Impudent little monkey, I like his spirit."

Edward had once complained that Nicholas was feeble and spineless. Now that he was confronted by a rebel of his own tough quality he did not seem particularly grateful for the change.

"I might have known that you would side with Nick," he grumbled. "I suppose you think I should leave him in that litter of papists."

"I never said so," she protested. Of course she
realized that Edward could not let his fifteen-year-
old son work in a house full of Catholics. "Why do
you accuse me of supporting Nick?"

"You make it your business to champion my victims. Tom, for instance."

"Tom! I've hardly mentioned his name."

He could not possibly guess that she had been
coming to renew her attack.

"No," he said, "you've gone beyond words,
haven't you? Making poor d'Aubais tramp around
London for you when he had many more important
things to do. I didn't recommend him to Walsingham in order that he should waste his days
hunting for my former secretary."

It had never occurred to her that Edward might
be quietly observing their efforts, and perhaps
laughing at their incompetence. Very much put out,
she could only ask, "How did you know?"

"That's part of my trade, to know what goes on."

"By planting spies," she said with a touch of
spite. He had made a fool of her, and she wanted to
pay him out. "I agree with Nick. You have too little
regard for the rights of ordinary people to mind
their own business."

"Possibly. But Tom Fletcher is not your business, Mary."

"That's nonsense. His future concerns us both
and how you expect him to survive——"

"Tom will survive without you trying to wet-
nurse him. A spell of hardship will be the best
schooling for that young man, and no more than he
deserves. And I assure you he won't starve."

Edward moved towards the study while he was

speaking. She followed him in, determined to continue the argument.

"Doesn't his repentance mean anything to you? Don't you care what happens to him, exposed to such temptations——What's that?"

Edward glanced at a thick bundle on the settle. "Blankets," he said briefly.

"Yes, I can see they are blankets, but who brought them downstairs?"

He hesitated, picked up a quill, and began to mend it with his penknife. "I told Ben to set up a truckle bed for me in here."

"You did what?" She gaped at him. "Edward—why?"

"I thought it more convenient, for the present."

"But why? Edward, you must tell me. Is it because I tried to help Tom?"

He did not reply, and went on chipping at the quill. He had a maddening habit of leaving a question to hang in the air, unanswered. She watched him, biting her lip. Whatever her private convictions might be, she knew she ought not to fight against Edward's decisions. God, in His inscrutable wisdom, had ordained that in all marriages the man was master. (She thought, irreverently, that God's wisdom was always inscrutable; sometimes it was positively opaque.) But she had been strictly brought up; she knew that her mother would have told her to swallow her principles and make a dutiful submission.

She said: "I'm sorry if I've let my judgment run away with me, and I promise you I'll try to be more —more amenable. So can't we call a truce?"

"You are mistaken—I'm not trying to force your

hand, and this has nothing to do with Tom. I propose to sleep down here because it will be less troublesome. You know the hours I have been keeping
lately. I don't wish to disturb you."

"Oh! Is that all? My darling, I never heard such
nonsense. Disturb me, indeed! Half the time you
don't even wake me, and I wish you would. I like to
be disturbed."

"Do you? Then I don't know what I am to say to
you, Mary." The note of desperate irritation jolted
her returning confidence. He also seemed acutely
embarrassed; his eye slid away from hers, and he
turned, beginning to shovel an armful of papers into the press. "Can't you learn to take a plain
statement of fact without always asking for chapter
and verse? I am going to sleep where I choose, and
that's an end of it. You won't gain anything by
being so confoundedly importunate."

Importunate—was that how she appeared to
him? It was the most cruel adjective he could have
chosen. When she had said that she liked to be disturbed she was thinking that it was worth waking
up in the small hours just to know that Edward was
there and that she had some share in his life, though
it was a passive one at present. She was not an ignorant girl of sixteen, expecting an overworked man
to make love to her when he was tired out. Anyway,
she had never dreamed of demanding love from
either of her husbands. There had been no need to
ask. In her experience the whole pattern of love-
making placed the initiative with the man, so that if
a woman was reduced to begging she became unnatural and contemptible. She felt as though Edward had stripped away all her defenses.

She stared miserably at his back, which was all

she could see of him. The wide and capable shoulders, in the elegant grey doublet, seemed as unresponsive as a wall.

"You are safe from me," she muttered. "I shan't pester you again." And she ran out, hurrying through the house, afraid of meeting anyone, wanting only to get to her room unseen, like a wounded animal scuttling to its lair.

Once there, she slammed the door, leant against it, and burst into tears. What had she done, what had gone wrong? Why had Edward turned against her? Because that plea of "convenience" was rubbish; he had never used it before, no matter how hard or how late he was working. He said there was no connection with Tom. Another woman, then? No, that wouldn't do, not while this conspiracy was in the wind. In spite of herself, Mary felt a spark of amusement at the idea of Edward pursuing suspects and sirens in different directions, hurrying between a mistress and the Secretary of State. Perhaps his long duel with the conspirators had brought on a quite irrational mood that was merely the result of frayed nerves? But she knew in her heart that this was not the solution; her native perception told her that he had some definite motive in pushing her aside, though she could not imagine what it was, still less how to cope with it.

She went over to the basin and bathed her eyes with rosewater. As the lotion tingled against her swollen lids she had the sensation of history repeating itself; this had happened to someone else in a story she had been told recently. Then she remembered Blanche Foyle, in the garden at Maringale, describing Edward's unkindness to his first wife. But it's not like that with us, she amended quickly.

He and Elizabeth weren't happy together, as we have been. He's told me a hundred times how much he loves me, and proved it. There's no comparison. And still she heard Blanche's clear voice: "Elizabeth never knew what she had done to displease him. That was what defeated her."

15

Next morning, while Mary was getting the three younger boys off to school, Nicholas slipped out of the house and went round to Paternoster Row. Half an hour later he was back, looking very dejected. All the excitement of battle had died out of him.

"Mr. Verney sent me home," he announced tragically. "He wouldn't have me in the shop. My father was one jump ahead of me, curse him. I might have known what he would do. He went round there last night, and now Mr. Verney is on his high horse, says he can't encourage me in an act of disobedience."

Mary did her best to comfort him. He mustn't take things too much to heart.

"After all, Mr. Verney is not the only musician in London. As soon as he has time your father will find you a new master—"

"And how long will he last? Until he turns out to be an anabaptist or an infidel, I suppose?"

"That's not very likely, is it?"

"Oh, there will be some snag or other, you'll see. My music will always be pushed aside. And why not? It's such a puny, trifling occupation, compared to his great concerns. That's what I mind most, and you none of you understand, not even Susan." He was suffering from a grievance which went deep

below the surface of childish bad temper. "When
my father let me study music I was so happy I
thought he knew how much it meant to me. That he
was giving me a life of my own, so that I could strive
for perfection and make him proud of me. That was
my vanity. He doesn't expect me to succeed. My
lessons are just a sop, a toy to divert me because I'm
going blind. Let poor Nick tap out a few more tunes
and forget that he's the useless runt of the litter,
the one that ought to have been drowned at
birth!" He was choking back the bitter tears in his
throat. "I don't complain about my sight, I don't
hanker after things I can't have. I simply want to
prove myself in my true vocation, without this chop-
ping and changing and senseless interference. But I
shall never get any proper support from him. All I
shall ever get is this damnable pity."

Once he had recovered from his outburst, he was
far too proud to go on exposing himself, so by the
time Edward came home to supper, Nick had
walled himself in behind a manner of stony civility
which bordered on downright impertinence. Edward treated him in the most deflating way: he pretended not to notice. This infuriated Nicholas, who
knew that none of the other children would have
escaped so lightly. His father was again being sorry
for him. It was the last straw. Since he had no work
to do, and nowhere to go, he nursed his wrongs with
a morbid intensity, hanging around the house all
day and adding to the general gloom.

With an unapproachable husband she hardly
ever saw, and a sulky stepson who was perpetually
underfoot, Mary felt she would go mad.

Poor Susan still looked guilty and subdued, and
that brought Mary's distracted mind full circle

round to Tom. He was still her chief anxiety. Because, however unhappy she or Susan or Nicholas
might be, they were none of them homeless and
starving.

Every time she walked along a London street
Mary hoped she might see him, and searched eagerly among the passing crowds. She was doing this
one morning on her way to the Poultry to choose a
fat goose, and perhaps her hopes were playing on
her nerves, for she kept thinking she recognized
him. Tom was darker than most Englishmen and
nearly as tall as Edward; it was extraordinary how
many dark, tall men there were in Cheapside to
raise her spirits at a first glance, and dash them
again as she drew close enough to see an unknown
face, pock-marked or bearded, the blank indifference of a stranger. She knew it was stupid, but
she kept imagining a likeness.

That man in front of her, for instance: he had the
same stretch of the shoulders, the same long,
springing stride as Tom. As she studied his back, he
swung to the left, avoiding the black brushes of a
chimney-sweep, and this revealed a different angle,
a tantalizing segment of dark hair and straight
nose, between the hat-brim and the high white ruff.
That profile seemed so familiar that her heart
began to thump with excitement. She passed the
Poultry, hurrying after her will-o'-the-wisp, who
wove his way through the busy streets with an ex-
asperating skill. If only she could catch up with
him. There were so many strollers blocking her
path as they gossiped and gaped. The peacock-blue
hat and cloak danced ahead of her. At the corner of
Lombard Street and Cornhill the young man
turned and stood still, waiting to cross the road.

Then she was certain—or almost certain.

"Tom!" she called out. "Tom!"

Several people eyed her curiously, and an elderly clergyman raked her with a disapproving glare. "Have you no shame, woman," he demanded, "that you go flaunting through the city after your paramour?"

A bunch of 'prentices nudged one another and giggled.

Mary shouted again, more loudly.

"Daughter of Babylon," groaned the clergyman.

But the young man in blue seemed quite oblivious. He stepped neatly between a couple of waggons and disappeared in the direction of Old Jewry.

Mary started to run after him, collided with a girl selling hot pies, and lost her chance of crossing as the heavy traffic lunbered on, barring her passage.

She watched the wheels grinding by, dull with disappointment. She would never track him down in that maze of little lanes. Slowly, she went back to buy her goose.

A moment's reflection brought some relief, for she began to think that she had been on the point of making a public spectacle of herself. The peacock gentleman could not possibly have been Tom: he was far too richly dressed. That cloak was the latest cut, there had been a flash of flame-coloured satin, the glint of a brooch in the hat. A prosperous young blade, with money in his purse and a definite object in view, very different from the description d'Aubais had brought her of poor Tom, so shabby and aimless. She must control her wild fancies; the wife of Walsingham's chief assistant couldn't go round accosting strange gallants and being mistaken for a daughter of Babylon. She grinned as she thought of the scandalized clergyman. What on earth would Edward say if he knew? And yet she could have sworn that it was Tom.

She had to discuss this episode with someone, and the first person available at home was Jane, who was sitting at the parlour table, writing out a French exercise. Etienne d'Aubais had selected one of his countrymen to give her lessons. Mary poured out her morning's adventure.

"What was the man wearing?" asked Jane.

"Oh, he was uncommonly fine, that's why I decided that it couldn't be Tom. He was dressed in blue, with one of those high, steep hats that have become so fashionable."

"And a coral ornament," said Jane dreamily, "to match the lining of his cloak."

"Yes." Mary gazed at her daughter. "How did you know? Jane—it was Tom, and you've seen him too!"

Jane got very confused. She plucked savagely at her quill, and her face, itself as bright as the tell-tale coral, was comically apprehensive.

"Oh Lord, why can't I hold my silly tongue? It was meant to be a secret. Don't be angry with me, madam; I did promise not to tell."

"You've no business to have secrets about Tom. No, I'm not angry, my pet, but since you've gone so far you had better let me have the whole of it. Where did you see him?"

"Here," muttered Jane.

"In this house? He hasn't been meeting Susan? She said that was all finished, and I trusted her—"

"It had nothing to do with Sue. In fact, he took care to come when she was out. He came yesterday, if you must know, and he watched you starting out for my uncle's. So I was the only one at home," added Jane, with a slightly defiant air which Mary understood perfectly.

The tension in the household had affected the younger children too, making them cross and unruly. Jane, never one to suffer fools gladly, had been rude to Cousin Eulalia and when the others had gone to visit the Freelands at Holborn she had been left behind in disgrace, with a dinner of dry bread and a penitential basket of mending. And, with the usual unfairness of life, it was Jane who had seen Tom.

"Tell me," said Mary.

"I was looking out of the window. I saw Ben stumping down the lane on some errand, and then a man came to the door and walked straight in without knocking. I couldn't see who it was. I knew my stepfather had gone to Whitehall, and the maids were all in the kitchen; I thought I should go and find out what was happening. There was no one in the hall; I ferreted around and then discovered him —Tom—in my stepfather's study, looking so sad that I wanted to cry. I rushed at him and hugged him, and I thought he was going to cry too. We were as merry as a funeral."

"What was he doing in the study?"

"Meditating on the good old days, I think. He misses all those dreary documents he had to copy, can you believe it? The truth is, he longs to be reconciled with my stepfather. He asked endless questions about him, and hardly spoke of Susan, except to say that he hoped you had both forgiven her. He says it was entirely his fault."

"Why did he come here if he knew we were out?"

"He wanted to fetch his books."

"Oh, I see. He didn't ask for his clothes? I have them packed in a chest upstairs."

"No, he says everything belongs by rights to my stepfather. But he needs the books for his work."

"What work? Did he tell you what he is doing, Jane? I can't understand how he comes to be so finely dressed."

"He's got plenty of money," said Jane, reviving. "He's working for a printer. Or a publisher. I forget which; it's the same thing, isn't it? Anyway, it has to do with the trade he learnt as a boy, and he can earn as much as he chooses, drink a bottle of wine a day and go to the theatre as often as he likes. And you should have seen his doublet—cut by an Italian tailor! I think he would be quite content if it wasn't for this miserable quarrel. Perhaps my stepfather will relent when he knows how industriously Tom is working."

She bubbled on, and Mary grew more bewildered. Tom's experience as a printer's apprentice had ended when he was eleven years old. What could that incomplete smattering be worth today? Not enough to pay for his new hat, let alone the rest of his wardrobe. And he was apparently living on the same luxurious scale—though he had refused to tell Jane where, which was odd, if he really wanted to make his peace with Edward. The evasions, the startling change of fortune, the obvious lie about his old trade, which could only have deceived a child like Jane—they all pointed the same way. Unable to make an honest living, Tom had been driven into one of those ugly professions that Etienne d'Aubais said were so lucrative. With a sick repugnance, Mary wondered which one he had chosen.

She was still wondering several hours later, as she sat in the little enclosed garden behind the house, embroidering a table carpet. The sheltered court drew the September sun like a magnet; there was a shimmer of heat off the paving-stones. Jane and Clemency shook the branches of the single fig-tree, hunting for fruit. Nicholas came out of the back door.

"There's a lady in the hall asking for you, madam. She seems very agitated." He screwed up his eyes against the light, which was, to him, so cruel. "I couldn't see her properly but I think she was the one we met last Christmas, who didn't know you were married to my father."

"Mrs. Quinton? What can she be doing here?"

Mary got up and followed him indoors, surprised and uneasy. This was confoundedly awkward. Edward had forbidden her ever to receive any Catholic visitors. Because of his objections, she had let her friendship with Eleanor Quinton lapse, after that one chance encounter in the street, and surely Eleanor must have guessed the reason, yet there she was in the hall, chattering to Susan.

"I'll remain here, in case your stepmother—she is your stepmother? You must be Mr. Garnham's daughter? In case she is too busy——"

"My dear Eleanor, I'm so glad to see you," said Mary, not quite truthfully, breaking into the high-pitched monologue.

They embraced, and Mary realized that her old friend was under some sort of strain that made her more incoherent than usual.

"Dearest Mary, I hope you don't mind—couldn't decide whether to approach you, and this house— it's a lions' den to us Catholics. Good grief, I

shouldn't have said that! Forgive me, I did not
mean to be discourteous. And I have a great favour
to ask you. But if you prefer it I'll go away."

"That would be a pity when you've only just arrived," said Mary, laughing in spite of herself.
"There's no cause for alarm. The lion is out at present."

They went into the garden. Eleanor exclaimed
vaguely at Jane and Clemency——what beautiful
girls they were, and how they had grown. Mary
sent them away, and settled her in the shade of the
fig-tree.

"You said I could be of some service to you?"

"Oh yes. If you would take my part. It's about
Richard."

"Your brother Richard?" The name conjured up
a flaxenhaired boy, seen at intervals over the years,
playing leapfrog in a Sussex meadow, riding after
his father's hounds. "Time passes so quickly, I suppose he must be nineteen or twenty now? And out
in the world, like the rest of us."

"Yes, he's in London. That's why I am so concerned, and I thought I might consult you, for Mr.
Garnham can have nothing personal against Richard. He is a member of the Established Church."

Gradually Mary pieced together scraps of
Eleanor's inconsequent rambling. The Quintons
had cousins living near Westminster with whom
they stayed when they came to London, and
Eleanor's favourite and much younger brother often
stayed there too. Sir Amyas Quinton was a respectable Catholic gentleman, but he had some dubious
acquaintances, including a plausible, shifty adventurer called Rashford, and Richard Brassey had
fallen under Rashford's spell. They were engaged in

some curious financial enterprise, and Eleanor was
sure they were heading for disaster.

"He sounds a most unstable ally for a boy of
Richard's age. But what do you want me to do?"

"If you could ask Mr. Garnham—he would be
bound to know—whether Richard is likely to be
prosecuted, and if there is any way I can save him."

"Oh," said Mary, taken aback. She could not
bring herself to say that she had no influence whatever with her husband; that he would neither confide in her nor advise her protégés. She did not want
to display her own wretchedness, and wished
Eleanor would go away and take her problems with
her. Though it was not Eleanor's fault, and she
seemed so vulnerable, with her worried, faintly
cowlike eyes, and her large hands fluttering. And
Richard, entangled by the temptations of London,
reminded Mary of Tom.

"What is it that you suspect?" she asked.

"Richard said—there was a cargo of sweet wine
—I think it was landed by night to escape the
monopoly tax. It's all a jape to him, he doesn't
mean any harm, but the justices would take no account of that. Suppose they sent him to gaol as a
common criminal—it would kill my father."

Mary's attention had wandered. There was a
small door in the wall, leading directly to Edward's
study. The latch had moved. That could mean only
one thing. Edward was going to open that door, he
was going to come out and catch her red-handed
entertaining one of the hated Catholics.

Now it was happening, inevitable as the sort of
accident that you watched in a frozen calm because
you couldn't prevent it. As he crossed the small

square of paving, Mary's mouth was dry, and she grasped the humiliating truth, that she was very much afraid of him.

She heard her own voice, stiffly keeping up the conventions. "Eleanor, may I present my husband. . . . This is an old friend of mine, Edward: Mrs. Quinton, who was our neighbour for many years."

She gave him a glance of silent entreaty. She hoped he would not fly into an immediate rage at the sight of a Roman idolator desecrating his garden—but with Edward you could never be sure. In fact he took the news quite impassively, and greeted Eleanor in his most urbane manner.

Eleanor was confused. His arrival had startled her, and she too felt frightened—of a man she knew only by reputation. Uncertain of her welcome, she began to explain.

"You must think it an intrusion, my visiting Mary, and indeed I don't know what my husband would say. He's at home in Derbyshire, or I should never have dared—I mean—nothing but the most urgent need would have brought me—Oh Lord, I'm making matters worse!"

This was too much for Edward's grave civility. He smiled—that sudden and charming smile which Mary had not seen for so long and mixed with her relief there was a pang of envy because it was not meant for her.

"What was the urgent need that obliged you to take this terrible step, madam?"

"I hoped to engage your clemency, on behalf of my young brother, if Mary would plead my cause."

"Well, I am here myself, so you won't have to

employ an advocate." Then, as she hesitated: "I promise you I am not an ogre, Mrs. Quinton. Whatever you may have heard."

"No, you aren't," agreed Eleanor, who was by now completely beguiled. "All those wicked slanders, I can't think why people are so malicious. . . ." Dimly aware that she was again being tactless, she launched out on the saga of Richard and his disreputable friend.

Edward was very considerate; he seemed to have endless time and patience. He reduced Eleanor's jumbled narrative into a clear outline, extracting names, dates and details, and Mary realized that this was one side of his professional skill: the sympathetic handling of nervous and incompetent witnesses.

Finally he said: "You can rest easy in your mind, Mrs. Quinton; there is no charge against your brother at present, and what you have just told me is all hearsay and guesswork, it could not be used in evidence. As far as I can see, the law cannot touch him."

"You truly mean that? Oh, Mr. Garnham, I'm so thankful! I've been in despair, thinking he might be arrested."

Edward damped her rapture slightly by telling her that someone ought to wean her brother away from Rashford, who was certainly a scoundrel. Eleanor thanked him again for this advice, and her gratitude was still echoing ten minutes later when he ushered her through the house and out into Warwick Lane.

"It seems superfluous to add mine also," said Mary, when he came back. "Yet I must thank you, Edward. You were so wonderfully kind to her. I didn't expect—I thought you would be angry when you found her here."

"You made that plain enough," said Edward, looking down at her from his great height.

"You might have misconstrued the situation. I'm not in the habit of receiving my Catholic friends whenever your back is turned."

"I know that, Mary. As to Mrs. Quinton, I don't suppose you had much choice; she's as persistent as a river in flood, isn't she? Poor creature. When a worthless young man gets into a scrape there's always some soft-hearted woman in the background, suffering far more than he does."

Mary swallowed this allusion without resentment. "You may call me a soft-hearted fool if you will; your own heart is not as inflexible as you pretend. You can show compassion, even to a papist, though I know very well what you feel about them."

"I doubt it," he retorted. "You are not placed as I am. Make what you can of my actions, but don't waste your time trying to assess my feelings. However you do it, the sum will come out wrong."

The flat contradiction brought her up short with a shock of pain. Just as she was beginning to feel closer to him he had eluded her again, stretching the distance between them quite deliberately, and leaving her more lost than she was before.

16

Mary wanted to consult Etienne about Tom. He came to Warwick Lane that evening, but she could not separate him from Edward, who carried him straight off to the study. After supper the men sat down in the parlour, drinking their sack.

Mary hung about in the hall, feeling impatient and ill-used. At last she could stand it no longer, and went into the parlour herself, with a lame excuse that she had mislaid her keys.

"They don't seem to be in here, madam," said d'Aubais, getting up politely to look behind the silver-gilt cups on the buffet. He glanced at Edward. "Now your wife has joined us, would it not be propitious to put our scheme to her?"

"Your scheme. I am not wholly convinced."

"You must agree it would be a safeguard."

Edward was cracking walnuts. "Are you proposing to bring your wife on this adventure too—as a safeguard?" he enquired with a hint of derision.

D'Aubais flushed. "That would not be practical. Margot is not—she does not possess the same equable temper as Mrs. Garnham."

As Margot was a hysterical trouble-maker, and they all knew it, Edward's remark, whatever it meant, was certainly malicious, and he had the grace to look a little ashamed of himself.

"What is this scheme," asked Mary, "which is to put my equable temper to the test?"

"Your husband says you will not agree to it."

"Why? Is it so very disagreeable? You might at least give me the privilege of deciding."

Edward prized a nut delicately out of its shell. It looked like a miniature skull. "Very well." He sounded reluctant. "I'll put it to you, Mary. We have to go tomorrow evening to a certain house not far from Westminster, to interrupt a meeting and detain the men who are holding it. We have cause to think that my movements are being watched. If I was seen to ride off in that direction at the crucial time, other interested people would be warned—I can't go into details—and those who got wind of our intention might slip through the net. Hence Monsieur d'Aubais's idea. He thinks that if we went by coach, and took you with us, dressed as though we were bound for a party of pleasure, no one would guess where we were going or try to run away until it was too late."

Mary listened, spellbound. This brought her closer to the heart of Edward's working life than she had ever been before, to the inner hub of action where a few chosen men on both sides juggled with destiny. Edward, a servant of the Privy Council, was one of the lesser jugglers. Once you got used to the unfamiliar plane on which these plots and counter-plots actually happened, d'Aubais's plan seemed perfectly sensible. Mary wondered why Edward expected her to turn it down.

"How dangerous are these conspirators?" she asked.

D'Aubais mistook her meaning. "There will be no danger," he assured her. "You would merely have to wait outside in the coach, and there will be soldiers——"

"I wasn't thinking of myself. Are they a grave menace to the State? To Her Majesty?"

"Yes," said Edward, in his most laconic manner.

"Then I'll come, if it will give you a better chance of catching them." She looked at Edward, hoping for his approval, ready to buy back his affection in this way if she could. A little warmth of gratitude would be better than nothing. Edward reached out to trim a spluttering candle. He did not comment. D'Aubais was studying him with a puzzled expression. Doubtful, Mary asked, "Is that what you wish me to do, Edward?"

"It seems the best arrangement we can devise. And you will be able to serve Her Majesty by taking a tedious drive into the country." He did manage a smile here, though it was curiously impersonal.

So the following evening Mary had the odd experience of putting on her best clothes for an imaginary banquet given by a non-existent host. A crimson dress, slashed with ivory; a gauzy, transparent cape that drifted over her shoulders like a cloud. (If this was worth doing it must be done properly.) A pearl and crystal chaplet in her dark hair, and more pearls swinging in a rope almost to her waist. The girls came to help her. Jane was full of awkward questions about the party; who would be there, and would there be a masque or a play? She wondered what they would have to eat. Mary wondered too. She supposed they would have to raid the larder when they got home.

Edward had borrowed the Radcliffes' coach, though the grooms were provided by Walsingham and had their instructions. Mary paused in the lane to say good night to the flock of children; she hugged Greville, reminding him to clean his teeth, just as Etienne d'Aubais arrived, announcing in a clear voice that his unlucky Margot was desolated, she had the migraine. Edward and Mary were loudly sympathetic. They had their audience. A group of casual onlookers had collected to admire all this finery; impossible to guess which was the enemy spy. At any rate his fears ought to be lulled. Edward was magnificent. The swaggering width of his emerald cloak and the glitter of his dancing-rapier exaggerated the long, tapering line of the legs in immaculate trunk hose. Anyone could see that he was in a holiday mood, handing his young wife into the coach with an air of tender devotion.

It was, thought Mary, a most accomplished piece of acting.

The fourth member of the expedition was already in the coach; another of Walsingham's underlings, called Robert Sykes. As the horses jerked forward he produced a roll of parchment which he rested on his knee. Mary eyed it with an unwilling fascination. That must be the warrant, signed by the Secretary of State.

Edward was in command, with Sykes as his lieutenant. Mary had been surprised that d'Aubais, a newcomer and a foreigner, was coming with them, but Edward had explained to her that they were hoping to capture a Spanish agent whom d'Aubais had known on the Continent.

The coach turned west along Fleet Street and passed Temple Bar. They drove through the village of Charing Cross and down the straight road which ran under the windows of Whitehall Palace. It was a dull, heavy evening and there was hardly any traffic, for the Court was at Nonsuch.

"It won't be long now," observed Mr. Sykes, his fingers beating a tune on the rolled parchment. "I hope those soldiers haven't given the game away."

"A company of halberdiers returning from a day's training? We took every precaution. And for heaven's sake stop brandishing that paper," added Edward.

"I'm sorry, sir," muttered Sykes.

The bulk of Westminster Abbey reared sombrely against the sulky sky, dwarfing the Parish Church of St. Margaret. They swung north, away from the river, leaving the town houses behind them and taking a devious course along the rutty byroads which wandered aimlessly between flat fields. It was countrified and pleasant here, the scent of grass and apples fresh after the sour miasma of the Thames. The colours paled into a neutral dusk. Mary had lost all sense of direction.

Presently Edward rapped a signal to the coachman. They drew up, screened by a grove of trees. A man appeared suddenly beside them, the light gleaming grey on his breastplate.

Edward leant on the window. "Have you anything to report, Mr. Bridges?"

"Nothing untoward, sir. I carried out your instructions, halted my men at Ebury Farm and gave them leave to fall out and take a rest. They then mustered discreetly in small groups, and are all deployed in their chosen positions, ready to move in when you give the word. We have the house surrounded. The Deputy Sheriff is due any minute."

"Has there been much activity?" asked Sykes. "Many visitors arriving?"

"I can't tell you that; I haven't been near the

main road. Mr. Garnham said we were to keep well hidden."

"No point in frightening them off," said Edward. "Well, you have your orders. Take your fellows round by the footpath and wait on events."

"Sir." The ensign saluted and stepped back into the undergrowth.

"I suppose we are wise," said Sykes as they moved on. "Going in unescorted."

"Cold feet, Robert? That's not like you. We're just paying a friendly call—until we make sure that our fattest pigeons are there to pluck."

"So long as Quinton doesn't get time to destroy any documents."

"Quinton!" Mary had been lolling against the cushions. She sat up sharp. "Did you say Quinton?"

"Why, yes, madam. Sir Amyas Quinton, he's the owner of the house where we are going——"

He broke off, as Edward rounded on him. "Who told you to prattle about our mission? Will you hold your gossiping tongue?"

"But I didn't think it was a secret from Mr. Garnham, sir. Considering she is here on the spot." Sykes was thoroughly aggrieved.

Mary hardly heard him. She was looking at her husband with a dreadful sense of foreboding. "The house where Richard Brassey is staying. Is that why you encouraged Eleanor to tell you all his private affairs?"

"Certainly not. There's no connection whatever."

She knew he was lying from the way he avoided her eye and the rough haste of his unconvincing protest. Besides, it was too obvious for any loophole. His unusual friendliness to a Catholic, all that probing for details about the smuggling exploits. And then, the very next day, this descent on the house where Richard was staying.

"How could you?" whispered Mary. "She came to you in good faith. She confided in you, she believed in your compassion and was grateful. How could you play such a filthy trick?"

"I tell you there's no connection. I haven't come all this way to arrest young Brassey. And an innocent man has nothing to fear——"

"Oh, hasn't he?" she flashed back. "That depends who is going to interpret his innocence."

She accepted a cynical grain of truth in his denial: a boy of nineteen would be very small beer; she didn't suppose his presence mattered much to Edward, one way or the other. But if he was there in the house he would be taken, along with the rest; they would all be taken because his sister had trusted the man who was married to her lifelong friend. I was the link between them, thought Mary, horrified.

"I won't be your accomplice," she said. "I'll warn them, I'll scream——"

"No you won't." Edward gripped her shoulder so hard that she felt the shape of his hand bite through to the bone. "Screaming will get you nowhere. This is no time for your whims and passions. We are here on the Queen's business, so stop acting like a child and try to behave yourself."

D'Aubais and Sykes, seated opposite them, were staring at their feet and pretending to be deaf. Their carefully blank faces swam before her with the swaying of the coach, Edward's callous voice chilled her to the heart, and she felt sick.

The coach stopped so abruptly that they all shot

forward and she nearly landed in d'Aubais's lap. Looking out, they saw that the road was blocked by a very fat yokel with a very fat pig.

"Lost your way?" enquired this worthy, grinning at the coachman.

"No, we ain't lost our way, and you'd better give us room and look smart about it, or you'll lose your pig."

The countryman scratched his ear. "I dunno where you think you're a-going. This lane's a dead end, fetches up at Ebury Hall, and you can't be going there, for Sir Amyas and the family's gone away, there's no one left save the caretaker. Happen your noble passengers is coming to eat their cheese and pickled onions with Joe Toddle." The fat man choked with delight at his own wit.

Edward swore under his breath. "What's that? Come over here, fellow. Did you say that Sir Amyas has gone away? He was here yesterday."

"So he was, your worship, so he was. He took wing early this morning, and all the other gentry with him."

"He's lying, sir," said Sykes. "It's a ruse."

"We'll see. Get that damned pig out of the road, Matthews, and drive on."

They creaked into motion. The house was round the next corner: a long brick building, a small mansion, about fifty years old. Though it was now getting dark there were no lights in any of the windows; their blind vacancy suggested that the pigman was right. There was a sort of passive sleepiness about the place, as though time was suspended while the owner was away.

The three men got out, and Sykes banged on the oak door, shouting, "Open in the Queen's name!"

He repeated the summons several times, self-con-
sciously, for the words echoed back with a mocking
distortion. And the house was hollow with silence.

At last they caught the shuffle of slippered
footsteps. Iron bolts rattled, and an elderly man in
shirtsleeves peered out, clutching a poker. He made
a clumsy bow when he saw the quality of the visitors, recoiled from the warrant, which he could not
read, and admitted that he was the caretaker and
that his unlikely name was Joseph Toddle. He said
that he was quite alone; Sir Amyas had left that
very morning for his estate in Oxfordshire.

"What did I tell you?" asked the man with the
pig, who had attached himself to the party.

Edward said: "This was a sudden decision. Did
he give you his reason?"

There was smallpox in the village, Toddle told
him. They wanted to avoid the infection. Edward
raised his eyebrows at this. Toddle, defending his
master, said he was none of your weak-kneed
croakers, he didn't run away from sickness as a
rule.

"But it's not for me to question what his worship
does," Toddle added virtuously. "All I know is,
they packed and went; Sir Amyas and her ladyship,
with the children, their nurse and governess, and
several gentlemen that's been staying here, young
Mr. Brassey and that Rashford . . . Yes, Sir Amyas
has taken his whole household, his musicians and
his cooks——"

"And his menservants and his maidservants and
the strangers what was within his gates," chimed in
the pigman, anxious to be helpful.

The Queen's representatives retreated a few
paces to hold a conference.

Mary heard Edward say: "We'll have to go in. He may have left some evidence behind in his haste. It's worth a hunt. Robert, go and get Bridges and the Deputy Sheriff; they can lend us a hand. We don't need the soldiery, let them stand easy."

"Very well, sir." Robert Sykes turned. There was a commotion in the shadows, a thud and a petrifying squeal. He had tripped over the pig.

Mary began to laugh.

It was the laughter of light-headed relief. The high drama had collapsed into a farmyard farce, and there was something so ridiculous about these officials, with their portentous warrants and their wily strategy, bringing a regiment of soldiers to besiege an empty house. Perversely unpatriotic for the moment, she was glad their plans had failed. Whatever Quinton and his friends had done, she felt a strange responsibility for them because, in her simplicity, she had let Eleanor betray them to Edward. So she sat in the coach, forgotten, and staved off the onrush of pain as best she could by indulging in a rather feverish amusement.

That mood passed soon enough, and then she was thinking hard. Could she have misjudged Edward? Could it possibly be a coincidence that the attack on the Quinton stronghold had happened the day after his meeting with Eleanor? No, that was too much to swallow.

She cast back to the interview in the little town garden, Edward harping on facts that were still obscure to her, though they must have meant a great deal to him. He was an expert at leading a witness. Using the smuggled wine as a decoy, he had lured Eleanor into various unguarded statements which, presumably, would complete his case against Quin-

ton. And if Richard was dragged into the dock too,
as he almost certainly would be, Eleanor would
learn that it was her well-meaning interference
which had put him there.

There were lanterns glimmering now inside the
house, moving from room to room. Ensign Bridges
had gone in some time ago, accompanied by a
brisk, irritable gentleman, the Deputy Sheriff of
Middlesex, annoyed at being called out on a wild-
goose chase. The man with the pig had got bored
and gone away. The grooms had taken the horses
out of the shafts and were walking them up and
down by torchlight. A bat, a tiny devil with black
wings, hurtled out of the smoky radiance and flew
straight at the coach, swerving aside with a mirac-
ulous inch to spare.

Mary wondered vaguely whether they would find
any more proofs of treason in the deserted house,
she did not really care. Since Quinton had run
away, he probably was a traitor, and she supposed
Richard was his dupe. Their guilt mattered less to
her than Edward's, for she thought he was guilty of
the most flagrant inhumanity. Of course she knew
what he would say to that—he would make the
eternal claim that loyalty to God and the State cancelled every other obligation. A bleak doctrine, and
anyway he had never grasped its true meaning: that
it was a supreme test of religious discipline. No ordinary man could forfeit his personal honour and
betray his friends without sacrificing a part of
himself and suffering a kind of death. Edward was
not an ordinary man. His friendship was something
he had offered to Eleanor in order to deceive her,
and the loss of his integrity seemed to cost him
nothing. He was content to do his country's dirty

work and take pride in the result. Well, someone
had to do it—but it needn't be my husband, she
thought miserably. He chose his profession, he
glories in it. But I can't. I didn't want to get in-
volved in this poisonous web of intrigue and persecution. I didn't realize what he was like.

"I should never have married him."

She spoke the words aloud, and they shocked her
as an open expression of ideas she had been sup-
pressing for some time. Ever since she heard the
story of his first marriage. No, the original doubts
went further back. She had been alienated by his
unforgiving and obsessive hatred of the Catholics. It
was not for her to judge him, but she could not
forget. She could not forget the way he had treated
his children, the way he had treated Tom. Their
own estrangement was simply the culmination,
showing that his feelings and his standards of behaviour were totally different from her own. He was
not so much an enemy; he seemed to belong to another species.

Yet according to the Church they were one flesh.
That was the central fact about their marriage. An
honourable estate, not to be undertaken lightly,
carnally or wantonly. And not, she decided with a
sudden clarity, to be undertaken by two complete
strangers, out to get the most suitable bargain their
money and rank could buy. Surely that wasn't how
God intended men and women to come together? It
was how matches were usually made; she had
meekly done what her family expected, and now she
felt that she had sold her birthright and cheapened
everything she had valued most in her years of happiness with Jack.

Sometimes in the past she had compared Edward

and Jack. Edward was the more accomplished lover, and she had let herself be conquered by pleasure, sensuous as a cat and as easily gratified. Resentful and ashamed, she discarded all those patient months when she had been trying to reach Edward through his mental barriers, and convinced herself that what she had felt for him was not much better than uncaring, anonymous lust.

She had begun to cry, the aching tears of humiliation. Her head throbbed, and she was weak from hunger, though she did not realize that. Presently someone came up to the coach, and she heard the grooms buckling the harness. She mopped her eyes hastily.

A foreign voice said: "You must be tired to death, madam. I'm sorry you have been left out here, we should have taken you indoors—but it has been an evening of disasters, you understand."

"Yes, I understand very well."

"Your husband wishes me to escort you home. He is still occupied with the Sheriff."

She was thankful that she did not have to travel with Edward. D'Aubais got in beside her and they set off on their journey back to the city, one of the servants walking ahead with a torch flare to guide the horses through the night.

"What will they do now?" she asked. "Will Edward go down to Oxfordshire after his prey?"

"So I imagine. Nothing can be settled until he has seen the Secretary of State."

"Well, I hope he bungles it again. Does that surprise you, monsieur?"

"No, why should it? You have been greatly distressed. We ought not to have brought you with us, and it was my fault, though I can't think why he didn't tell me that you were friendly with some members of the family."

"Can't you? I can. He didn't wish you to know how he got his information. I don't suppose Walsingham cares how his vultures collect their carrion, but I think you have a more exacting conscience."

D'Aubais sighed. "My conscience is often torn to shreds. In matters like this we have to do things we would rather avoid."

"The end justifies the means? That's Edward's watchword, he borrowed it from the Jesuits. I can't see why he objects to them so strongly, considering how well he imitates their methods."

There was a short pause. Then d'Aubais said in his gentle way: "Don't be too hard on Edward, madam. He is, I think, undergoing a deep spiritual conflict that we can none of us wholly appreciate."

"Indeed? That sounds very noble. I could feel more pity for Edward's troubles if I knew what they were."

"I can tell you one of them," said d'Aubais. "You realize, no doubt, that Quinton must have been warned that we were coming to arrest him. Edward thinks that he will be held responsible."

"Why should he be? Even Edward can't prevent other people's mistakes. If that Sheriff talked, or the soldiers——"

"They were none of them notified until this morning. Quinton left home at seven o'clock; that means the news leaked out last night, at the very latest. In fact it was probably two or three days ago, for none of the other conspirators walked into our trap. Clearly they had all been warned. But by whom? The case against them was known to a mere handful of men in the whole of England. All honest

servants of the State who are also far too ex-
perienced and discreet to give away their secrets by
accident."

"Well, someone's tongue must have slipped.
Why should Edward be singled out for blame? He
certainly doesn't gossip."

"Because there remains one more source that our
adversaries may have tapped. So far the only written record of this business is a report that Edward
is compiling for the Secretary of State. He keeps it
locked in his study, but when we were discussing
the matter just now he admitted to me that on one
occasion recently he went out and left it lying on his
table. He thinks that someone may have read it,
perhaps taken a copy."

Mary digested this. A most unpleasant thought
struck her. "Are you trying to say that Edward suspects me?"

"But no, madam! What a horrible suggestion.
He did not consider that for one instant, I assure
you. It never entered his head."

"I'm glad to hear it. You can never be certain
what Edward will think. I might seem the most likely culprit, for who else is there? You can't count the
children, nor the servants, who are all illiterate.
And I don't fancy Cousin Eulalia as an enemy
agent."

"In your own household there is no one. Edward
believes that an outsider may have got in and ran-
sacked his papers. He reproaches himself for being
too lax. A house like yours, in a London street, with
no special guard, and the door on the latch so that
you can all come and go as you please—the fellow
could have slipped in unseen and no one the wiser."

"It seems very far-fetched to me." Mary had become sufficiently absorbed in the problem to shake

off her own miseries and concentrate. "Even supposing your outsider was lucky, and hit on the one day when Edward forgot to lock up his report, I still don't think he could have come and gone invisibly. The house is full to bursting, there are people passing through the hall all the time, up and down the stairs, into the kitchen. . . . A stranger wouldn't even know the way to the study. I grant you that anyone who knew his ground would have stood a better chance, but I can't think who——Oh, my God! Oh no! It couldn't be. He is the last person——"

"Who, madam? Who is the last person?"

"Tom," she said slowly. "He did come, two days ago. (I meant to tell you, but I haven't seen you alone until now.) He chose a time when we were all out except Jane, and she found him in the study. He wanted to know everything Edward was doing, but wouldn't say where he was living himself. Worse of all, he has a great deal of money all of a sudden, and no proper reason to account for it. This is the most damnable thing to suspect—but what other answer fits so well?"

Etienne took her carefully through Jane's story. It all added up to the same ugly conclusion.

"Do you remember," she said, "describing those 'devious byways' that are open to a man when fate turns against him? You said that spying was one of them. I paid no attention then, I should have said that Tom's principles were too strong. I still think so. It's incredible that he should change into a traitor overnight."

"Very few men do that. It's a matter of circumstance; most spies are made, not born. Your purse is empty, you pass on a harmless scrap of knowledge and receive a handsome present. What could be wrong in that? Then something a little more venal is required, and so on until you've gone in so deep you can't retract."

There was a depressing silence. Mary was devoted to Tom; he mattered far more to her than Richard Brassey, who had faded into the background. She thought that he was essentially made of good stuff, but he was young, he had been weak over the entanglement with Susan, and Edward had brutally destroyed his self-respect. She could imagine him, friendless, embittered and destitute, a prey for any agent who was clever enough to handle him.

D'Aubais said: "I don't think they can have corrupted him beyond redemption, not in a few short weeks. If we could get hold of him we might help him to break loose and make a fresh start. I'll try again tomorrow."

The coach lurched wearily on, at a walking pace. In this half-world nothing seemed quite real, Mary even felt divorced from the cramped discomfort of her own body. She was numb from the successive shocks she had received that evening. They had left her hopeless, defeated. She could not help Eleanor and Richard, she could no longer build up any illusions round the wreck of her marriage. There remained a moral duty to find Tom; to plead, argue and threaten, anything to rescue him from a squalid and disgraceful career that would probably lead to the gallows. They might already be too late. From brooding over him, her mind moved logically to the person who was responsible for all these disasters.

"If we lose Tom," she said flatly, "I shall never forgive Edward as long as I live."

17

Etienne spent the next few days doggedly haunting the fashionable taverns; he had no time to come to Warwick Lane.

Edward still slept in the study of his own house, and ate his breakfast before disappearing for the day; his withdrawn and brooding presence was sensed rather than seen. He had not gone to Oxfordshire after Sir Amyas Quinton; for some reason the arrest of the Catholic conspirators seemed to be hanging fire.

Mary was left to her own devices, and to the children, who were not much comfort to her.

Greville came home from school clutching a gingerbread man; he said a gentleman had given it to him in the street.

Horrified, his mother demanded some more details about this gentleman. Greville, licking the gilt off the gingerbread, said that he was very old, with a bushy beard and a beautiful coach, full of presents for little boys. Confused by Mary's insistent questions, and by something he did not understand, he then burst into tears and ran out of the room.

"Dear God," said Mary, aghast. "I thought the child was safe to go that short distance alone. I warned him not to speak to strangers. If I could only be certain . . ." She turned to Harry and Rog-

er, who were doing their Latin at the parlour table.
"Has he said anything to you?"

Harry raised his head and looked at her through
Edward's grey eyes, with an amused superiority
that also reflected Edward.

"Don't get in a fantigue, madam. It was a fairy-
tale. There isn't any predatory gentleman."

"What do you mean? Someone gave him the
sweetmeat."

"He picked up a groat in the churchyard yesterday, when we were coming away from Evensong,
and spent it at the cookshop."

"He found someone else's money and kept it!"
Mary's instant relief was flooded out by a new indignation. "That's as bad as stealing—on con-
secrated ground, too. And you let him do it. Harry,
how could you? You know right from wrong, even if
he doesn't."

Harry shrugged. "They say finding's keeping.
How were we to trace the owner of one solitary
groat?"

Roger nudged his stepbrother. "Why did you
have to tell her?"

"Because I don't want the office of escorting our
sweet young innocent backwards and forwards to
school every day," said Harry.

He returned to his Latin.

Mary smacked Greville soundly, and gave him a
lecture on the future fate of thieves. Afterwards she
found herself dwelling on the attitude of the older
boys, which was much more disquieting. Perhaps
she had been hard on the six-year-old Greville,
whose crime was mostly due to ignorance, but he
had to be checked, or what would he become, exposed to the careless morality of the big brothers he

worshipped as demigods? What distressed her most
was Roger asking, "Why did you have to tell her?"
Roger, whose guileless honesty a year ago had been
almost embarrassing. All that was changed—and
how many lies had he told her on his own account?
He and Harry were growing impudent and slovenly; they were often in trouble at school. Harry had
corrupted Roger, there was not much doubt of that,
and all Edward's children were accomplished liars.

What Harry needed was a regime of steady, even-
tempered discipline and constant supervision. The
man who ought to supply it was too self-absorbed
for anything so laborious; he made matters worse
by veering erratically between iron severity and
neglect.

Musing on Harry as a subversive influence, Mary
realized unhappily that she was not much better
herself. She had felt it necessary to put Jane on her
guard.

"Your stepfather may ask you if any unwarranted person has come to the house lately. It
would be wiser not to mention Tom."

"I'll be dumb as a post," said Jane, but there was
a faint inflexion of surprise, and she gave Mary a
long, speculating glance.

It was an odd sort of mother who encouraged a
very pretty and lively daughter of thirteen to deceive
her natural guardian. Anyone could guess where
that might lead, a year or two from now.

We are each of us being infected by the blight,
thought Mary. Even the docile Clemency was a
worry in a different way. She was languid and
washed out, and she had a poor appetite. Though
she pretended to blame the smoky London air,
Mary knew that Clemency, always too vulnerable,

was suffering from the emotional climate indoors.

None of the Dacres can thrive in this house, she thought. I wish to heaven I'd never brought them here. Which was the sequel to her other unceasing self-torment: I should never have married him.

Two more days crept by, and there was still no news of Tom. On Wednesday Edward came home to supper, so at half-past five the family was united in the parlour. Nicholas managed to start an argument by telling Susan how much he had enjoyed himself last night at the Goose and Gridiron.

This was the Mitre, near St. Paul's, where the Society of Musicians held their concerts; their sign, which hung outside, was actually a Lyre and Swan, but everyone used the facetious nickname.

Edward overheard as he was probably meant to. "You're too young to go drinking in taverns. And what the devil do you mean, slipping off without permission?"

"I wanted to hear some proper music again. Do I need permission for that? Or am I to be starved of everything I love, for fear the dulcimer-player might be a secret papist?"

"Don't be a fool, Nick. If you are starving for music, you can at least make some of your own. We've heard a great deal about your thwarted ambitions, but very little sound of practising lately."

It was true that Nicholas was too apathetic to play; disillusion had soured his pleasure. Determined to nurse a grievance, he said that it was monstrous they hadn't got an organ, and as for the virginals upstairs, they rattled like a box of nails.

"Very graciously put. And what's wrong with the lute I gave you? It won't hurt you to give the virginals a rest, and you'll never get far until you improve your skill as a lutenist."

"To be sure," said Nicholas, crumbling his bread and gazing towards Edward who was, for him, a dim outline at the head of the table. "You'd prefer to wean me away from the virginals, wouldn't you, sir? I dare say you think my choice too womanish."

So far Edward had treated Nicholas with a kind of irritable forbearance. Now there was a glacial hardening in his expression which his family knew for a danger signal, even if Nicholas couldn't see so far.

Susan rushed into the breach, nervous but valiant. "Why should it be that women generally play the virginals and men the lute? The virginals are equally difficult, and the finest musicians don't despise them. All the great masters write for the keyboard."

"My dear Sue," drawled Nicholas, "that's another distinction. The masters are common fellows; they do for money what we do for pleasure. Hirelings tap away at the keyboard. Gentlemen play the lute."

Mary said, "Get on with your supper, Nick, and stop baiting your father."

Nicholas was so astonished at this peremptory firmness from his stepmother that he did what he was told. Edward was astonished too, and not at all grateful.

"When I need your support in controlling my children I'll remember to ask for it. Until then I advise you to curb your passion for interference."

Mary was helping Harry to some more lentils. Grimly, she scooped up another spoonful, aware that everyone in the room was uncomfortable and that they were all on her side. The children must know that she and Edward were barely on speaking terms, but they had kept up a decent public civility until now.

The usual brisk chatter had died away. The children munched their dried fish, a dull meal; it was against the law to serve meat on a Wednesday. Not for any narrow popish reason, but because the end of religious fasting had nearly ruined the nation's fishermen and exhausted the supply of cattle. So the Protestants still had their compulsory meatless days.

A late wasp, which had been lurking in the snug folds of the arras, came out and flew towards the smell of food, buzzing drowsily. Clemency and Greville squealed and jumped about as a matter of course.

"He won't sting you if you stay still," Edward told them, not unkindly.

The wasp hovered over a dish of stewed apples. Jane flapped it away, and Mary caught sight of Roger's face. Roger loathed wasps. He was not afraid of being stung; it was the fat, black and yellow bodies with their nipped-in waists that disgusted him. He flinched visibly.

"What's the matter with you?" asked Edward.

"I don't like the ugly creatures, sir." Roger appealed to his mother. "Could I go out till it's been killed?"

"Certainly you can't go out," snapped Edward. He could put up with a mild panic from the little ones, but not from a boy of eleven. "I never heard anything so faint-hearted."

"It's hard to conquer these aversions." Mary

tried to placate him. "Jack couldn't abide snakes."

"And what's that supposed to prove? Some doctrine of heredity?"

Mary had a confused idea of what she meant; these strange instinctive quirks had no connection with ordinary courage. Jack, who was terrified of snakes, had been recklessly brave throughout his short life, and he had died a hero. It was no good explaining to Edward. She watched while he and Susan tried to stalk the wasp, which was weaving its way around the fruit. It made a spurt towards Roger. He swung his legs over the bench and scrambled free, almost unseating Harry.

"Roger, go back to your place," said Edward.

Roger stayed where he was.

Edward got to his feet. "Very well, then. I'll carry you if I must. You are going to be taught a lesson in self-command, you damned little coward."

Something snapped in Mary's heart. She jumped up and pushed her way between them, challenging her husband.

"Let him alone," she said. "He doesn't need your teaching. I'm not concerned with what you make of your own children, but I can depend on the parentage of mine, and no boy of Jack's will ever be a coward."

She saw the fury break in Edward's eyes, remote as a blaze of lightning. Then his hand swung deliberately, and he slapped her hard across the mouth.

She scarcely understood the impact of pain as she stood there, exploring her swollen lip with her tongue, and staring up at the stranger in front of her. She felt stunned. Then she was brought back to reality by Roger, who had forgotten the wasp and was flinging himself at Edward.

"You hog! You brute! How dare you hit my mother!"

"Roger—no!"

She grabbed him by the belt, frightened of what Edward might do to him.

Edward surveyed them with acute dislike. "I'm sure Dacre would have been proud of you both," he said, and walked out of the room.

Then it was a bedlam. The two youngest children were crying, Susan was comforting them, Roger was saying he felt sick.

Clemency reverted to the past. "I want my father," she wailed. "I wish my father wasn't dead. I wish we'd never come here. I want to go home to Sussex."

"So do I," muttered Jane.

"I don't blame you," said Nicholas.

Mary found that her lip was bleeding where Edward's signet ring had cut it. She wiped off the blood. None of the children knew what to say to her, so they sensibly left her alone, and huddled round the table. It was old Eulalia who came up to pat her on the shoulder and offer condolences.

"My poor lamb, don't take it too grievously. All men indulge in bouts of cruelty when they are crossed. We have to endure our trials as best we can."

Eulalia had poured out to Mary the detailed humiliations of her marriage to a lecherous drunkard, and she now felt they were sisters in tribulation.

Mary turned aside and leant against the chimney-piece above the empty hearth trying to grapple with her despair. It wasn't just the misery of the last few minutes. Too much had gone before.

She could still hear the children talking in the room behind her, and they were echoing her thoughts.

"My father told me no gentleman would strike a woman," declared Roger.

"He was mistaken," said Nicholas. "He never met my father."

"What's gone wrong?" This was Jane. "Why has Mr. Garnham altered so? He wasn't like this before."

"Who are you to judge?" retorted Harry. "You've only been here a year. My father has had good spells and black spells all our lives. Though come to think of it, these last weeks have been the blackest ever."

Mary was aware that Susan had approached her and was waiting quietly, not liking to intrude.

"Is that true?" she asked. "What Harry says? Is your father being more—tyrannical than usual? I thought I was making a happier home for you and the boys, but it seems I am doing more harm than good."

"You have done us infinite good," said Susan. "You know that, madam. The fact is, my father seems to be strangely unfitted for marriage, and his discontent is visited on the whole household. I did tell you once how badly he treated my mother," added Susan with a hint of reproach. "I don't think you believed me."

"I believe you now," said Mary.

She retreated to her bedchamber and paced up and down for ten minutes, in a frenzy of resentment which she mistook for rational thought. Then she reached a decision.

When she entered the study, without knocking, Edward was at his desk, counting some money. He rose immediately. She saw that he was very pale.

"I owe you an apology. It was a disgraceful way to act, and I deeply regret it. I shall never repeat the performance, I promise you."

"You won't get the chance," she assured him. "I didn't come for your apologies. I came to tell you that our marriage is over and I am leaving you."

He looked at her as though the position was reversed and she had hit him.

"Leaving me? That's impossible, you can't leave me. You are my wife."

"We can arrange a deed of separation. It's true we shall still be bound by the laws of the Church, but they don't compel us to live under the same roof."

"You've nowhere to go."

"I shall return to Sussex, to my eldest brother George, at Down Park, or to my father-in-law."

"If you mean Sir Roger Dacre, he is no longer your father-in-law."

"We won't quibble over that; he still has an interest in his grandchildren. Either he or George will take us in."

Edward was fidgeting absently with the coins on the table, building a little gold tower. His hand trembled slightly. She wondered what he was feeling. Wounded pride, probably. A masculine possessiveness about his legal chattels. There was no indication of anything softer. All warmth and spontaneity, all the signs of love, had died out of him some time ago, and this ultimatum had not revived them. But that did not make any difference: she was his wife, and she had no business to talk of leaving him.

"You would be putting yourself entirely in the

wrong." The tone was aggressive. "I've given you
no grounds for desertion. I'm sorry for what happened this evening, and I've said so, but, after all,
you did provoke me. A man is entitled to chastise
his wife, and a single blow——"

"You showed a most becoming moderation,"
said Mary in a voice of silk. "I know your rights as
well as you do, sir. If you had ever chosen to correct
me privately and for a serious fault I must have sub-
mitted without complaining. Was it so outrageous
to tell you that you don't know how to deal with
Roger? And can you quote any divine authority for
slapping my face in front of my young children?"

She had him at a disadvantage, and she made full
use of it.

"Speaking of rights and duties, you have an odd
notion of fulfilling yours. A husband who refuses to
share a bed with his wife can scarcely set up as an
example. You have deserted me. Don't think I'm
leaving you on that account," she added hurriedly,
in case he did. "I'm going because, try as I will, I
can no longer respect you. As a husband, a father,
a public servant, I find you egotistic beyond bearing. You let your actions be ruled by malice and
vengeance, and what's far worse you glory in them.
When I think of how you sent Tom Fletcher away
penniless, how you deceived Eleanor Quinton, I feel
ashamed—and chiefly because there is no shame in
you."

At the beginning of this diatribe Edward had
made one movement of incredulous protest, but he
heard her through in silence. His eyelids had come
down, giving him that masked look which was so
baffling. He was breathing rather hard, but if she
had pierced his self-esteem he did not show it.

"Have you done tearing my character to shreds?" he asked.

"There's one more matter I must try to make plain to you. I may be wrong in leaving you, after the vows we took, but I have my children to consider. I am appalled by what I see happening to them in this house. If you don't know what I mean, think back to what they were a year ago—and compare them with your own sons and daughter. I am devoted to those three, and they are none of them growing up as they should. I've done what I can for Sue and Nick; Harry won't let me get near him— he's too like you. It's on my conscience that I ought not to abandon them. But I can achieve nothing for them as things stand, and at last I've realized that while I stay here and quarrel with you, their lives are even more wretched than they were before. If you want to ruin your own children I can't stop you. I wish to God I could."

She waited for the expected outburst. None came. Edward simply took no notice. He was arranging a pile of ledgers on his desk; she would not have known that he was listening but for a certain tautness about the neck and shoulders.

"Is there anything you wish to say?" she asked.

"No. Nothing that could satisfy you, madam, now that I know the full extent of your hostility. It's not worth bandying words. Make what plans you please. I shan't stop you."

Mary was conscious of victory and defeat at the same moment. So this was the end. Riled by his indifference, she fired a parting shot.

"We can't undo the knot that binds us, yet that doesn't greatly matter. I've no desire to look for another husband, and as for you, Edward, I think it's very fortunate you can't marry again. You've made two wives miserable. That should be enough for any man."

She left him, not waiting to see how he took this final sally. There was a sort of triumph in having found the most telling phrases for what she wanted to say. Vanity carried her up the stairs; at the top she gave in to a sense of anticlimax. It had been too easy, too negative. She counted for so little with Edward that he did not value her even as an opponent. The merest token of a struggle, and he had let her go. Well, that was what she wanted, wasn't it?

She heard footsteps in the hall below. Edward's limp, more pronounced than usual. Was he coming after her? She peered over the banisters. He crossed her line of vision, head bent, with the stiff, irregular gait of a sleepwalker, and plunged into the street.

It was no use loitering here. She had plenty to do, and the prospect daunted her. I shall have to pack all my clothes, she thought with dismay. And that wasn't the half of it. A woman who was rising thirty, with four children, a maid and a waggonload of furniture, could not slip out of her husband's house dressed as a page, like the eloping heroine in a ballad. They couldn't possibly leave here tonight, and they couldn't travel down to Sussex without preparation. Perhaps her brother Guy, at Holborn, would give them a temporary shelter tomorrow— unless he tried to send her back to Edward. Guy had strong views on the subjugation of wives. Then there were the young Garnhams to think of, and she had a genuine pang of guilt there. She must talk to Susan. . . .

She was in her bedchamber some time later, wondering how to divide the household linen, when

Benjamin, the servingman, rapped and stuck his head in to say there was a fellow asking for the master; very insistent, he was.

"Mr. Garnham went out a short while ago."

"He says he's got to see him, madam."

"Can't Master Nicholas—— Never mind, I'll come."

The caller turned out to be a grotesque little man with a bulbous head and stumpy hands, the fingers webbed like ducks' feet. He tweaked off his cap respectfully, gazed at Mary in childlike disappointment, and said, "You're not Mr. Garnham."

She decided that he was half-witted.

"I am Mrs. Garnham. My husband is not here. Can you give me a message for him?"

"There *is* a message, that's why I come. He was a-wanting to get the news, and I was to give it him, for his ears alone. Now he's not here, I'm fair mazed what I should do. If you're his lady-wife I reckon your ears is the same as his. One flesh, that's in the Good Book."

"Yes," said Mary, to whom this reminder was extremely ill-timed. "You can safely confide in me. Who is the message from?"

"He'll know who it's from. I wasn't told no names. Are you listening, lady?" He screwed up his eyes in an effort of concentration, and recited fluently: " 'Nine o'clock. Rose Lane. Blackfriars. The exchange must be made tonight without fail. There will be no further chance before the skies fall.' That's it. And another piece I was to add: 'Hoping his worship's family may long continue happy and prosperous.' Do you want I should say it over?" He did so, word-perfect.

"Nine o'clock at Rose Lane in Blackfriars," repeated Mary, rather dazed. The message did sound urgent, in spite of the unimpressive messenger, and Edward had apparently been expecting it. He had gone out, directly after their encounter, perhaps more disturbed than she had given him credit for. So if he had forgotten a previous commitment it was partly her fault. Mary did not like the spirit in which Edward practised his profession, nor his personal war against the Catholics, but she realized that his work was vital, and she did not want him to make a critical blunder because she had distracted him.

Fetching her purse, she gave the little clown a present for his pains, and asked if he could return an answer to the man who sent him. He shook his head, muddled and childish again, for it was clear that he had a freak memory in a crippled brain. He did not know the gentleman's name, nor where to find him.

Vaguely uneasy she watched from the doorway as he trotted off. Probably Edward would be back soon. It was just after seven. She wondered who would be in Rose Lane at nine, and guessed that it was one of those brave secret agents who risked their necks by enlisting on the other side. They had to watch their step night and day, and somehow manage to report the plotters' latest moves. "The exchange must be made . . . before the skies fall." There was a note of desperation there. And that unnecessary flourish about his worship's family suggested a code.

The little messenger—was it his simplicity that made it safe to employ him?—was passing the Bell

Inn. There was already a torch flaring outside the Bell, an invitation to comfort and good cheer in the approaching dusk. She saw the stunted figure plainly in the arc of light. And the other man who stepped out of the porch and followed him down the lane.

It was Tom.

18

When she saw Tom everything went out of Mary's head except the desire to catch him. Her long cloak was hanging over a settle at the back of the hall. Fetching it, she swung it round her shoulders and ran into the street.

By the time she got there he had vanished. She hurried down Warwick Lane, searching the way ahead with anxious eyes stretched. It was still light enough to see through the drowned grey haze of an autumn evening, and luck was with her, for at Amen Corner she got a glimpse of that familiar yet elusive back in the distance. The odd little man who had brought the message must be somewhere beyond him again.

A week ago, in Lombard Street, she had scared Tom off by shouting his name. She was not going to make the same mistake twice. She padded silently after him. At the bottom of Ave Maria Lane he cut across the main thoroughfare, leaving the Cathedral on his left. Mary was too far behind to see which direction he had taken. Right-handed to Ludgate or on towards the river? She paused, uncertain.

An insidious voice said, "Are you willing for a little sport, sweetheart?" and she felt an exploring pinch on her thigh.

"Keep your paws to yourself," snapped Mary,

much too indignant to be frightened.

The prowling gallant was startled; the haughty, well-bred accent was not at all what he had expected. He let her go with a stammered apology.

Mary was across the road before she realized that she could hardly grumble at such treatment. Virtuous young women did not wander about London at seven in the evening. She was suddenly aware that all the people round her were men, and several of them seemed to be eyeing her hopefully. She knew she was flushing and her face felt strangely naked. Surely she had a mask somewhere? Yes, in the lining of her cloak. She tugged out the black velvet strip and put it on. That was better than nothing. But in the meantime Tom had got away from her, probably for good. She could have cried with vexation.

She was walking at random down one of the streets that led to the river, and then she saw him, some way off but going quite slowly. She quickened her pace, struggling to overtake him.

Down St. Andrew's Hill they went, along Carter Lane and down Water Lane, between leaning houses that nearly met overhead, over broken paving slimy with refuse. Mary's brain was working as fast as her feet. Tom was still spying on Edward and his colleagues, shadowing the man they used as a messenger.

She broke into a trot, oblivious of the hoots and ribaldry from a group of louts who flattered themselves that she was running away from them.

Round the next corner and into a patch of open ground, framed by high walls, with a maze of alleys filtering off at five different angles. And there was Tom, a few yards away from her, gazing as though he was the one who had now lost his quarry.

She stumbled forward and seized hold of him, panting, "I've got you at last!"

Tom was nearly knocked off his balance by this apparition, who seemed to be a small, slim girl he had never seen before.

"What the devil . . ." He peered closer. "Mrs. Garnham! How did you get here? You can't be alone at such an hour?"

"I chased you all the way from Warwick Lane. I must speak with you, Tom."

"I should be honoured, madam—on any other occasion. The fact is, I am somewhat engaged at present." He hesitated. "I suppose I ought to take you home. You should not be roaming the streets without an escort." But he was preoccupied, scanning the people who were moving to and fro in the crowded alleys.

"I don't see the little fellow with the webbed fingers," said Mary crisply. "You may as well give up the pursuit. I should tell you, Tom, I know what you've been doing these last weeks."

This was an error in tactics. Tom stepped back. Another second, and he was going to make a dash for it.

"You try that," she said, "and I'll scream. I'll scream loud enough to raise the watch. Those burly citizens over there—they'll come to my rescue. I'll swear you were molesting me."

"You wouldn't dare, madam. Consider the scandal——"

"I don't care a fig for the scandal; you're not escaping me till I've had my say."

"We can't talk here," he muttered, sulky in defeat.

The wall in front of them surrounded a large garden. There were many isolated gardens scattered about the town, belonging to the Livery Companies, the Inns of Court, the Bishop. Mary could not identify this one, but she saw that someone had left the gate ajar.

"We'll go in there." She took his arm.

Tom murmured something about trespassing on private property.

"And what else were you doing that morning in my husband's study?"

"So Jane told you?"

"She let it slip without meaning to."

They were walking on shorn grass beside a grove of trees. Beyond the walls the light of London cast up a faint glow in the sky, but here the advancing night was a deep, mysterious blue. Someone, probably the same careless gardener, had left a bonfire of autumn leaves to smoulder. They sat down on a bench, the pleasant warmth stealing round their ankles.

It did not occur to Mary that this was not a very wise place to choose for confronting a paid spy. The spy was only Tom, the boy who had lived in her home, almost another stepson; she had darned his stockings, got him to do odd jobs of carpentry, spoilt him with extra slices of his favourite pie. He seemed to accept the old relationship, for he leant forward, prodding the fire with a stick, his manner diffident and respectful.

"You must think very ill of me. Indeed I hoped you would never learn what I was doing, but since you know the worst can we get the sermon over, madam?"

"Oh, Tom—what am I to say? You may have

been desperate for money; was there no other means of getting it? I would have given you some gladly. Monsieur d'Aubais and I have been scouring London, trying to find you. I don't feel fit to condemn you; I've never been poor and hungry. Even so, it is a terrible thing to betray your country."

"To do *what*?" Tom sat up with a jerk.

"That's what it must lead to in the end. I dare say that some of your scavenging may do little direct harm, but where are you to draw the line? Once you start selling to the enemy, you are putting yourself in their power. From then on you have become their tool."

"Who do you call the enemy?"

"For pity's sake, Tom! Who would you expect to be the enemy?" She was maddened by this sudden change of front. He had come meekly into the garden, prepared to listen to a homily, and now he was being stupid, obstructive, making it impossible for her to help him. "Who bought your new clothes? Don't tell me you made your fortune working as a printer; I'm not so simple as Jane."

"Not as a printer. For a printer."

What was the difference? Presumably he wrote something that other people printed; that still didn't answer her questions. She was pretty sure that young, unknown authors didn't make money very quickly. Of course he might be using his specialized knowledge to write anonymous attacks on the Council—Edward's former secretary, still taking too much interest in Edward's affairs. That would just be another well-paid form of betrayal.

He was watching her; the uncertainty told him something, for he said with a kind of astonishment:

"This is blind man's buff! You haven't the faintest notion how I am employed. You might as well admit it, madam."

He got to his feet.

Mary said: "Tom, I can't keep you here by force, but if you go I shall be obliged to give my husband those facts that I know already. And I should warn you that there are reasons why he is bound to have you arrested."

This might in fact have been enough to send Tom out of the garden and out of their lives for good. Enough to save his skin but nothing else. Instead he stayed where he was, a disgruntled and badgered young man who gave her, for the first time, a faint inkling of hope.

"What do you want me to do?"

"Tell me how you get a living. Even if it isn't honestly come by, I should rather know the worst."

"Would you? I wonder." He sat down again, scrabbling among the dead leaves with his foot, reluctant to begin. "I may as well be hung for a sheep, I suppose. . . . You know that I was once apprenticed to a printer called Zadok Rowley who was sent to prison for libelling the Queen? He printed one of the scurrilous stories about her and Leicester. They cut off his hand and took away his licence, but when he came out of the Clink he still went back to his old trade. Not libelling Her Majesty—that was a folly he certainly regretted—his true talent lay in producing a supply of curious and highly spiced works that were never registered at Stationers' Hall. He has a secret printing-press, and you'd be surprised how much he can charge for the damned stuff. I was. I went to see him when I was down to my last borrowed shilling, not knowing where I'd sleep the night. I guessed long ago what he was doing, and I asked if he would commission me to translate a few of the rarer classics. The ancient authors are a gold-mine, though you can hardly call it virgin gold. Rowley thought it a tremendous jape. He said it would soothe the consciences of some of his more scrupulous readers if they could claim they were studying the valuable writings of a Cambridge graduate. And they are valuable—I make him pay through the nose for them. It's not everyone," said Tom in a brittle, contemptuous voice, "who can serve up filth on a silver plate. I ought not to mention such matters to you, but you would insist, and if you are too disgusted with me——"

"My dear Tom, don't be a fool! I'm sorry you've been driven to this, but it's not such a terrible crime. I was imagining something infinitely blacker."

Her sense of relief, almost of anticlimax, was checked by Tom saying repressively that it was no light matter. He was grateful for her forbearance, but it was lucky, he said, that she did not really understand the nature of the books he was talking about.

Mary agreed meekly that it was probably just as well. She realized that Tom, like a good many young men, was apt to cherish strange illusions about the ignorance and almost excessive purity of any older woman he happened to put on a pedestal. Having had five brothers and two husbands, she had been given a fairly robust view of the world's vices, including the ones they would not indulge in themselves. She knew that the appetite for lewd books was a pitiful and degrading perversion, but she also knew quite well that Tom had not been corrupted by it. And he wouldn't be, provided she could help him to break loose and make a new start. After all her suspicions, she found no difficulty in accepting his story, because in his grudging shame there was the unmistakable ring of truth. If he had to account somehow for his ill-gotten gains, this was the very last profession he would invent. He would far rather claim that he was a gambler, even a cheat.

This was partly explained by his next, tentative remark. "Madam, need you pass this on to Mr. Garnham? He thinks I am sufficiently depraved already. After what he said of my leading Susan astray, I can guess the conclusions he would draw."

"You can set your mind at rest; I shall say nothing to my husband." A promise that she found only too easy to make.

Tom brightened. It was pathetic that he cared so much what Edward thought of him, even now. A moment later he asked: "Did you suspect me of spying simply because I looked so rich? What am I supposed to have done?"

This was an awkward question. There was a strong temptation to tamper with the answer. Mary found she could not lie to him. She had accused him, and she owed him an honest explanation, however difficult it might be.

It was far more difficult than she expected. He listened, incredulous. She could almost feel him freezing into antipathy beside her.

"You were told that a spy had gained access to your husband's papers, and you immediately assumed that I was guilty of the most ungrateful malice towards the man I love more than I ever did my own father. You thought I could betray Mr. Garnham—to say nothing of the small matter of selling my country to the enemy."

"I am truly sorry," said Mary. It was she, not Tom, who was on trial now.

"Do I take it," he enquired, "that Mr. Garnham shares your opinion of me? Why haven't I been arrested?"

"Mr. Garnham knows nothing of your visit to Warwick Lane. And I dare say he would have shown more sense than I have. Tom, will you try to understand? I knew you were in desperate straits for money, and when you became so prosperous, I was fool enough to be swayed by outward circumstance. I should have known you better, but I thought you had been weak, not wicked. I wanted to give you another chance."

"Then you shouldn't have done so," he retorted. "You should have denounced me. There are things which no degree of poverty can excuse. As for being weak or wicked, heaven knows I have plenty to answer for: making love to my master's daughter, translating lewd books—those are faults for which I would ask your charity. This other matter is entirely different. If I were the villain you suspected I should deserve to hang at Tyburn."

It might have been Edward speaking. He went on insisting that he couldn't prove his innocence, while she assured him that no proof was necessary. She had to repeat this a good many times before he was mollified.

"You might well have thought I was spying this evening," he said presently. "I saw someone who reminded me of the days when I used to accompany Mr. Garnham on his missions, and that roused the

hunter in me. I've felt infernally out of touch, not
knowing what progress he was making. I was never
privy to any State secrets, but I knew what was in
the wind when I was dismissed, and I thought that
affair would have come to a head by now, unless
something has gone wrong."

Mary had a flash of insight. She knew, as though
he had said it aloud, that Tom had been comforting
his loneliness with a dream, a wonderful dream in
which he uncovered the Catholic plot, bearded the
ringleaders single-handed, and probably saved
Edward's life into the bargain. Afterwards he would
be thanked by the Secretary of State, the Queen,
and, of course, a contrite Edward. Poor Tom. It was
both funny and pathetic.

She had missed part of what he was saying.
". . . This little fellow hangs about the taverns
where the malcontents foregather and runs their errands. Not from any evil motive; he has the mind of
a child, that's why they call him Simple Simon.
And he is blessed with a marvellous gift: he can
learn off a set of words and repeat it perfectly——"

"Good grief!" said Mary.

"Madam?"

"Simple Simon—he's the man who came to our
house? The one you were following? He gave me a
message for my husband, and when I saw you go
after him, everything was forgotten; I never wrote it
down."

"Was it of any great importance?"

"It sounded so to me. He was to meet the sender
down here in Blackfriars at nine o'clock."

"It's not far short of that now."

"What am I to do?" She gave Tom the gist of the

message, ignoring his faint protest. She had gone back to trusting him implicitly, and was thankful to do so. "I wondered—you know better how these things are managed—could it come from a loyal agent within the enemy camp?"

"Very likely. He might well use such means, rather than a letter, if he was being closely watched. No one takes much note of Simple Simon. Well, what's to do? I don't see how Mr. Garnham can keep the appointment. If you went back to Warwick Lane, and he came down here—there isn't time. He'd be half an hour late at the least. And he may not even be at home . . ." Tom cogitated. "I don't like to think of that poor fellow waiting in vain. Suppose I was to go instead?"

This might be Tom's dream in a rational form: the chance of reinstating himself by doing Edward a good turn. Unfortunately there was an objection.

"I should be grateful," she said, "if you could repair the damage I may have done. But, Tom, Walsingham's people must know you have left my husband's service; do you think you would be accepted as an envoy?"

"You mean, they all know I was kicked out in disgrace," said Tom accurately. "I should hardly inspire confidence. No, that plan won't work."

"How would it be if I was to come with you? I expect I should be recognized as Edward's wife."

"You?" He was startled. "I couldn't take you on such an adventure. I couldn't expose you to the threat of danger; what would Mr. Garnham say to that?"

He wouldn't care in the least, thought Mary. She said, "Supposing you went by yourself, I should have to walk home alone, and there would be dangers of another kind."

There was some sense in this, and after a little hesitation he agreed to take her with him to meet Edward's anonymous friend.

They stamped out the embers of the bonfire, leaving the dark garden for the fitful glare of the streets. Tom knew the way to Rose Lane, which was near Carmelite Street, in the borderland where fashionable Blackfriars merged into notorious Whitefriars, the criminal district of Alsatia. Even approaching from the respectable side, the streets grew more narrow and stony, and the lanterns in the doorways more irregular. Tom spoke only once during their short journey.

"I didn't ransack your husband's desk, but I'd give a lot to discover who did."

It had not occured to Mary that there was still a mystery and a villain. Someone had got hold of the information that sent Quinton scurrying from Ebury Hall. Someone, presumably, who had read Edward's report. It was not a pleasant thought.

They reached the single entry to Rose Lane. There was no suggestion of country gardens and June sunshine about this squalid passage, a mere chasm between two tall ranges of buildings, which came to an end fifty yards down against the wall of an ancient church. The lane was unfit, but they got their bearings quite easily, for there was a lantern hanging on the church door straight ahead.

Tom and Mary stopped at the opening of the lane. A man with a guttering torch was loitering near an alehouse on the opposite side of the street; there was no one else in sight. They trod cautiously down the cobbled alley; it was greasy underfoot, and there was a strong smell of cats. Mary's muscles contracted with an old fear of enclosed spaces and darkness which she remembered from childhood games of hide-and-seek. She was trying hard to hide her nervousness from Tom.

As they drew near the church, the dim light seemed bright by contrast. At first they thought the place was deserted, but a muted shuffle slewed them both round, and they saw a human shadow edging into the furthest corner.

If this was Edward's agent, it was natural that he didn't want to be observed.

Addressing the shadow, Mary said, "Will you tell me, sir, have you invited a friend to meet you here at nine?"

"Not I, madam. You are mistaken." It was a half-educated voice, hoarse and somehow unpleasing.

This was an absurd deadlock, neither side prepared to be completely frank until the bona fides were established. She decided to test out a phrase from the original message as a kind of password.

"I can assure you that his worship's family continue happy and prosperous."

This had an instant effect. The shadow emerged from the corner: an elderly man, ferret-faced behind a sparse beard.

"He never sent you here! Or did he? Have you brought the—credentials?"

"We've come empty-handed," Tom began to explain, "but I hope you will trust me to carry a message."

The answer was a snarl about traps and treach-

ery, and a lunge forward. Mary caught a tell-tale
glitter and realized that the man had a drawn
sword under his cloak.

She cried out, "Tom, take care!"

After that everything happened very quickly.
Dodging the raised sword-arm, Tom met his ad-
versary head on. They grappled together. Tom, so
much younger and tougher, got possession of the
weapon, but he did not use it. Instead, he gave the
man a contemptuous punch in the chest which sent
him spinning. He fell down and lay on the ground,
doubled up in a paroxysm of gasping.

"Get up, you fool," said Tom, flexing the sword
between his fingers.

"He's hurt," said Mary.

"Not he. Thinking out his next move."

"Air," croaked the husky voice.

Mary twitched the lantern off its hook and put it
down. She knelt in the dirt and lifted the stranger's
head on to her lap, tearing apart the thickness of
cloak, doublet and ruff. The heart-beats under the
coarse shirt came in a shallow cataract, racing
against suffocation, and there was a bluish tinge
round the mouth and nostrils.

The stranger stared upwards, beyond her, at the
young man he had tried to kill. "Might have known
. . . dirty coward . . ."

"Save your breath," Mary advised him.

There was not much breath to save. She felt the
last heave and flicker within the exhausted body;
the mouth shrank from the teeth in a rigid and terrible grin. The eyes were fixed as marble.

"He's dead," said Mary.

"He can't be. I scarcely touched him."

"His heart must have been failing already. One blow was enough to finish him. It wasn't your fault."

She was still cradling the head which had become, literally, a dead weight.

"Did you recognize him, Tom? What was he, do you think? An assassin, or one of our agents?"

"I don't know. Not an effective assassin, and besides, they hunt in pairs. He asked for credentials; it wasn't till I spoke that he took fright, though why he flew into such a rage—I suppose he must have mistaken me for someone else. What a needless way to get killed." Tom scowled unhappily. "I caused his death; at any rate, that's what they'll say. He may have been sick, but he hit his head as he fell, and there are other bruises and the marks where I gripped him in our struggle. Anyone who came down here now would say I was his murderer. Madam, we'll have to leave him and go."

Mary closed the dead man's eyes. It was the only thing she could do for him. "The Lord have mercy upon you," she said softly, "and forgive us our trespasses."

She stood up, very conscious of her own shortcomings. Her stupidity in forgetting the message, and what Edward called her passion for interference. Their coming down here had led to a tragic misunderstanding; this poor stranger had got himself killed by a man who meant him no harm, and she was responsible.

Tom leant over the corpse, fumbling through the clothes.

"It's no use," she said. "I've seen death too often to make a mistake."

"I've got to search him."

It was the trained action of a man who had lived in the atmosphere of plots and counter-plots which surrounded Mr. Secretary Walsingham.

He removed a wedge of paper wrapped in a kerchief, and returned the sword to its sheath. Then they left the dead man lying where he had fallen, and tiptoed up the lane.

Rounding the corner, they bumped into a man who was carrying a torch. He held it high, and they were dazzled by the flame, their guilty faces petrified in that awful, revealing brilliance. Blinking, Mary clung to Tom's arm. They pushed past the invisible torchbearer, and paused, listening to his footsteps in the night.

"He's going down the lane. Oh, Tom, do hurry."

"Not too fast, madam. We mustn't seem to be fugitives."

A minute later they heard a sound of running, shouting, banging on doors.

"He's found the body," said Tom. "He's raising the alarm."

They were in a long street which suddenly seemed much too well lighted. Soon, much sooner than you could have expected, the cries of "Murder! Foul play!" were drawing near. Shutters were flapped open, a party from a tavern came out to stare. And the calls of the pursuers were very close. "You take this side, Will, and I'll go round the back. Dickon's fetching the constable. Stop any strangers you see, they can't have got far."

It seemed impossible to go on; Mary's legs felt like dough. Tom whisked her into a doorway and pressed his face against her shoulder. She was so small that she was completely engulfed. By a piece of quick thinking he had magicked them both into something as commonplace and static as a tree: a pair of lovers kissing good night. Clasped in that queer, passionless embrace, Mary found a measure of security.

Will or Dickon, whoever it was, lumbered heavily by. A little further on they heard him stop, at a question barked by a voice that was used to command. A great deal of talking. Tom moved his head a fraction to see what was happening.

"Some local dignitary," he whispered into Mary's ear. "He's bringing out his whole household, armed with cudgels. Now what's he going to do?" More talk, and a lot of portentous striding about. "Curse his guts, he's posting the servants across the end of the street. We shall have to turn back."

That left them with no means of escape. They were cut off between the river and the impenetrable horrors of Alsatia. And if they stayed here, in the area round Rose Lane, sooner or later they were bound to be stopped and questioned. And the man with the torch would recognize them both.

Mary was trembling. Tom gave her a comforting squeeze.

"Take heart. There's a place where we can stay safe for an hour or so, till the hue-and-cry has died down. You have only to walk a hundred yards. Lean against me as you are now; we must keep up the pretence, it serves very well."

They sauntered off, lovingly entwined, and apparently too engrossed to notice the unusual excitement in the street. No one paid the slightest atten-

tion to them. Tom led her up the first turning into
an enclosed yard, where there was a house with the
door ajar, and candles in the hall. Mary supposed it
was an inn, though there seemed to be no one
about. She was too dazed to be curious.

Tom rapped on the lintel and whistled. A servant
appeared dressed in black. After a murmured con-
sultation, Tom produced some money. They were
taken upstairs, into a small room with a table and
two stools, and a looking-glass of polished metal.
The painted arras had a rather peculiar design of
nymphs and satyrs, and the air was fusty with stale
scent.

"This will suffice," said Tom. "And you can
bring us some wine." As the man left them, he
added to Mary, "No—don't take your mask off
yet."

Now that the door was closed, she caught sight of
an alcove, and filling the alcove, blatant in its rad-
dled finery, was the most enormous bed. Then she
realized what sort of a house this was.

She looked at Tom, and saw that he was
blushing.

"I'm sorry, madam. This is no place for a lady of
your virtue. I'm well aware how unseemly you must
find it, but we had to go to ground somewhere, and
I could devise nothing better. I'll take you home as
soon as that rabble down below have got tired of
searching for us, and in the meantime there will be
nothing to offend you here; they are very discreet.
Though I dread to think——"

"Yes, you dread to think what Mr. Garnham
would say."

Mary laughed. It was the laughter of taut nerves.

She tried to stop when the man came in with the wine, but he was not interested. He had served too many couples in that house, he did not listen any more.

19

Tom set down his cup, remarking that they still had to examine the papers he had taken off the corpse.

"They may indicate what sort of a man it was I killed." He unwrapped the kerchief; there was only one document inside. "This is in Mr. Garnham's hand. So he was an agent, though he shouldn't have been carrying his orders. Strange—I can't make head or tail of this."

"Would it not be in cipher?" suggested Mary. She moved along the table to look. "The letters are very ill-formed, aren't they? And the lines are so uneven. His old pain in the wrist must have been troubling him when he wrote that."

The foolscap was tightly folded. Tom smoothed it out, and they saw the signature at the back: *Edward Garnham. 29th October, 1558.*

"Fifty-eight!" exclaimed Mary. "Why, that's nearly twenty years ago."

What was so memorable about the date? Of course, it was the year of the Queen's accession. In late October Queen Mary, sour and disappointed, was sinking into her last illness. Princess Elizabeth was at Hatfield, waiting for her star to rise. And Edward was in Newgate Prison, under sentence of death.

Mary's heart received a warning, swifter than any logical reason could travel through her brain. She sat down again, gripping her hands in her lap, without knowing why. Nicholas, Tom, Susan, Eleanor Quinton—all those people whose troubles had obsessed her—vanished under the shadow of a nameless premonition.

Tom turned the paper over and began to read.

" *'I, Edward Garnham, of Maringale Bois in the County of Essex, setting forth this statement of my own free will, do humbly confess that I have sinned exceedingly against Almighty God and His Holy Church, in that I have entertained, and seduced others to follow, certain vile Lutheran heresies and pernicious blasphemies, which I hereby renounce and forswear . . .'* Do you know what this is?" asked Tom, in a strangling voice.

"Yes," said Mary. "It's a recantation."

"He recanted," whispered Tom. "Denied everything he held most sacred. He didn't—he wasn't—all that we've ever thought about him—it wasn't true."

Too numb to be conscious of her own feelings, she watched the knowledge grow in the face of a young man who had lived on the legend of Edward's valour far longer than she had. He was almost in tears.

"So that's why he didn't burn. Don't you see? It wasn't the old Queen's death that saved him. He broke down, after his trial, and wrote—this."

He pushed the paper aside, but it drew him irresistibly. He picked it up and read it persistently through to the end, with a dry mouth, stumbling over some of the phrases, for the recantation was dreadfully complete. Each Protestant doctrine and practice which they had been taught to cherish was in turn derided and torn apart by an apostate who in his final paragraph showed himself beaten, servile, begging for mercy from the men who had driven him to this betrayal.

When Tom had finished reading they could neither of them look at the other, but sat in silence, grappling with a private sense of shame.

At last Tom said brutally: "I prefer the honest lechery which brings me in my living. I can get through that without vomiting."

His original grief had passed, leaving a cold and implacable contempt.

"I suppose they couldn't have converted him? He was young and alone; their priests are very cunning. He may have actually believed . . ." Mary's words trailed off. She had heard Edward discoursing on religion; he was a Protestant by conviction, no one had ever fogged that brilliant intellect with doubts. And he hated the Catholics; she was beginning to realize exactly why he hated them so much.

"He isn't a secret papist," said Tom. "He hasn't been serving Rome all these years; I'm positive of that. He's enforced the laws of England with an exemplary zeal. No—he hasn't the guts to make a successful traitor. He wrote this obscene rubbish simply to save his own skin."

"Yes, I'm afraid he did. . . . But isn't that the lesser evil? Tom, we shouldn't judge him too harshly. Could you endure to be burnt alive? I know I could not. And there were others who recanted, too. Archbishop Cranmer, for instance."

"He redeemed himself and died bravely. Archbishop Cranmer," said Tom, "didn't survive to spend the next nineteen years trading on the glory of a martyr's crown he wasn't entitled to wear."

It was then that Mary realized the full enormity of what Edward had done.

Tom got up and walked about the room. "It's the hypocrisy I can't stomach. He was a poor renegade who couldn't stand the fires of Smithfield. Very well. As you say, I might have done no better. But how could he set himself up as the shining model of a Christian, condescending to teach us our duty from the heights of his exalted sanctity? Look at the way he treated his children: Nick was a weakling and Sue was a deceitful slut—you speak of judging harshly, madam, but who was he to judge them? Nothing but a common swindler who'd cheated his countrymen from the day they set him free and hailed him as a hero."

"It's not so simple." Mary had been thinking very hard. "I understand now why he was so severe with the children. He was terrified of seeing his own faults reborn in them. That's why he said that Susan came of tainted stock."

Tom was following his own train of thought. "What a misguided simpleton I've been! I worshiped the ground he trod on. That night at Maringale he called me a peasant; I wasn't fit to touch the daughter of an honourable gentleman like Mr. Edward Garnham. Honourable—God save the mark! And after you took Susan indoors there was much more in the same vein. I had nothing to plead in my defense. He told me to go, and I trudged off through the forest. I lay down in the bracken and wanted to die, because I had been unworthy of his trust. After all he had given me I hadn't been able

to match his peerless integrity. How could I have
been such a fool? Or he such a damned pharisee?''

Tom had always idolized Edward. Edward's re-
cent harshness had made no difference. All Tom
had wanted was his forgiveness. But now the idol
was reduced to clay, a chipped and dirty clay at
that, and the change in Tom was so extreme that it
was almost physical. There was a hectic bitterness
about him; he had reverted to the wry intransigence
of his London ancestry, though without losing his
acquired poise. He looked like a lone wolf, a solitary
adventurer,.who would never put his faith in anyone again.

It was a measure of Edward's flagrant dishones-
ty, the harm he had done in deceiving this boy.

"One thing's settled," said Tom. "That fellow
was no loyal agent. I don't know how he came by
this paper, but I can guess what he was trying to do
with it. He was an extortioner, bent on selling it
back to the author at a very high price. Hence the
meeting in Rose Lane, and all those dark hints in
his message. We needn't shed any tears for him. I
can swear that his death was an accident, and I
doubt if they'll prosecute me after I've laid the facts
before the Secretary of State.''

"The facts?" repeated Mary blankly. "You don't
intend going to Walsingham with Edward's confession?''

He stared at her. "Why, yes. What else can I do?
I have no choice.''

She had not thought so far ahead. "Edward's recantation was a sin, not a crime. Doesn't that lie
between him and God? The State has no concern
with such a matter.''

Tom was not going to leave her with this comfort-

ing illusion. "You and I may believe that he wrote
this recantation in fear of his life, never meaning a
word of it. Our opinions carry no weight. The
evidence that counts is here in black and white,
above his signature. Walsingham's principal lieutenant was at one time a professing Roman Catholic. How can anyone ignore that?"

She did not answer.

"You say he has committed no crime," added
Tom. "What of his stolen reputation? And the pension he receives from the Queen? He's had a mint of
money out of her, in nineteen years, on false pre-
tences. Are you asking me to hush that up and become an accessory to a fraud?"

"You've grown confoundedly moral, all of a sudden, considering the way you earn your own living."

Tom flushed. "That's hardly a just comparison.
Because he is your husband——"

"And your benefactor. Have you forgotten? Well,
perhaps you may be allowed to forget. There's no
more I can say in mitigation. But before you set out
to ruin him have you considered that his whole family will share in the disgrace? Nicholas, Harry, Susan—don't you owe a special debt of chivalry to
Susan?"

"You know I don't want to hurt Susan," he burst
out. "Poor girl, I've caused her enough misery already. I don't want to hurt any of you. And I'm not
aiming at revenge. I simply want to speak the truth,
as a subject of the Queen. And the truth is, Edward
Garnham is unfit to hold office, and you know it.
Also, if I must be frank, I've no great wish to take
over the vacant role of martyr and let myself be con-
victed of murder, without telling the story that

would clear me of malice."

"If you are arrested you will have to speak. But why should you be? Provided we can get away from Blackfriars tonight, no one will connect you with that odious little man. You had no motive and we weren't seen at Rose Lane, except by that one fellow with the torch. How is he going to find you again, out of the whole population of London?"

Tom stopped his restless pacing. "Is it possible that you haven't understood? No, after all, you are not so versed in intrigue as I am." He propped himself on the stool beside her. "Listen, madam. Now we've guessed what the dead man's profession was, we can account for the fellow with the torch. Extortioners invite murder; for that very reason they are doubly careful in all their dealings. No one in such frail health would have met his victim alone without some kind of safeguard. He'd have stationed a satellite nearby, out of earshot maybe, but able to witness any attempt at violence, ready to intervene if the need arose. That was our torchbearer."

—"Then why didn't he intervene? Oh, I see. He was round the corner, waiting for Edward."

"Yes. He was there when we arrived, but he kept well clear of us then. He wasn't expecting a woman. On our return, we walked flat into him and gave him a good, close view. The result was, he went immediately down to the church, discovered the body and raised the alarm. For this is the point: a group of criminals who were threatening your husband would probably have been studying his ways for some time, and the chances are that any one of them would recognize me as his former secretary."

Mary was disarmed. Assuming that Tom knew

what he was talking about, there would soon be a warrant out for his arrest. She could not ask him to keep his mouth shut and go to prison as a gesture of outgrown gratitude to a family that had cast him out, a man he had come to despise.

20

When Tom and Mary finally left Blackfriars no one attempted to waylay them. He escorted Mary home and saw her safe indoors. He would not come in; he was determined to avoid his deposed hero. Mary did not blame him. She, too, dreaded meeting Edward.

The person she did meet, fretting in the hall, was Cousin Eulalia, a loose robe over her nightdress and her hair in plaits.

"Oh, Mary! Thank heaven you are come back. What possessed you to run off in that incontinent way? I've been distracted—the children—crying themselves to sleep, poor little souls."

For once Mary was not interested in the children. She said coolly that she was sure Susan had taken good care of them, and asked, "Where is Edward?"

"Oh! We had another disturbance. Mr. Garnham's been like a cat on hot bricks all the evening, waiting for some message that never came. And then, more than an hour ago, two men arrived to enquire whether he had news of Tom Fletcher. There is no end to the folly that young man can get into; it seems that he has killed somebody in a brawl. Mr. Garnham went out immediately—to view the corpse, I fancy. A melancholy task. Well, that is what comes of raising people above their station. I always said that Tom had bad blood in him. . . ."

She prosed on. Mary was engrossed in her thoughts. So Tom had been right. They were after him already, and of course Edward had been consulted straight away, as Tom's former patron. I must see him directly he comes in, she thought. She got rid of old Eulalia, and decided to wait for Edward in the study. It was no use going to her bedchamber; he would certainly not come to her there.

There was a minor annoyance when she discovered that the study door was locked and the key was missing. It seemed rather late in the day for these precautions. Uncertain what to do next, she remained planted in the passage. And then she heard it, that very slight sound from inside the study. Faint and undefined, something between a sigh and a sob. Nerves jumping, she called: "Edward! Are you in there?"

Absolute silence. She stooped to the keyhole and in doing so saw a thread of light under the door. But the keyhole itself was blocked—by the key. The study was locked on the inside.

He must have returned to the house while Eulalia was upstairs. Having found the extortioner dead and that damning sheet of paper gone, he had crept into his only refuge like a hunted animal.

"Edward." She rattled the latch. "Do let me in. I've been with Tom in Blackfriars—I have to speak with you."

The words vibrated in a hollow of emptiness. Yet the room was not empty. She could almost feel the man on the other side of the door, holding his breath, willing her to go away. Her husband, a self-made outcast who could no longer show himself to another human creature.

A wave of coldness swept over her, and she was terribly afraid. She had been frightened in the street with Tom; this was twenty times worse. She had got to reach Edward within the next few seconds.

She could not force the door. If there was another way in—and there was. The door that led into the garden. He might have forgotten to lock that. As these facts flashed through her mind, she was down the stone passage and into the kitchen. The rats rustled behind the wainscot, and Benjamin snored on his pallet in the buttery. She brushed past the scrubbed table, dragged at heavy bolts. The paved court now, and the night air. A sharp turn, and a mute prayer as she felt for the wooden panel. Oh God, let it open. The door flew wide, the light rushed to meet her, and what she saw in that room was indelibly clear.

Edward was standing in the centre of the floor. He had taken off his doublet and ruff; the sleeves of his white lawn shirt were rolled to the elbow. In his right hand he held a dagger, and the wicked edge of the blade was just quivering across the vein in his left wrist.

Mary screamed, and flung herself at him so violently that the dagger spun through his fingers and landed two yards away. She dived to grab it from the rushes, and straightened up, gripping it tightly behind her like a child hiding a toy.

"You fool," she said. "Is that all you can do— slash your wrists?"

She heard herself nagging, a petulant shrew.

Edward looked at her. "You know, don't you?" he said quietly.

She nodded. It had suddenly become impossible to speak.

"You were at Blackfriars. I was certain of it when they described Tom's companion." His voice faltered on a note of anguish "Why couldn't you let me die?"

There were hollows scooped out under his cheekbones, and a pallor so ghastly that he might have been dead already.

"You won't mend matters by dying. Edward, I know you are in great trouble, but that's no cure."

"I wasn't hoping for a cure. I was running away, as I always do. From one hell to another. I betrayed my Master—well, suicide is the proper end for Judas."

You're no Judas, she thought. Peter, perhaps. A Peter who had heard the cocks crowing for nineteen years.

He had turned away from her and stumbled into a chair, resting his arms on the table.

"Will you go now?" he asked. "You've no need to mount guard over me. I promise you that I shan't kill myself tonight, nor as long as your children are in the house. If you have any mercy to spare for me I beg you to let me be alone."

It was a hard plea to resist. In spite of it, Mary stood her ground. This time she was not going to be driven out of Edward's private sorrows.

"You've been alone too long. Now I know the truth, there's nothing to prevent your talking to me."

"No. I can't talk to you."

She made herself persist. "I may not be the person you would choose——"

"That's not the reason. Mary, don't you understand? I'm too ashamed."

Mary did not know what to say.

"There is nothing singular in your weakness," she ventured at last. "You were—not brave enough to burn at the stake. Neither am I. So why should you scruple to confide in me? I cannot judge you."

"You would have gone to the stake," he said. "I've seen so many of your kind who were tempered in the furnace. They are my perpetual judges. Our noble army of martyrs was not a race apart—you know that, you've read Foxe's book. A few were endowed with special gifts, the vicar here at St. Sepulchre's and my friend Green, of the Inner Temple. The majority were poor men, simple men, women as gentle as you are, girls not much older than Susan. I saw a young maidservant at Smithfield once: a little, stunted creature, no man would have looked twice at her. I stepped back from the heat of the flame, it was so great. She stood within its compass like a bride; I shall never forget her serenity." Edward paused. In his voice, as he spoke of the martyrs, Mary recognized a longing so intense that it was painful to hear. He said: "That child was one of God's saints, while I—what was I? A juggler with words, a Bachelor of Arts, playing with religion as though it was a game. I could dissect every line in the Gospels according to the rules of theology, but I did not value my Saviour's love one quarter so high as I valued the air in my lungs and the comfort of my own pampered flesh."

"You do yourself an injustice," said Mary. "You did not always set such a high price on your comfort. Wasn't it that very fact which undermined your strength, so that you couldn't bear the torment of martyrdom? Your health had been vitiated on the rack."

"How do you know that! I've told so many lies, how do you know I didn't squeal at the first twist of the screw?"

"My dear Edward, you carry the proofs on you to this day." Lying in his arms, she had felt the knots of scarred tissue under the bare skin; she had never dared to comment on them. "And you didn't betray your companions. They all survived, and swore that your loyalty had saved them."

"Well, I had just enough manhood for that," he admitted grudgingly. "I didn't see what the outcome must be. It's a strange thing, yet everyone will tell you the same: when you are undergoing torture you don't think ahead. Each minute has to be endured separately; the hours of respite pass in a blessed haze; the following morning hardly exists."

Now that she had lured him into talking, he was anxious to go on. Mary sat down on the truckle bed, arranging herself so that she was out of his line of vision. She realized that a purely verbal contact was all he could stand at present.

"After five spells on the rack," he said, "they paid me the compliment of thinking me invincible. They abandoned their questions and formally accused me of heresy. I've been told that I made a good impression at my trial; it was no more than play-acting, for I was half stunned. I didn't believe this was happening to me. When I was back in my cell, under sentence of death, the fearful knowledge broke over me like a wave. I was barely twenty-two and my life was over. I was about to die in the most horrible agony. To go through that carnage and be literally consumed by it. Men under torture say they want to die. They don't mean it. There's a universe of difference between pain and death. Every fibre in my body ached and throbbed, yet it was still my body, and I was inside it. The thought that I must perish in the fire, lose the world of sense and touch I loved so well—heaven itself seemed a poor consolation, and in my frantic greed for life, the very promise of heaven had grown dim. I huddled in my cell, crying out against my destiny, ready to sell my soul to the devil, if he could get me a reprieve. And that is what I did.

"They sent me a priest. He came prepared to reason with an obdurate Protestant. I was past reasoning; faith and pride had gone to the winds. In him I saw my one way of escape. Supposing I made my peace with the Catholic Church, was it too late for my life to be spared? He told me they would need a detailed rejection of my errors. I agreed with every point of doctrine that he raised; I pleaded youth and ignorance, implored him to intercede for me. I was—abject. Did you read the whole of my recantation?"

Mary's reply was inaudible.

He wiped the sweat from his forehead. "I wonder you can stay in the same room with me. When I recall that orgy of grovelling falsehood I am so sunk in shame—even so, the first version was insufficient. I was ordered to make it more humble. I obeyed, like a whipped schoolboy, and did my lesson again. After that I was left in possession of my life, for what it was worth. It should be very precious, considering what it cost me."

There was a long pause. Eventually Mary asked, "What happened then?"

"For a while nothing. I was in no state to care, for I had fallen into a low fever, brought on, I think, by melancholy. I worked out the exact sequence later, and it was ironical enough for a Greek play. My priest hurried to the Court, in fine fettle at having secured so notorious a convert, to find all the great people there shaking in their shoes. The Queen's doctors had just declared that her disease was mortal: three weeks at the most, and England would have a Protestant soverign once more. I imagine that no one wanted to hear of any new-made Catholics; they were too busy wondering how we should set about converting them. No doubt they thought we should emulate their filthy bonfires—well, never mind that. Papists of every degree were beginning to scamper for cover, and one of them was Perridge."

"Was he the priest?"

"No, the gaoler who had charge of me; he had been a constant witness of my humiliation, and the only one, apart from Father Green. He asked me to speak up for him when the Protestants came to power. He said he had always been kindly disposed towards me, and in a spirit of goodwill he had torn up my recantation. He showed me the scraps of paper, with a few phrases that I could recognize, and then consigned them to the privy."

"But how was that possible? The document we found this evening——"

"It was a trick. I told you that I had been compelled to write a second version; the paper I saw him destroy was the earlier draft. He got hold of the other, too, and kept it against a rainy day; he was a thorough-paced villain. He was also an unjust steward who had robbed many of his prisoners, and he very wisely fled to the Continent before they were able to bring him to book.

"Queen Mary died on the 17th November. Directly I was released, James Radcliffe's parents had me carried in a litter to their house in Chancery Lane, where Mrs. Radcliffe and her daughters nursed me like angels. No one mentioned my disgraceful act of cowardice, and I was grateful for the charity which refrained from heaping reproaches on a sick man. My father and mother arrived from Essex, and it was when my mother wept and spoke of miracles that I grasped the truth—my recantation had never been made public. They thought I was a hero.

"I could not shatter their illusions, then and there. They were so proud of me. They thanked God for giving them a son who was an example to all Christians. I lay in bed, stupefied, wondering what I was to do. I decided that I must broach the matter to Mr. Radcliffe or James, and in the next few weeks I did try to tell them, but each time I began they mistook the cause of my distress, and begged me not to dwell on my sufferings. They said these memories were impeding my recovery. Every day it grew harder to disclaim the part for which they had cast me. My friends all admired me so generously that it seemed—I know this sounds the most specious hypocrisy—it seemed discourteous to tell them that they were making fools of themselves, though I can't expect you to believe that."

"I can picture how it was," said Mary thoughtfully. "You could not bring yourself to hurt them."

"Up to that point I had the shreds of an excuse. Had it rested there—but my undeserved fame had spread too far. I received letters from a host of dis-

tinguished men, offering me advancement of whatever kind I chose. The Queen granted me a pension.
My father was overjoyed. His life had been nar-
rowed by poverty, by the continual struggle to hold
on to Maringale and maintain the rank of a gentleman in the teeth of my grandfather's debts. He
foresaw a very different picture for me. I could re-
build the family fortunes, rise to the top of my profession—and I saw my chance as clearly as he did.
I had simply to go on wearing the guise of a would-
be martyr, and I was bound for the heights.

"I was tempted, and I committed my second sin,
not so black as the first, yet more contemptible, for
I was no longer in danger of burning. I was corrupted by ambition, and to feather my own nest I
let myself be hailed as the champion of a creed I
had vilified and abused."

Mary thought he had been corrupted by his love
for his parents. He could not bear to spoil their happiness, or to deprive them of the better days they
were counting on, after a lifetime of hardship. She
remembered all the improvements at Maringale,
which had begun with his rise to prosperity. Whatever his faults, he had been a good son.

"I was mad," he said, "to think I could get what
I wanted through lies and blasphemy. God is not
mocked."

Not while He leaves us a conscience as His ministering angel, she thought. And yours has been an
avenging fury. She allowed herself a glance at her
husband. He was still leaning on the table, shivering in his thin shirt. She got up and fetched his
doublet.

"Put it on."

He did as he was told, unusually docile. He

looked lost, defenseless, like a boy whose wilful independence had landed him in a disaster he hadn't reckoned on. Like the boy who had broken down in Newgate Prison. At least he was no longer afraid of talking to her directly. Mary went to throw a log on the fire, and then settled herself on a cushion beside his chair, not touching him, but very close.

He began to tell her about his first wife.

"I ought not to have married her. A man as solitary as I am has no right to marry. The knitting together of two free spirits becomes impossible. You've found that, Mary, by bitter experience. You said yourself that I had made both my wives miserable, and when I think what I have done to you——"

"Never mind me. I should like to know more of Elizabeth. I have heard that she was discontented; perhaps it was partly her own fault. Young girls expect so much."

"She expected the moon, poor Elizabeth. She was beautiful and spoilt, the darling of a doting family. She could not interpret my moods, nor understand how my unresting conscience drove me to work sixteen hours a day, when she wanted to be hunting or dancing. After all, I was trying to expiate my sins, not hers; she had some reason to feel resentful. And there were the nightmares.

"I had been plagued by them, intermittently, since I came out of prison: those hideous dreams of burning; I had woken in the darkness, to find that they had no substance outside my own hag-ridden brain. I did not know, until I had a wife to tell me, that I performed them aloud. I shall never forget Elizabeth's rousing me because I was shouting out all manner of nonsense—that was what she called it. I asked her what I'd said, and she repeated the gist of it, parrot-fashion. My heart turned to ice. I had made what amounted to a full confession of my treachery.

"She was a simple creature, and she had missed the point. Yet even Elizabeth would fit a meaning to these dreams if they happened too often. They follow a regular pattern; an outbreak of recurrent nightmares, lasting several weeks, and then a long lull. While the spell was on me, I should not be safe to pass a night in the same room with her. I did try to manage without sleep, and the strain on my health was too heavy——"

"Edward!" Mary had made a discovery about her own marriage. "You had a nightmare at Maringale in the summer. When I came back to London you starved yourself of rest, and then you moved down here—so that's why you wouldn't go to bed with me!"

He turned to her, his eyes tragic and beseeching. "There was no other reason, Mary, I assure you."

"Why didn't you tell me?" The words were stillborn, for she realized that Edward had been physically incapable of telling anyone. Certainly not his first wife, who sounded foolish and rather pathetic, no strong partner for any husband, and completely at sea with the tormented man she had married.

They had made the best they could of a bad job, but Elizabeth's temperament was not equal to the aridity of neglect. She had been unfaithful to him. Mary, who had heard this story from Blanche Foyle, listened to Edward's version of it. He had been extremely angry; Elizabeth had outraged something in his essential male possessiveness that

went very deep. All the same, he had tried to behave
well. He had not beaten her or locked her up, as
plenty of men would have done, and he had stood
by her loyally; there had been no open scandal.

Elizabeth longed for a more positive reconcil-
iation, she needed a comforting reassurance that he
could not give, and it was unlucky that her tearful
entreaties touched him on the raw.

"She would insist that nothing was altered, that
if I had remained in ignorance, I should have seen
no difference in her. What was that to the purpose?
A fact is a fact, whether anyone knows it or not. She
did not like to think of herself as an adulteress, any
more than I like to think of myself as an apostate, so
she made this pretence of reshaping the past as
though it had not happened. That was what I could
not stomach. However much I have deceived others,
I haven't deceived myself. Her feeble protestations
fretted my temper, and I was cruelly unkind to her.
She was afraid of me—many people are; I believe
my manner is too cold and forbidding. So we struggled on. I think she loved me, and I was not indifferent to her; we were the victims of that disappoint-
ing kind of affection which can create pain without
healing it. By guarding our tongues, we did in the
end achieve a certain degree of harmony, but we
were never truly comfortable together. After she
died I swore I would never marry again."

"What made you change your mind?"

"Circumstance. And Francis Walsingham." He
was fidgeting with his signet ring and frowning. "As
a widower, I discovered an easy means of making
my lot more bearable. One evening I was across the
river in Southwark; I'd been on some mission or
other for the Council, and as I returned through the

dusk, there were handsome, painted fireflies in all the windows, calling their seductive invitations. It came to me that I was thirty-four years old; I'd drudged through twelve years of slavery, trying to expiate a sin that could never be undone. Experience had taught me that I could not hope for a happy marriage. . . . That was the first time I went into a brothel as a customer. It wasn't the last. To start with, I went because I wanted a woman, any woman. Soon I began to search for something besides lust. When a man pays a harlot to entertain him she is ready to suit his varying moods, laugh when he considers himself a wit, coo like a dove when he is sad. She listens to all he says, without presuming to question what is left unsaid. To these women I was no more secretive than any of their lovers. The barriers that existed were taken as a matter of course. I had long lost the art of close friendship; I was terrified of giving myself away, also I knew that my friends' regard was based on a false notion of my character. With men and women of my own kind, I was constrained; over in Southwark I felt free. I could bask in a climate of confiding ease, be frank and outspoken on subjects which I had the right to choose, without feeling obliged to bare my soul. No one would trespass on my privacy, or take offence if I shut up like an oyster. And I was spared the danger of talking in my sleep; a mistress can't complain because you don't spend the whole night with her.

"I met a girl I liked better than the rest—not a common whore, a courtesan who would deal honestly with one protector. I grew fond of her, she was warm-hearted and merry. I count my time with Jill as the least of my transgressions."

Mary was appalled. Not by his amorous adventures, which she took in her stride. It was the thought of this proud and fastidious man, forced to assuage his loneliness with the only companions who could make no demands on him, because he was paying them. She did feel a stir of gratitude towards the girl Jill, who had been warm-hearted and merry. Perhaps their desire for each other had been genuine.

"Why did you part from her?"

"The hounds of righteousness hunted me down. I had been watched, as we all are. Walsingham trusted my discretion, and allowed me to live as I pleased, but when my visits to Southwark finally seeped through to the Lords of the Council he could hardly defend me. Their lordships said that a man of my profligate habits should not be employed on the Queen's business. They said it was neither seemly nor safe. I don't blame them. I had never gossiped to my mistresses, but how could they be sure of that? Walsingham told me that unless I wished to lose my Crown appointments I had got to mend my ways. He advised me to marry again.

"My career was vital to me; it had become both a lifelong dedication and the rock which supported my family. I had to accept his ruling. I said goodbye to Jill, and then I came home and did something I'd never done before: I sat in this room, with a bottle of *aqua vitae*, and drank myself insensible. The next morning I faced my dilemma. I couldn't exchange one vice for the other. If I went on drinking I should soon start to babble, not merely the Queen's secrets but my own. Yet I couldn't go on as I was, imprisoned in a comfortless house, where my children, dearly as I loved them, simply added to my anxieties. I must get out of my trap, though it meant walking into another. There was nothing for it but a second marriage."

Edward had become so absorbed in his memories that he seemed to have forgotten Mary's identity. He glanced down at her, with a sudden compunction, and said: "I ought not to be telling you these things. To suggest that I married you as an alternative to drinking and whoring! I might have had the grace to keep that motive hidden. Though I suppose it doesn't matter now."

"It would never have mattered," Mary assured him quickly. "We were strangers when you first approached my brother, and there are worse reasons for such a bargain. It's laid down in the Prayer Book that marriage is a remedy against sin."

"I've always considered that a most uncivil definition," said Edward, with an echo of his old, astringent wit that was like a blow to the heart.

"I did not choose quite blindly," he said, after a moment's pause. "I was looking round for a bride, with no great ardour, and I happened to call on your brother when he was entertaining visitors from Sussex. The talk was all of Mary, and how fortunate the man would be whom she took for her second husband. I asked who Mary was, and they gave me a portrait of such a paragon—surely, I thought, this woman could bring me a measure of content, give my children the loving care they need so badly, and turn my house into a home."

Mary's mouth quivered. She said with an attempt at lightness, "Young widows are always cried up in the most extravagant terms."

"Yes, I took their eulogies with a grain of salt. Then I met you. And I felt like the Queen of Sheba

—the half was not told me. But I still shouldn't
have married you."

"My dear——"

He ignored her outstretched hand and sat staring
at the fire. "I hurt everyone who comes near me,"
he whispered. "Mary, I am most truly sorry for the
wrong I have done you, making you so wretched
and dragging you down in my fall. I am in no way
fit to be your husband, let alone the stepfather of
Dacre's children."

Simultaneously, their minds leapt back a few
hours, to supper in the parlour. She now saw exactly why he had slapped her face.

"There's no point in making mountains out of
molehills," she said, before he could speak. "We
neither of us behaved very well. I ought to have seen
that you were being driven beyond endurance.
Were you trying to buy back that paper? You
haven't yet told me how it cropped up again. The
gaoler who stole it, Perridge—is he still alive?"

"Not now. He died this evening, in Rose Lane."

"So that's who he was." Mary was possessed by
a sick and savage hatred. "I eased his dying breath,
and said a prayer for him. I wish I'd cursed him on
his road to hell."

"No, you don't," said Edward. "You have the
supreme gift of loving your enemies. Unlike me. Not
that I rate them all at Perridge's level. Any honest
papist would have handed my signed statement
over to the priests. Master Perridge had other fish
to fry. The Dominican father who achieved my
'conversion' retired to the Catholic parts of
Yorkshire and died not long after, so Perridge had
the sole claim to a valuable secret, if ever he dared
to come and use it. The fear of his own black record

has kept him abroad all this time. At last his avarice overcame his caution. Tempted by the hope of a luxurious old age, he returned to England under an assumed name. That's not as easy nowadays as you might suppose; he did it by attaching himself to the Ebury Hall conspirators. They are financed from the Continent. One morning in August, when you were still at Maringale, he accosted me in the street. He'd changed a good deal, and his beard was grey, but I recognized him directly I heard his voice. It was a voice that had plagued me too often in my dreams. My God, it seemed like another nightmare, as he drew a folded paper out of his purse and showed me my signature, and the whining degradation of that final paragraph. He asked me whether my former views on doctrine needed refreshing. Or perhaps I could still recall what I had written? I could have strangled the little rat. He laughed, and said: 'You won't attack me in the open street. I am willing to part with this precious manuscript for eight hundred pounds in gold. In the meantime I shall lodge it safely where you cannot reach it, and if I am killed or arrested before the purchase is concluded, it will go to the Secretary of State.' "

"So great a sum! Edward, how could you pay him?"

"I had to, or be ruined. I saw him twice afterwards, and begged him to reduce the price, but he was adamant. These last weeks, when I haven't been chasing conspirators, I've been besieging money-lenders. Approaching each one with a plausible reason and a moderate request, for fear it should get about that I was in debt. It was a slow and difficult method, but what else could I do? I haven't a penny to spare, outside what we live on,

and I couldn't sell so much as an acre of the land in
Essex without raising a storm of conjecture. I had to
borrow the whole amount from the usurers. There
was no other way."

"There was my dowry," said Mary.

"Well, I may be a cheat and a trickster, but I
didn't touch that."

"I wasn't implying—I thought we held all things
in common."

"That doesn't mean I can rob you without your
consent. In any case, we were going to need your
dowry while I pinched to pay off my creditors. I've
mortgaged all my property, up to the hilt. The
night I rode down to Essex, I'd come to fetch the
title-deeds."

"And that was when we discovered Susan with
Tom."

"Finding out their intrigue was like seeing myself
reflected in a glass. My pious daughter, who was
just such another whited sepulchre. A deceiver and
a liar. Tom too; I'd brought him up, and even he
had caught the infection. I lashed at him with every
scathing accusation that came into my head. I
treated the boy abominably; is he very bitter
against me?"

"Not at your dismissing him. He's taken this other matter hard." She hesitated. "He's gone to Walsingham with your recantation. I did my best to stop
him, but he wouldn't listen."

"Stop him? Good heavens, you couldn't stop
him. If only I'd never sent him away. Once I recovered my temper, I decided to get him back on his
old footing—as soon as I'd settled with Perridge; till
that was done, I had no time or inclination to spare
for anything else. By the same token, I meant to

give more attention to Nick, and choose him a new music-master. Now it's too late. They will repudiate any offer of mine. Not that I can help either of them now. Tom's lucky to be rid of me. Poor Nick is going to be damned with the consequence of being my son. And I fought so hard to preserve him and Harry from having their name dragged in the mud. When I think of the extremes I went to—you haven't heard the worst of them."

What more could there be, Mary wondered, her heart sinking.

"You remember our drive to Ebury Hall? Well, you are hardly likely to forget it!" He saw her stiffen, and said: "In all this inventory of crimes, there is just one I can ask you to acquit me of. I didn't take you out to watch Eleanor Quinton's relations being dragged off to prison. They were none of them in the faintest danger that evening."

"But you didn't know that when we started. You couldn't possibly have guessed that someone had warned Sir Amyas."

"I didn't guess," said Edward. "I warned him myself."

"*You* warned him!" Her brain was spinning. "You contrived the escape of a man you were supposed to arrest for treason! I don't believe you."

Edward flinched. Up to now Mary had shown no sign of the horror he seemed to expect, but this last revelation was such a profound shock that her very astonishment condemned him.

"It was a monstrous thing to do," he admitted, "though not quite so bad as it sounds. I haven't allowed the Queen's enemies to escape scot-free, I've merely delayed the reckoning."

It was the delay which he needed. All the time

that he was struggling to pay Perridge, there was
another, hidden relationship between them which
the extortioner never realized. Edward was getting
nearer and nearer to the point when he would have
to arrest the Quinton conspirators and their
hangers-on. Perridge was one of them, chiefly for
his own convenience. If he was pulled in, he would
certainly produce the recantation, out of sheer spite
if nothing else. The one hope was to buy him off
before the arrests were made; he would be glad
enough to abandon his friends and get out of the
country. Edward knew that only his greed was
keeping him in England.

Edward had the promise of a final loan which
was to be available today, and then, last week,
Walsingham had insisted that the net must be
drawn when the plotters met at Ebury Hall on
Thursday. This was a definite order; they had plenty of evidence, and he couldn't understand why his
lieutenant was being so cautious and dilatory.

"I was at my wits' end," said Edward. "Nothing
would dislodge Perridge till he had the money. Except perhaps the knowledge that they were all going
to be arrested for treason—and there was a limit to
the depths that even I could stoop to. I didn't know
where to turn. And then your friend Eleanor came
to my rescue."

"I can't think how."

"She poured out the affecting story of her scape-
grace brother being led into trouble by the precious
Rashford; he was another of the more venal underlings. Quinton's collected a pretty crew of villains
around him. Well, I took my chance. I wrote an
anonymous letter to Sir Amyas, telling him that the
High Sheriff was preparing to descend on his house

and interrogate the occupants about a matter of smuggled wine. What would you do, if you received such a letter, and discovered that the smuggling had indeed been going on under your nose, that the threads of evidence were entangled with your own plot to overthrow the Government? And if the Queen's officers were due to arrive the same evening that you'd planned a meeting of the chief conspirators?"

"Cancel the meeting. And possibly run away, though I don't see what good that did him."

"I think he was afraid of what we might get out of his servants. And I dare say he was anxious that the smuggling fraternity should have time to disappear before we caught up with him. Now, I hear, he's returning to Westminster prepared to meet anyone. No doubt he's had news of what happened on Thursday, and he may have found it reassuring. A small unescorted party that called and went away again. You'll remember I was careful to keep the soldiers in the background."

"Yes, I see. But what do your colleagues make of it?"

"At first they were inclined to believe that our whole strategy had been betrayed. Everyone was asking who was the spy in our midst. I even felt obliged to invent a red herring by pretending that my private papers had been tampered with. As it happened, the chairs in here had been shifted one day, and a few of my books disarranged—that's what gave me the idea. I dare say the boys were fooling around when I was out."

It wasn't the boys, it was Tom and Jane, thought Mary, but she did not interrupt him.

"Now that we can observe the chief conspirators

going on with their plans, Walsingham doesn't
know what to think, but they won't slip through his
hands again. We have word that they mean to meet
at a house in Tottenham, and this time we shall
reach out and seize them.

"That is, Robert Sykes will seize them," he
amended. "I shan't be there. I shall be in prison
myself."

"In prison?" she repeated. "Edward, must it
come to that? Surely there can't be a law against
recanting under duress——"

"There's a law against receiving a pension you
haven't earned. I've been milking the Treasury for
years. And they've a graver cause to prosecute.
Once they've perceived the connection between me
and Perridge and Quinton, they'll guess who sent
that warning. Although I had no evil design, although I've done no damage in the long run, I can't
deny that I abused a position of trust and helped a
wanted man to evade capture. That's a felony; I
think they can charge me with misprision of
treason."

Mary did not know what misprision meant, and
was frightened to ask. She gazed at him in silence.
The fair head was bent, the fine profile decimated
by the lines of suffering and defeat.

"My course is run." He sounded very tired. "I
hadn't the courage to confess in cold blood; now it's
out of my choice. I could almost welcome the release of owning the truth at last—if it wasn't for you
and the children."

21

Mary was waiting in a small parlour at the back of Mr. Secretary Walsingham's house in Seething Lane. She had been waiting for nearly two hours. Edward had been summoned here at the crack of dawn, and she had insisted on coming with him, to be left alone with her fears while he was closeted with Walsingham. What would they do to him? she wondered, her mind dragging round in the same circle for the hundredth time, so numb with apprehension that she hardly noticed the domestic noises of the house: two servants arguing, a little girl practising on the virginals, the footsteps of the busy hurrying clerks. And when the door finally opened she did not notice that either.

A voice said, "Mrs. Garnham."

Mary jerked to her feet in confusion.

"This is a bad business," said the Secretary of State.

He was dressed as plainly as a puritan, grave and dark-skinned, the man the Queen called her Moor. In spite of his air of austerity he had an easy manner which had a disarming effect even on his opponents; it was part of his stock-in-trade. Mary eyed him nervously and embarked on a speech she had been rehearsing.

"I know you have just cause to be angry, sir. I can't defend what my husband has done, but indeed he has suffered for it. I hope you will remember what a heavy price he has already paid for his—his mistakes, and be merciful if you can."

"He doesn't ask for mercy. Which is why I've come to find you. The fact is, I need your help."

"My help?" echoed Mary.

"I want the added weight of your influence to prevent him proclaiming his wretched story from the roof-tops. He's set on making some sort of open confession, and he's got to be stopped."

Mary gaped. "But don't you want him to confess? I thought you would insist—I've been praying that you might not send him to prison; I didn't think anything could save him from being publicly disgraced."

"Your prayers are likely to be answered," Walsingham told her caustically. "For there can be no retribution. Your husband has presented me with a stalemate; strange he did not see that for himself."

"I must be very stupid, sir. This is Greek to me."

"You know that the name of Edward Garnham is dear to all English Protestants. He has become a symbol, a living link with our brothers and sisters who were faithful unto death. What are people going to say if his legendary valour is exposed as a sham? You can guess with what relish the papists will seize on his shabby imposture, and the effect it will have on the waverers, the doubters, the mockers. Soon there will be rumours flying round that Garnham wasn't the only renegade; that Foxe falsified his book, glossing over many similar recantations; that half the so-called martyrs died unwilling and terrified, while the other half never died at all. No one under thirty has a clear memory of those bloody days, and the young are always ready to suspect what their elders tell them. Our Church is still so new, it hasn't much historical witness to set against the embalmed mythology of Rome. Queen Mary's persecuted victims are our saints, and we can't afford to have them brought into disrepute because one impudent liar managed to assume a share of their glory.

"If he publishes the facts," continued Walsingham, "Garnham will be doing the greatest harm that anyone can render to a noble cause. He will be making our pretensions look ridiculous."

And you will be the chief laughing-stock, thought Mary. The wily Secretary of State, who was famous for knowing everyone's secrets, completely taken in by the man who had been his trusted lieutenant for years.

He might have been fooled by Edward; he was quite acute enough to read Mary's expression, and he smiled rather bitterly.

"Yes, I cut a ludicrous figure, don't I? You think I am an interested party, and you are right."

Mary blushed. "I didn't mean to be uncivil—"

"It's of no consequence. But my interests are not purely selfish. If my judgment is discredited my work will be hampered and my advice unheeded— and I happen to know that there is no one available who can serve England so well in my particular office."

This was said without conceit, and Mary accepted it. Walsingham was too precious to the State; any lessening of his power might lead to a national disaster.

"So you don't mean to proceed against my husband? You'll ignore the letter to Sir Amyas Quinton?" She stopped, afraid that she had given away the most damning of Edward's manoeuvres. Perhaps he had been able to keep that hidden after all. She was relieved by Walsingham's calm reply.

"The letter was written under a temptation which won't arise again. Provided we lay hands on Quinton next week—and I've little doubt that we shall—I can overlook that subterfuge. Are you so amazed, madam? I have forgotten worse lapses, when policy demanded. It's an art that all statesmen learn to practise."

She felt herself thawing into warmth and hope. "Then he won't be ruined? He was so despondent last night he frightened me . . ." Her confidence died down as she recalled what Walsingham had said earlier, and why he wanted her help. "Are you telling me that it's *Edward* who is threatening to make a scandal?"

"He is determined to own the truth for all the world to hear."

"But that's incredible! After struggling so hard to keep it dark—" She paused, considering some of the things Edward had revealed last night. Was it so incredible? The solitary guilt, the play-acting, had been a constant mental torture. He could not summon the courage to confess of his own accord, yet in the past few hours, when discovery was certain, he had found a bleak consolation in the idea of shedding his disguise, however painful the result. Perhaps he had gone too far over the brink to change his mood and withdraw.

"What do you want me to do?" she asked.

"Make him realize the waste and folly of his present course. You have claims on him which he can't evade. Come, I'll take you to him."

Walsingham led her through an ante-chamber to a long low room where there were books and stacked papers, chests with heavy locks, maps hanging on the walls and a great terrestrial globe. Edward was standing in front of the massive table, pale as a ghost in the morning light; he gave the impression that he had not moved all the time he was alone. He threw an incurious glance at Mary and returned to his inward contemplation.

Walsingham placed a chair for Mary, and then sat down behind the table. Edward remained standing at attention, like a dishonest servant who was about to be disciplined for cheating his master—and that, of course, was the humiliating point.

"Well," said Walsingham. "You have had a chance to reflect. I thought it fitting that your wife should join us, since your future concerns her too. Have you come round to my opinion?"

"No, sir." The voice was subdued, but there was a stubborn edge to it. "I'm sorry. I can't go on lying, and it wouldn't serve your purpose if I did. No good comes out of evil. I can't keep up the pretence any longer; I must clear my conscience."

"I marvel that you care to resurrect your conscience at this late date," remarked Walsingham, with a sarcastic inflexion which made Mary want to hit him. "It has been most conveniently buried these nineteen years."

"The stinking corpse of my conscience, then," retorted Edward, "which others have dug up for me. I am in no position to sue for favours, yet the one favour I am asking is granted to the basest criminals. I have lost everything—my integrity, my livelihood. You can break me at your will. Surely you won't deny me the chance to make my peace with God?"

The two men stared at each other. Walsingham was about five years older than Edward, and they were a complete physical contrast. Intellectually, they were equals, and they had worked together very closely. There had been a genuine liking and respect on both sides. Edward must be sadly conscious of losing that also.

Walsingham sighed. "I am not standing in your way. If you need spiritual guidance you have only to go to a parson—"

"And what good will that do, when I can't comply with the conditions? You have to 'make restitution and satisfaction according to the uttermost of your powers, for all injuries and wrongs—'"

"Don't quote the Prayer Book at me!" snapped Walsingham, exasperated. "I know the exhortation as well as you do. What are these conditions that trouble you? What restitution were you intending?"

"I've been drawing a pension that I never earned. I ought to return the whole sum to the Exchequer."

"That would be impossible," exclaimed Mary. "You couldn't replace the revenue of so many years."

"Not without beggaring myself and leaving my children to starve. I must simply pay back what I can. At least I can renounce any further charity from the Crown. You will acknowledge the force of that, Mr. Secretary. You reminded me a while ago that Her Majesty cares little for the finer points of theology; you maintained she would rather have a live agent than a dead martyr. Do you think she would be so forbearing towards that agent if she knew he had been steadily defrauding her Treasury? You can hardly say that she doesn't care about money."

Walsingham did not reply. He had been thwarted too often by the Queen's well-known passion for economy.

"If you cover up my depredations," said Edward, "they will be on your conscience also. Besides, you'll have to explain why I am dismissed from the Government service. Even supposing you allow me to resign——"

"You go too fast. I am not dismissing you and you are not going to resign. You are far too useful to the State. That's another reason why you can't make this declaration."

"Useful to the State? A man who traffics with the enemy!"

"Who once delayed the ends of justice without perverting them. There is no need to exaggerate. I am dealing with men, not archangels; you are no more fallible than the rest, and you know it. And don't start telling me that you obtained your place by trickery. You've kept it by merit alone. The labourer is worthy of his hire."

Edward brushed this aside. "That doesn't include my pension, nor my false reputation as a hero. Can't you understand, sir? This stolen property is like a millstone round my neck. I must get rid of it or perish."

Mary had been watching and listening, unwilling to join in the argument until she had grasped the motive behind Edward's compulsion to strip himself of everything he had won at such a high cost. Walsingham appealed to her now.

"Let us hear your opinion, Mrs. Garnham. Do you think your husband can wipe out the wrong he

has done by letting his sins be visited on his whole
family? For that is what it will come to. Do you
believe that God demands such a sacrifice?"

Edward shifted unhappily, and Mary saw that
this was the one plea that might move him. He
would do almost anything to protect his children.
Then she remembered what he had already done to
protect his parents from the pain of his original failure. It was not ambition or greed but affection
which had started him off on his career of deceit.
That was the sacrifice which should never have
been made. Like most women, Mary had always
thought that she valued human claims higher than
abstract ideas of honour, but here something inside
her rebelled. She was not going to extort any compromise from Edward. He must be free to work out
his own salvation.

She said: "I agree with my husband, sir. I don't
think that good can come out of evil. . . . Edward, I
still hope you may not feel it necessary to make your
story public, but if you are firmly persuaded that
this is the only way you can find peace, then I
should not wish to prevent you. And I think the
children are quite old enough to see the true meaning of your dilemma. We shall all stand by you,
whatever happens."

"I thank you," murmured Edward. "That is very
generous."

Walsingham looked extremely annoyed, as well
he might. He had fetched in Mary as an ally, and
she had turned against him.

They seemed to have reached a deadlock. Edward stayed frozen in his unnerving stillness, and
the silence became oppressive.

Abruptly, Mary asked, "Can you tell me, Mr.

Secretary, why was my husband given a pension?''

The men glanced at her and then at each other. In each of those clever faces she saw the same verdict: all women are bird-witted, they can't master the most elementary reasoning.

She persisted. "When a man is sentenced to death and afterwards reprieved is it the custom to give him a pension as well?"

"No," breathed Walsingham, his eyes narrowing like a cat's. "No, by God, it isn't! You put me to rights, madam. The pension—I can refer to the exact terms—was granted as a compensation for his previous sufferings on the rack. By refusing to speak he preserved the lives of several leading Protestants, while sustaining great injury to his health."

"Permanent injury," Mary pointed out. "He is often afflicted with swollen joints. He has a recurring dislocation of the shoulder."

"Yes. And a slight limp, although he conceals it so well." They were discussing Edward as though he was not there. Walsingham leant back in his chair, olive-skinned and bland, addressing him with a touch of triumph. "You fool, there was no need for these qualms. The recantation doesn't affect your pension, one way or the other. You don't owe the Queen a penny."

Edward was not at all grateful for this information. The unkind thought crossed Mary's mind that he was developing a taste for martyrdom after all. He scowled, saying: "You can't settle all my debts so easily. I've lied consistently for my own profit. For years I've enjoyed a spurious reputation——"

"Have you?" asked Mary. "Have you enjoyed it, Edward?"

He was taken aback. "You know what I mean.

The word may have been ill-chosen."

"An odd choice indeed," commented Walsingham. "We've all noted your distress when anyone ventures to praise your past achievements. I put
it down to modesty; now I see it was the sharp pang
of guilt. Which poses a question of moral
philosophy—can a man profit from a sin whose advantages he hates like poison? I think not. And
where there is no gain there can be no restitution.
There is nothing you need renounce, neither money
nor fame. This frantic desire for confession is based
on a fallacy."

"I don't want money or fame," protested Edward. "I want to speak the truth."

"What you want is neither here nor there. I
would not willingly trample on your religious
scruples, but your wife has shown you they are
groundless. It's a pity you didn't consult her
sooner; we'd have been spared a deal of trouble. In
secular matters you come under my authority, and
you'll do what you are told."

"Yes, sir," muttered Edward, all the argument
knocked out of him.

"What happened in Newgate Prison will remain
a secret between us three and young Fletcher—he
won't blab, since I'm taking him into my service;
he'll see the wisdom of keeping his mouth shut. So
we come to a reckoning." Walsingham surveyed
Edward from head to foot with a cold appraisal.
"You expect and deserve to be punished; you have
no right to complain at the poetic justice of your
punishment. You allowed yourself to accept the
glory that is due to a martyr, and however much
your unwarranted crown may pinch, you will have
to wear it for the rest of your life."

The man in front of him did not move an inch.

Defeated on every issue, there was nothing left for him but stoic obedience.

Walsingham stood up. "I'm sorry, Edward," he said, more gently. "God knows, I find no pleasure in hurting you. Your reputation is not your own to throw away; it belongs to the State. . . . Mrs. Garnham, your husband is in no fit case to continue in harness at present. Take him down to the country and see if you can bring him to a rational frame of mind."

Edward did not say a word as they walked home. It was a shrewd windy day, and the painted shop-signs were banging and creaking overhead. She was cold, and he must be cold too. They had neither of them slept or been able to swallow much breakfast. She studied him anxiously; he looked as if he had been through a long illness. Or as if he was going to be ill, she thought with foreboding.

The house in Warwick Lane was sombre and quiet. Mary had packed the children off to Holborn, where one of her nephews was providentially having a birthday. They gravitated towards the nearest room, the parlour. Edward cast himself wearily down on a bench. Still he did not speak.

"Is it so terrible?" she ventured at last. "Surely Mr. Walsingham has convinced you that there is nothing you have to do in the way of restitution, so can you not come to terms with your conscience?"

"It's too late for that. I'm finished. These last weeks have brought it all home; I've been forced to see myself too clearly, and I can no longer endure what I see. How do you think it feels to go through the world without a single friend, knowing that every show of affection or trust is meant for a man who never existed? Anyone who could read my true character must hate me."

"Edward, that's nonsense! I don't hate you."

"Don't you? I've given you every cause to. But that's old history; we needn't dwell on it." Making an effort to sound casual and composed, he asked, "When do you mean to start for Sussex?"

For a few seconds Mary could not remember why she was going to Sussex. Then she was stricken. "You can't have thought—what sort of a poor creature do you take me for? I'm not going to leave you now!"

"Why not? You promised to stand by me if I was disgraced, and I'm grateful. Indeed, I don't think your courage would let you desert a sinking ship. However, since Walsingham is determined to keep my hulk afloat, you have no call to remain and the sooner you go the better for you and your children."

"But everything is changed——"

"Why should that prevent your going? You decided to leave me yesterday and you didn't know the sum of my infamy then. I won't impose on your pity——"

"This has nothing to do with pity. Nor duty either. When I said I was going I was in a rage, I thought you were as hard as iron, and as merciless. If I'd had the smallest inkling of the agonies you have suffered do you think I am so dull that I couldn't have made allowances?" Edward was looking at her as though she was talking a foreign language. "Has it never struck you," she asked, "that weakness and failure are easier to forgive than implacable righteousness?"

He did not answer. This was certainly a language that he could not understand.

"You don't know much about forgiveness, do you?" she said.

For that, she decided, was his real trouble, his

ingrained heresy. Unable to forgive himself, he had shut his eyes to the whole process which alone made a Christian life tolerable, or even possible. Etienne had grasped the essence of this, when he said that Edward was unlike the other martyrs because he couldn't repeat St. Stephen's prayer. (Poor Etienne, was he still scouring the taverns for Tom? It seemed a century ago that finding Tom had been so vitally important. And now she wished she had never found him at all.)

Edward had withdrawn into that remote indifference which she had learnt to dread. He seemed further off than ever; last night's outpouring of confidence was dammed up by his despair, and she was sure that he longed to be rid of her, of his children, of every human contact.

The idea of being unwanted had daunted her so often, but she had lost her useless pride. She went to him and touched his shoulder, willing herself to meet the pain of being rejected.

"Let me stay with you, love. Don't shut me out."

She felt the muscles stiffen under the cloth as he braced himself against the comfort he had never dared to ask for. Then his resistance broke. He turned, with a clumsy violence, half rising to kneel on the bench, gripping both her hands.

"Help me, Mary," he whispered. "Help me to conquer my devil. There's no one else who can."

"I'll help you," she said softly.

He clung to her as though he was drowning. She stared down at their clasped hands. The white rim of his cuff had slipped back a little and there was a faint scratch across the vein in his wrist. And she recognized the dark temptations of his particular devil and knew what the battle was that she would have to fight.

EPILOGUE

On Christmas Eve, 1578, an elegant young man on a fine bay horse was riding through the forest towards Maringale Bois. His steep-crowned hat was set at an exaggerated tilt, and his boots were of Spanish leather; even his fur-edged cloak had an exotic swagger, for it had been made in Paris, where Mr. Thomas Fletcher was attached to the English Embassy.

He had been over a year in the Queen's service, first at Ludlow, with the Council of Wales, acting as a clerk to the Lord President; then he had been transferred to France.

And today, he thought wryly, he was stepping into the past. A most unwilling step, forced on him by the cunning of Sir Francis Walsingham. Tom, arriving in London with despatches from the Ambassador, had reported in Seething Lane. Sir Francis had received him affably, and asked him, since he had no other duties on hand, to carry an urgent letter into the country. Naturally he had agreed, and then he had been told where the letter was to go. Being an ambitious public servant with his way to make, he could not possibly back out. Of course, it was easy to see what the Moor was after; it must irritate him to know that two of his followers were not on speaking terms.

Not that Tom had been able to indulge in the pleasure of meeting his former guardian and cutting him dead; so far their paths had not crossed. But he had ignored two letters from Garnham, and perhaps Walsingham knew that. He considered it disgraceful that Garnham was back in his old employment, successful and admired. He had been suspended from office for several months; they said he had been ill. Tom knew better.

The floor of the forest was thick with fallen leaves. The naked trees lifted their branches to the sky; it was uncannily still. And very different from that warm summer night, sixteen months ago, when he had left Maringale on foot, stumbling along, forlorn, too dazed to know where he was going. Somewhere about here he had thrown himself down in the bracken, and wept—yes, actually wept—over the things Garnham had said to him. He had believed them all, because he had believed, frantically, in the wisdom and integrity of his hero.

He had not seen Edward Garnham since that night. In a few minutes he was going to see him again. He would have to be formally correct, but formality could be the deadliest weapon of all.

The narrow chase ended and the sunlight parted the trees. There was the familiar stretch of grass, with the moat and the Manor beyond. Tom had an odd sensation at the pit of his stomach. As he drew closer he saw a group of people at the front of the house, and a handcart loaded with holly and ivy. They were engaged in the Christmas ritual of decorating the outer walls with evergreen.

They were too absorbed to notice him as he crossed the bridge. Children and gardeners; Jane plaiting a wreath. A long-legged boy (good heavens, was that Harry?) perched on the top of a ladder, looping one of the garlands round an upper window-sill. His father was holding the foot of the ladder and shouting directions.

"Not so tight there. Give it a bit more play. . . . Mind what you're at; I don't want a holly-bush on my head."

He sounded so happy, thought Tom resentfully. He had reached the forecourt. Jane saw him, and shrieked: "It's Tom! Oh, Tom!" She ran to greet him.

Tom dismounted, very much aware of Garnham, who had turned quickly, the laughter still alight in his brilliant grey glance. His exhilaration ebbed, he came forward, doubtfully.

"My dear Tom, we thought you were in France." He spoke with obvious constraint. "You are truly welcome."

Tom bowed. "I am here under orders, sir. As a messenger from the Secretary of State."

He produced Walsingham's letter and gave it into the hand which had been stretched out to him.

"I see," said Garnham, evenly. "Well, it's good that you've come at all. Clemency, run and fetch your mother."

Tom was surrounded by children. Jane, Harry, Roger and Greville—they were all inches taller. They pelted him with questions. Garnham stood aside, absently tugging at the seal of his letter.

"How splendid you are," breathed Jane, devouring him with her great, dark eyes. He noticed that she had become extremely pretty. "Such a grand gentleman, Tom. Is this what comes of living in Paris?"

"You are easily deceived, my dear. It takes more than Paris finery to make a gentleman."

Her puzzled frown gave him a pang of contrition, which was not removed by Greville, who demanded, "Have you brought us any presents?"

He should have stocked up some foreign trifles for the children; they had never done him any harm.

"My greedy son on the grab again." And there was Mrs. Garnham; he had forgotten how tiny she was, and that young fragile air which was so deceptive. She seized on him without ceremony. "Dear Tom, this is the best of times to arrive. Now we shall have you for Christmas."

"I regret, madam, I must be on my way immediately."

"Will you not stay?" asked Garnham.

"I fear it will not be—convenient. As I informed your worship, I did not come of my own choice."

He had the satisfaction of seeing his shot find its mark.

"You may change your mind after dinner," said Mary.

Tom was about to make it plain that he did not wish to dine at Garnham's table when another member of the family appeared at the front door.

"Nicholas!" he exclaimed, diverted.

"Who is it?" asked Nicholas, turning his head. He seemed to be listening with a most intense concentration. His movements were curiously contained. Tom saw that he carried a stick, which he tapped on the brick path in front of him. He realized that Nicholas was now quite blind.

This was such a shock that Tom lost command of the situation. He was almost tongue-tied when Nicholas was led up and hugged him with impulsive delight. Not that it mattered, for Nick was perfectly at ease and ready to do all the talking. By the time Tom had regained his poise he found he was engaged to stay for dinner.

They went indoors. Everything was just the same. At Maringale they had always kept up the old-fashioned custom of the whole household eating their midday meal together in the hall. The twenty-odd menservants and maidservants were assembled at two trestles. The family trooped up to the dais, washed their hands at the ewry board, and sorted themselves out at the table. Garnham said grace and everyone sat down.

Tom's wits were working again. He surveyed the company: Mr. and Mrs. Garnham, both his boys, the four Dacres, old Eulalia Sims. One person was missing.

For all his considerable assurance Tom found it a little difficult to mention her. Mrs. Garnham came to his rescue.

"We hope to see Susan over the holiday," she said. "She is only a few miles away, at Ravestock, attending on Lady Foyle as a waiting-gentle-woman."

"At Ravestock?" he repeated, surprised. "How does that suit her, madam? I shouldn't have thought it was much to her taste."

He could not imagine Susan, timid as a wild bird, among the Foyle peacocks, but her stepmother assured him that she was well established, and Roger weighed in with a schoolboy's opinion.

"You'd hardly know our old Sue; she's rigged out like a maypole these days, drenched in scent and paint. And if you can believe it, she's got a proper, live suitor at her heels, mooning about love and that rubbish——"

He broke off, rather red in the face. Tom suspected that several of his relations had kicked him under the table. Roger had never been famous for tact.

Garnham was cutting up a plate of venison for Nicholas, who sat beside him.

"Are you keeping up your music, Nick?" asked Tom.

"Lord, yes—I'm hard at it. I'm studying for my Bachelor's degree at Oxford."

Tom was left speechless. Nicholas at Oxford—it was more incredible than Susan at Ravestock. So incredible that he wondered if the boy was lashing out with a grim sort of joke. Whoever heard of a blind undergraduate?

Mary Garnham said, "Nick has been very fortunate——"

"Fortunate?" interrupted her husband. "It was pure merit." He addressed Tom, enthusiasm breaking through his reserve. "One day last year, while Nick was working for Miles Verney, a customer came into the shop while he was playing the virginals. He seemed pleased with what he heard, and stayed on, asking for more. A few months later this stranger came to call on me. It was Dr. Michael Browne, the organist, and he wanted me to let Nick study with him. When he learnt how matters stood —that it was impossible for Nick to live in College —he offered to take him into his own house and smooth out every obstacle. Dr. Browne has a wife and three daughters who all sing like nightingales, and between them he is so spoilt and petted that very soon there'll be no ruling him."

It sounded like a fairy-tale, even down to the three beautiful daughters. Tom said at once how glad he was to hear of Nick's golden prospects. And

of course he was glad. Delighted. He was especially
fond of Nick, who certainly deserved a reward for
his uncomplaining courage. Yet in the back of his
mind Tom felt a conflict of emotions he did not wish
to examine too closely. Fate was favouring Garnham, as usual. A musician with a university
degree was immensely superior to an ordinary paid
fiddler. His son would be able to follow his profession and remain a gentleman. To be sure, a Garnham of Maringale could always parade his ancient
lineage—even when he lied and cheated like a common thief.

As Tom's animosity deepened the conversation
languished. Garnham lapsed into a silence and
hardly touched his food. His family was infected
with a nervous anxiety that was almost tangible.

Mrs. Garnham kept the ball rolling with scraps
of gossip about their various friends. Tom must
know that Monsieur d'Aubais was making himself
invaluable to the powers in London. Madame was
the same as ever.

"She can afford two serving-wenches now," remarked Jane. "She abuses them roundly, and they
retaliate, the rude Cockney peasants. Poor Madam, she is in a continual state of umbrage."

Tom accorded this a polite and distant smile.

Greville regarded him across a plate of quince
cheese. "Did you know that I have a half-brother?"

"What's new in that? You have two—stepbrothers." Tom hesitated, perceiving the difference.
He looked enquiringly at his hostess. "Is there—
does he mean——"

"Yes, we have a lusty boy, just turned six weeks.
He's fast asleep upstairs, or you'd have had good
warning of his presence. It's a particular joy to

Greville, not to be the youngest any more."

As he murmured the necessary congratulations Tom thought bitterly: even here he has his triumph. This serene and entrancing creature had given him a child. Although she knew his miserable secret, she had heard every line of that grovelling recantation, and it had filled her with disgust. As well it might, for she had a magnificent spirit herself; she had been as brave as a lion that night in Blackfriars. It was wicked that she should be tied to such a husband. Yet in spite of it all she seemed blissfully content. What fools women were.

The females of the family were exclaiming: fancy Tom not knowing the biggest news of all; they thought he would have heard. They overwhelmed him with details about the baby. He was the image of his father. He weighed heavier and roared louder than any other baby. He was called Francis, said Cousin Eulalia, after his august godfather.

"Are you telling me that *Walsingham* is his sponsor?" demanded Tom. This was too much. He turned to Garnham with a calculated insolence. "I must felicitate you, sir. I fancy you can't have expected such a signal honour?"

Mary Garnham brought the meal to an end by asking Nicholas to say grace.

The benches were pushed to the wall; under cover of the noise she spoke to Tom.

"For God's sake, have you no pity? Can't you spare him a scrap of kindness?"

Tom was not quite tough enough to withstand that reproachful gaze. He muttered something incoherent and turned aside, to find himself confronting Garnham, who said: "I'd like a word alone with you, Tom. If you please."

"I've a long ride ahead of me, sir. There can be no purpose in delay."

"I shan't keep you above ten minutes."

Tom had meant to leave at once, but the children were blocking his passage; Jane was following the conversation with an innocent curiosity he found rather disconcerting, and he could not escape without causing a tedious amount of comment. He gave in and allowed Garnham to take him to the small bookroom which looked out over the moat.

Here nostalgia hit him like a tidal wave. It was in this room he had first read *Morte d'Arthur,* sprawling on the rushes, bewitched, during a wet August, while the mentor who had introduced him to the riches of Malory sat writing at the table. Later, it was Tom who had sat at the table, pen flicking across the paper, while Garnham walked up and down, dictating. There had also been a few unnerving encounters, when the high-spirited boy had needed a reminder of his guardian's authority. And good grief, thought Tom, if I had ever dared to be impudent in those days I should have come here shaking in my shoes.

Just because he was not shaking, because he held the upper hand, he was doubly conscious of the topsy-turvy world which had swung off balance the night he discovered Garnham's recantation, and he felt a surge of fury towards the man who had injured him in a way he did not begin to understand.

He remained obstinately at the edge of the room, every nerve in his body hostile and suspicious.

"What good do you expect to come of this? If you imagine you can win me over——"

"You may set your mind at rest," said Garnham. "I don't intend to weary you with a specious defense of my past crimes. I know very well what you think of them, and you are right. They are indefensible. There is just one matter that I want to make plain, for your sake, Tom, not mine. The night I drove you out of this house I was already embroiled in my secret dealings with Perridge. I was caught fast in the net, my judgment distorted——"

"I believe you, sir. Concern for your safety would banish any other consideration."

He ought to box my ears for that, thought Tom. But he won't. He's a broken reed; once you've exposed the sham, there's no fight left in him. Obscurely he was angrier than ever with Garnham for letting him behave so badly.

Too angry to recognize that what he mistook for weakness was a deliberate self-denial, and that there was a bleak dignity about the man who would go through a most humiliating ordeal in an effort to right a wrong which was haunting his conscience.

Garnham leant against the chimney-piece, stooping a little under the low ceiling.

"Most of what I said to you that night was directly inspired by my private misfortunes. I want to be certain you understand that, it's important that you should." He looked across at the handsome young man he had taught and encouraged for so many years. "You are covering the foothills quickly; I think you are going to climb a long way. When you find the girl you wish to marry the chances are she will be as well born as Susan. It distresses me to feel that you might be held back by some totally unnecessary doubts. Doubts which I must have planted. You need not suppose that the insufferable slights I cast on your breeding are a fair measure of what you have to expect. I assure you it is not so. I objected strongly to your dallying with Susan in the moonlight; any father would have done the same, and you are too honest to shrug off what I said to you on that score. But when I implied that you were unfit to marry the daughter of a gentleman, I was merely relieving an inward wretchedness that had nothing to do with you. I talked a great deal of ugly nonsense, knowing it to be false in every conclusion."

Tom drew a long breath. "Did you suspect I was brooding all these months because you called me—what was it? A peasant who belonged to a dunghill?"

"I was afraid you might be."

"You flatter yourself, sir. It's true I was brought up to take everything you said for gospel. Since coming to know you better, I have—shall we say—recanted."

He paused, but Garnham did not reply. That one word had done its work.

"We've nothing further to discuss then," said Tom. "I'll bid you goodbye, sir."

Garnham continued to stare into the fire. Tentative, aware that he was risking a further brutal snub, he asked the questions he should have asked the first time his protégé left Maringale. "Have you anywhere to go, Tom? How are you placed for money?"

Tom had raised the latch of the door. "I shall fare well enough. I may not be so rich as you are, but what I have was come by honestly."

He swung out of the room, to find that Mrs. Garnham and Jane were standing at the open door, gaping at him with incredulous dislike.

Very much put out, he muttered that he was starting back to London.

"We shan't attempt to stop you," snapped Mary. She pushed past him and went to her husband.

Jane whispered: "Tom, how could you? How could you be so cruel?"

Tom ignored her. He marched into the hall to fetch his cloak and gloves. The table had been cleared and the trestles up-ended. A sweet, plucked melody drifted down the staircase: Nicholas practising a Byrd almayn. The younger boys were hanging more garlands around the house; Tom could hear them calling and laughing. The sky was overcast and it would soon be dark. He wouldn't make London tonight. He could go to the inn at Epping, and ride on tomorrow, drink himself into the necessary state of good cheer and then sally out in search of a woman. It would be a strange way of spending Christmas.

I have plenty of friends, he assured himself. There were a number of colleagues, or old Cambridge companions, who would gladly have asked him for the Twelve Days, if they had known he was in England. But there wasn't a single house where he could arrive unheralded at any hour of the day or night, knowing for certain that he would be welcome.

He was pulling on his gloves, in a kind of dull melancholy, when he became aware of Jane hovering beside him.

"Tom, what's happened since you've been away? Why are you so changed?"

"It's not I who have changed."

"Oh yes, it is. The last time we were together— do you remember that morning in London, when

you told me you were working for a printer? You
weren't angry then. You didn't blame my stepfather for dismissing you. And after all, you did give
him some cause; rolling in the hay with Susan."

"Susan and I did not roll in the hay," said Tom
austerely. "You shouldn't use such terms about
your stepsister. And if you think I bear him a
grudge over that you are barking up the wrong tree,
my dear. I have a far graver reason for avoiding Mr.
Garnham."

"So it has to do with that scandal he got into? I
thought as much. They hushed it up, and pretended there was nothing amiss, but we all guessed.
Except what it was that he'd done—we never did
know that. Tom, can you tell me——"

"No, I can't. I swore an oath that I'd keep my
mouth shut. But no one could make me swear to go
on treating him as a sainted paragon. When a
man's actions are thoroughly contemptible he can
hardly complain if he meets with contempt."

"That's a fine piece of logic!" Jane flung herself
down in the window-seat, with the undirected
energy of a childish temper she had not quite outgrown. "He is not to defend himself, these actions of
his must remain veiled in mystery, and I have to
take your word for it that they were contemptible.
Who made you his judge? How can you aspire to
judge the man who brought you up and cared for
you and taught you all you know? Haven't you a
grain of modesty or thankfulness? If he is des-
picable, what are you?"

He gazed down at her, beset by some very unexpected sensations. Fierce in her loyalties, his little
Nut Brown Maid of two summers ago, she had acquired a stormy beauty which held out a dazzling

promise for the future. Tom did not want her to despise him. He wanted to justify himself, and to reclaim his own share of her loyalty, which had suddenly become very precious.

Before he could speak, she challenged him again. "What is it to you if my stepfather took bribes——"

"Edward Garnham never took a bribe in his life!" said Tom with a sense of outrage which was decidedly inconsistent.

"Did he not? We thought it might have been that. Well, whatever he's done, my mother and Sir Francis have forgiven him, so why can't you?"

"There's no similarity. Walsingham had a political motive for being lenient. And Mrs. Garnham would always be a dutiful wife."

"A dutiful wife! Is that how you see their marriage? God give me patience! Women don't love by order, Tom. Even you must know that."

He was taken aback by her sweeping scorn, and by something that lay behind it: a maturity of outlook which made him feel that this half-grown girl of fourteen was in some ways older than himself.

"I dare say you think my mother so simple that she can't see any fault in her husband? Just on account of his being her husband?"

"I never said that," he protested. "She has a keen perception of right and wrong."

"Yes, and she has had plenty of wrongs to forgive, let alone this matter you are too infernally discreet to mention. I know she was very unhappy for a time; he used her so unkindly. I saw him hit her once—he slapped her face in front of the whole family. I hated him then, and I think she hated him too. Susan was persuaded that she meant to leave him.

But then this trouble broke over him like a deluge. He was sent for, to Seething Lane, and we were packed out of the way. Afterwards we came down here to Maringale, and he fell ill."

"What ailed him?" asked Tom. He had firmly believed that it was a diplomatic illness, invented to hide the fact that Garnham had been exiled from London in disgrace.

Jane considered. "I suppose you'd call it a sickness of the mind. He had terrible dreams, as though he was burning at the stake. Susan heard him crying out in his sleep; she said it sounded as though he wanted to burn. I can't understand that, can you?"

"Yes," said Tom, half reluctant. "Yes, in a way I can. Go on. What next?"

"He fought to stay awake, to resist the dreaming, and as a result he went to the other extreme; he couldn't sleep at all, and that was worse. He couldn't eat, either. Clemency and the boys had gone to the Foyles at Ravestock, but my mother kept me and Sue at home to help with the nursing. Not that she let us help, in the end, for she did it all herself. He couldn't bear to let her out of his sight. She never took her clothes off for three days at a stretch. I think she was afraid of what he might do. I overheard them talking once; he was asking her to lock up his razors."

"Oh, my God," muttered Tom, now really horrified.

"I shouldn't have repeated that," said Jane. "You are so set against him, you'll say he was wicked and a coward."

Tom had reasons, unknown to Jane, for thinking Garnham a coward. Strangely enough, he did not apply them here. His mind was in a turmoil. Not having seen Garnham for over a year, he had conjured up a picture of that odious play-actor escaping scot-free, enjoying his exalted position as much as ever, and cynically indifferent to the lies that had got him there.

But if Garnham had suffered so acutely, if remorse alone had driven him to the brink of suicide, that opened up a new aspect of his character. And an aspect of Tom's character too; one which he did not like to contemplate.

He sat by Jane in the window-seat. "Tell me more. Mr. Garnham has fully recovered? From what I gathered in London——"

"Yes, gradually he improved; Susan says it was a miracle—if any miracle could be so slow and tedious. I think it was my mother's doing, and she didn't get him on his feet again by being what you call a dutiful wife. She did it by love. None of your die-away, poetic fancies, either, but a sturdy, vigorous love that can thrive in any climate. For there's no denying, he can't have been the sort of husband she was expecting when she married him."

Nor the sort of man I thought he was, when I was a boy. The unspoken echo rang in Tom's brain. I loved him too, in quite a different fashion, granted. But wasn't that the second closest degree of loving, the bond which had united him to his adopted father? No, he was never that—Tom made the correction without finding much relief in it; the distinction was merely academic.

Jane, having whipped up her feelings, was now wishing openly that he had never come back to Maringale. He had ruined everything. They were happy before, they were looking forward to such a

joyful Christmas, and now it was spoilt. Her stepfather would sink into one of his black moods—
there had been signs of it at dinner—and they
would all be wretched. Tom listened, getting more
and more uncomfortable.

"There's nothing I can do."

"Yes, there is. You can see him again and tell
him you are sorry."

"Jenny, I can't!" exclaimed Tom, appalled at
the prospect.

She misunderstood him. "You don't have to alter
your views of this dire secret which seems to cause
you such offence. But surely you ought to express
sorrow for being so unmannerly—so lacking in filial
respect?"

It should have been amusing to hear Jane preach
a sermon on filial respect; it was not her most noticeable virtue. Tom passed over the comedy, clinging to his feeble objection.

"I am not Mr. Garnham's son."

"It's the one thing you've always wanted to be,"
retorted Jane, with a shrewdness which caught him
like a kick in the ribs. "And I think you owe him
more than his sons, for you had no claim on him—
what he gave you came from the true goodness of
his heart. You used to recognize that. Why, it was
you who set up as his champion when the rest of us
found him harsh and overbearing. You would insist
that he was perfect."

You would insist that he was perfect. Did that
explain the deathly bitterness of his disillusion? The
man who had come to the squalid printer's shop,
and carried off the little, frightened 'prentice into
another world—he had been like a god. The almost
legendary figure, who seemed to do exactly what he

liked, even had a godlike quality in his blazing fairness, his autocratic splendor. Right from the start Tom realized it now, his love for his protector had been tinged with something which was dangerously near to idolatry. Was that why the story behind the legend had failed to rouse his compassion? An idol was either a powerful despot or a senseless lump of clay—you could not, in any circumstance, pity an idol. You could and should pity a fellow-creature whose weakness had made him tragically vulnerable. This failure to pity was in itself a weakness and a betrayal.

He was so engrossed in his thoughts that he forgot about Jane, until she disturbed him by bursting into tears.

"Go to my stepfather," she sobbed. "Darling, sweet, Tom, I pray you to go, for my sake. You don't want me to die of misery?"

"No, no," he said, harassed. "How can you be so foolish?"

"Ask him to let you stay for Christmas," she gulped. "Otherwise you'll go on quarrelling, and we shall lose you for ever, and I shan't be able to bear it."

She sounded so doleful; she was hardly more than a child. On second thoughts it was the un-childish side of Jane which had provoked this outburst, though he was not sure if she knew it. Poor pet, he longed to take her in his arms and soothe her, but restrained himself, remembering Susan. The girls in this house were the very devil.

Routed, he said he would do anything she wanted, if she would promise to stop crying.

Jane stopped, without any visible effort. She mopped her eyes, which were brighter than ever,

clutched his arm and announced that they would go
to her stepfather immediately. Apparently she
meant to act as Tom's escort.

The bookroom was empty. One of the servants
told them that the master and mistress had gone
into the garden.

"We'll find them there," said Jane, who was now
bubbling with confidence. She dragged her prisoner
by the sleeve.

Before they had reached the end of the terrace
Tom was extremely apprehensive. The force of several quite new ideas was compelling him towards
this interview, but as he struggled to adjust his
mind he was struck by a disagreeably vivid impression of his performance during the last two
hours. He had been the most intolerable lout. All
other implications apart, what could have induced
him to behave so atrociously to any man twenty
years older than himself? Edward Garnham might
have been chastened by remorse; even so, the
leopard could not change all his spots. Perhaps he
had felt obliged to put up with Tom's impertinence
—he was hardly likely to overlook it.

As Tom and Jane rounded the corner of the
house they saw the Garnhams pacing up and down
by the yew hedge; she was talking persuasively, he
limped along beside her. Cold weather often
brought on his lameness. The halting foot recalled
to Tom a fact he had conveniently managed to
forget; the actual suffering that this man had endured to overcome before his will finally broke. So
much for the few remaining shreds of self-esteem;
now Tom knew there was nothing for it but a most
complete retraction.

Garnham and his wife had turned; they stood

still. The two couples faced each other across the grass. It was a moment of paralysing awkwardness. Tom's courage had quite gone; he wanted to run away. It did not strike him that his former guardian was just as anxious to run in the opposite direction.

Instead, Garnham stayed where he was, rigidly impassive. Jane gave Tom a push.

They advanced over the lawn, which seemed to have grown much larger. The last few steps were the hardest. He came to a standstill.

"I was wishing to speak with you, sir. If you will permit me——" His voice had got stuck in the upper register; he coughed, and tried again. "I am aware that my conduct has been—has been very remiss, and I want to withdraw anything I may have said—that is, certain things I did say, deliberately, to cause you pain."

This was even more difficult than he had expected, especially in front of an audience. He couldn't deal with that shabby sneer about recanting. He did not know how Garnham was taking his apology, being unable to raise his eyes above the furls of a dark red cloak, and a charcoal-grey doublet. He swallowed, and went on.

"I won't attempt to offer you any excuse. No act of yours could have warranted—and I've been wildly at odds in my reckoning there, which makes it worse—in any event, it wasn't for me to condemn you. I have been arrogant and ungrateful, as well as uncivil. . . ."

His words trailed off uncertainly, to be met by a chilling silence. Tom ventured to glance. Garnham was wearing his masked look. Once the animation was cut off those heavy eyelids and unyielding features were inclined to seem impervious. Tom was too confused to recognize blank astonishment, or the wariness of a man who had been badly hurt. He waited, expecting to be slaughtered on the spot.

Jane saw fit to thrust her spoke into the wheel.

"Go on," she prompted. "Can you stay for Christmas?"

She ought to have seen that his case was hopeless. But Tom was so demoralized that he plunged grimly on.

"Mrs. Garnham was kind enough to invite me, and I wondered whether—I am sure you would not consider—I have forfeited the chance of being your guest."

"You can never be a guest in any house of mine."

Tom bit his lip. It was the final expulsion from paradise. He had not understood, until this moment, how desperately he longed to be back in the family circle. The aching loneliness gripped his heart.

Then, to his amazement, Garnham smiled.

"Not a guest, Tom. You can make us very happy if you come home."

"Oh," said Tom. For the next few seconds he was too stupid to say anything else, slumping there like a dolt, while the warmth crept into his veins, and he savoured the experience of coming home. Of having a home to come to. He pulled himself together. "You are far too generous. After I snarled at you like a savage dog—indeed I am truly sorry, sir."

"Yes, I know you are. So am I sorry, in another connection. We are a pair of miserable sinners, Tom, so let's call it quits. This is Christmas, not Lent."

He couldn't have achieved that lightness a year

ago, thought Mary. The ability to cast off his own overshadowing memories and give Tom a respite from emotion.

Edward had taken his arm. "My dear boy, I have a thousand things to say to you, and I want all the latest rumours from the Continent. Which reminds me," there was an appreciative gleam, "what a fine Italian plotter we have in Mr. Secretary. Hustling you down to me on Christmas Eve with a letter about the appointment of coroners. Did you ever hear of such a paltry device?"

"Coroners?" Tom grinned. "Was that it, sir? He might have chosen a more beguiling topic."

They strolled off together towards the path that led to the forest. Tom, promoted to the status of a junior colleague, was being treated to a ribald comment on the interfering habits of Mr. Secretary Walsingham.

Mary watched them go. She was distracted by a plaintive enquiry from Jane.

"I wish you'd tell me, madam; what did my step-father *do?*"

"Something very terrible; he destroyed Tom's faith in human nature. Don't fret, Jenny. You've patched it up again."

Later in the afternoon it came on to snow. Mary, sticking a candle into the leafy nest of a kissing ring, paused and looked out of the parlour window at the children dancing through the airy white swirls, the flakes landing on their heads and shoulders as softly as a shower of feathers. They were bringing in the last consignment of greenery.

Edward and Tom returned from their walk in the forest, collected Nick and retired to the bookroom, where they ensconced themselves like lords, idling in luxury round a great fire, while the rest of the household got on with the work.

Presently Mary went upstairs to feed her baby. It was the most fundamental delight, the rhythmic pull of pleasure as he drew the milk from her breast. The fluff on his paper-thin skull rose and fell with his even breathing. He was lapped in animal contentment, far removed from the excitements of his half-brothers and -sisters; strange to think that a few Christmases from now he would be the noisiest of the pack.

She had laid him down in his oak cradle when Edward came to find her, accompanied by Tom, who would have to be fitted out with borrowed clothes, as he had brought none with him.

"That's easily done," said Mary. "Tom, come and meet Master Francis Garnham. Is he not a beautiful boy? And wonderfully like his father?"

"Do you think so, madam?" Doubtful, Tom peered at the pink, swaddled bundle. "I should not wish to commit any further discourtesy——"

"I thank you," said Edward. "You assuage my vanity. Women pay the strangest compliments."

His hand crept down to stroke the baby's cheek. He was touchingly proud of his new son.

When she was alone with Tom, providing him with tooth-soap and one of Edward's shirts, Mary sensed that he was a little on his guard. He probably thought that she resented his behaviour more than her husband, and he was right. But he had made amends, and she did not want to spoil his homecoming, so she kept up a flow of brisk chatter. They soon got round to Susan.

"I can't yet picture her at Ravestock," he said. "Who is this suitor Roger thinks so poorly of?"

"Roger doesn't hold with courtship. As to the suitor, it's William Chaucer, Lady Foyle's son by her first husband. Hence the charm of Ravestock."

"Oh, Will Chaucer's a good fellow. They should be well matched."

Mary agreed, thinking of the large, sweet-tempered young man who had taken Susan under his wing directly she arrived in his mother's house. It was partly due to Tom that she had found the courage to go there, freed from the obsessions of her childhood. Mary wondered, with a certain anxiety, whether he was plagued by any lingering and useless day-dreams.

Some acute observation during supper convinced her that he wasn't.

The party broke up in good time, with the prospect of many late nights ahead.

Mary took a candle and went to inspect her preparations for the feasting. The larder was crammed. Sleek capons and lute-shaped hams dangling from the beam. Great coffin pies. A barrel of oysters. Jars of mincemeat and bowls of forcemeat. Dark, fruity pudding mixed in a basin, and the Twelfth Night cake. Little savoury kickshaws. Racks of apples from the orchard. Oranges and lemons, brought from London. Nuts and medlars, tarts and jellies. And the comfits: birds and fishes and coneys, moulded in sugar and painted with cinnamon and saffron. There was a rather drunk-looking duck; Clemency had made that. And underlying the pungent spices the good, fresh smell of warm bread in the bakery.

There should be enough, thought Mary. Yet there were so many hungry mouths, such a swarm of visiting neighbours and tenants. . . .

"You would never live it down," said an amused voice behind her.

"Live what down?"

"Starving us to death in the Twelve Days."

"Fool," said Mary, smiling.

Edward kissed the back of her neck. He had been doing what she had once predicted—reading her mind—but she hardly noticed. That kind of exchange came so frequently now.

They wandered into the firelit kitchen.

"Well, you have recovered your lost boy," she said. "Are you content, sweetheart?"

"Yes, my cup is full. He has indeed been lost, poor lad. Thank God we can try to make it up to him—by giving him back his home, I mean; there's nothing else he needs. My troubles did some good to Tom, at least, for they brought him to Walsingham's notice, and his course is set fair."

"Would he be an acceptable son-in-law now?"

"Certainly. When a man is forging ahead like Tom, there's no profit in quibbling over his ancestry. But what's that to the purpose? Sue is as good as promised to young Chaucer."

"We have other girls to provide for." She laughed at his bemused expression. "My dear Edward, I wonder why Walsingham employs you. I'm speaking of Jane. Didn't you see how they were sparring throughout the evening?"

"Jane! She's a mere infant."

"She's fourteen, and she'll be ready to marry young, as I was. Oh, not for a while yet; Tom will have time to get firmly established. I think there's a true affinity between them. Hasn't it dawned on you that it was Jane who brought him to his senses this afternoon, which was more than you or I could do?"

Edward said quietly, "If Jane can enslave a man as completely as her mother, Tom will be nearly as lucky as I am."

No one could be luckier than I am, she thought, held close in the crook of his arm, his strength and tenderness possessing her. She was not conscious of anything contradictory in this belief. The idea that hers was an unusually difficult marriage had simply disappeared under a flood of gratitude for the best parts of it.

For Tom and Jane, too, there could be the satisfaction of a well-made partnership. And one thing more. If he married Jane, Tom would become Edward's stepson-in-law. The nearest approach to being his son.

Edward moved over to the window and pulled open the shutter.

"It's stopped snowing."

She joined him, and they gazed on to a land of glacial purity. The layer of snow had crusted on the yew hedge and the terrace wall; the ground shimmered under the frosty radiance of the stars. Christmas Eve, drawing towards the hour of the Nativity.

"Do you think the cattle are kneeling down in the barn?" she asked. "Or is that a popish fancy?"

"It's what my old nurse taught me. She was a Roman all her days, God rest her."

He could speak temperately of the Catholics, there was none of the old venom. As far as policy and doctrine went, he was unchanged, and he would still pursue his country's enemies with an untiring competence. But with no tinge of malice. The innocent were no longer damned by their faith; it was even becoming possible to meet some Catholics as friends. When you came down to it, Edward had hated them not for what they had done to him, but for what they had made him do to himself. Not for the rack, but for the self-inflicted wounds, and when those were healed there was no more compulsion to hate.

He had made his peace, learnt the hard lesson of acceptance. He had been forced to accept the truth about himself with humility and detachment, in place of the raging despair which was entirely useless. If there must always be a faint ache of regret, he could accept that too, patiently, not letting the past tyrannize over the future. The future mattered so much more now, it was implicit in that final, overwhelming gift, unwelcome for so long, because he was afraid of it, because it was spoilt and corrupted. Now at last he had come to accept that too, eagerly and with both hands. The precious gift of life.